The Imagined Life

The Imagined Life

ANDREW PORTER

Alfred A. Knopf   New York   2025

A BORZOI BOOK
FIRST HARDCOVER EDITION
PUBLISHED BY ALFRED A. KNOPF 2025

Published by Alfred A. Knopf,
a division of Penguin Random House LLC,
1745 Broadway, New York, NY 10019.

Knopf, Borzoi Books, and the colophon are
registered trademarks of Penguin Random House LLC.

Library of Congress Cataloging-in-Publication Data
Names: Porter, Andrew, 1972– author.
Title: The imagined life : a novel / Andrew Porter.
Description: First edition. | New York : Alfred A. Knopf, 2025.
Identifiers: LCCN 2024038538 | ISBN 9780593538050 (hardcover) |
ISBN 9780593538067 (ebook)
Subjects: LCSH: Families—Fiction. | LCGFT: Novels.
Classification: LCC PS3616.O75 I49 2025 | DDC 813/.6—dc23/eng/20240823
LC record available at https://lccn.loc.gov/2024038538

penguinrandomhouse.com | aaknopf.com

Printed in the United States of America

2 4 6 8 9 7 5 3 1

The authorized representative in the EU for product safety and compliance
is Penguin Random House Ireland, Morrison Chambers, 32 Nassau Street,
Dublin D02 YH68, Ireland, https://eu-contact.penguin.ie.

For my mother and father

Part
1

1

When I first embarked on this project a few years ago—this search, if you will, for the truth of what happened to my father—my wife, Alison, warned me about the dangers of getting too close to something I might not want to know. She reminded me of what had happened when she'd gone through her own mother's journals shortly after her death. About half of the stuff in there, she said, she'd wanted to know, and about half the stuff in there she hadn't. In the end, she felt that her mother's image, or at least the image she'd always had of her mother, had been diminished, changed. She'd been humanized is what I think she meant, and I suppose that sometimes, despite our best intentions, this isn't something we always want.

In the case of my father, though, I wasn't actually that worried about what I might discover. I'd never held him on a pedestal, never believed him to be a great man. I knew that he was flawed, knew that he had made a lot of mistakes in his life, and besides, I had grown up amidst the collapse of his career, the spurious allegations that ensued, the rumors and hearsay. These scandalous stories had been as much a part of my youth as the Brea Mall and skateboarding and my girlfriend Julie Enderton's red VW Bug.

They were part of an ongoing debate that was forever changing and shifting, revising itself, growing more and more absurd and elaborate as time went on. In some of the most bizarre versions of this story my father was portrayed as a borderline lunatic, a man who could fly into a rage without the slightest provocation, a man who had once given his students alcohol during office hours, a man who had supposedly poisoned the cat of a colleague over his policy stance. The absurdity of some of these claims was so extreme that I almost had to laugh at times and probably would have, had my father's fate been different or had the outcome of his tenure case been more favorable. But, as it was, these stories, like so many other things about my father, became embedded in my psyche as a kind of parallel narrative of my life, a fictionalized version in which my father was the campus pariah and I, by association, his son, destined to inherit his shortcomings and flaws. For a long time this fictionalized version of my father's life held such a heavy place in my mind that it almost felt like a prophecy of sorts, an inescapable fate, and it's only now, forty years later, that I can say with some degree of certainty that almost none of it was true.

The small plot of land that my parents owned on the west side of Fullerton is now home to a twenty-four-hour car wash, and though I don't go home very often anymore, when I do, it always saddens me to pass by it and remember what it had once looked like. Back then, when I was growing up, there had been about eight to ten houses on our street, all 1950s style ranch houses with large front yards and swimming pools in the back. Our house had looked identical to the two on either side of it, an inconspicuous beige structure with a slightly sloping roof and two large palm trees on either side of the front porch. What distinguished our house from the others, though, was the garden, which my mother took care of with a kind of zeal and passion she showed toward few other things in her life.

At that time, we had a stately perennial bed at the front of our yard filled with gardenias and hibiscus, white oleander and plumbago, daylilies and juniper, and out back, behind our pool, there were avocado trees and jacarandas, cascading blooms of bougainvillea and lantana, birds of paradise, morea irises, Mexican bush sage, and jasmine. I knew the names of all of these flowers because I'd helped my mother plant them, had stood beside her as she mixed the dirt with some kind of weird concoction of bone meal, alfalfa, chicken manure, and peat. As my father sat inside, grading papers in the kitchen, my mother would give me gentle instructions about where to stand or what to water. She always took the process of gardening very seriously and never more so than when she was putting in something new. Meanwhile, my father, perched at the kitchen window, would be staring out at us, shouting words of encouragement or sometimes weird phrases that seemed to have some kind of special meaning to my mother, phrases that she'd typically roll her eyes at or sometimes shrug off with a smile. My father was always trying to make my mother laugh, speaking in that private language of theirs, and my mother was always trying to pretend he wasn't funny, though he could be very funny and often was when things were good.

On nights when he wasn't too busy, my father would sometimes even come out and join us in the garden, sitting by the side of the pool with a glass of wine or a beer, occasionally smoking a cigarette as he paged through the evening paper or one of his Robert Ludlum novels. Back in Pennsylvania, which is where we'd lived before we moved to California, my father had always worn corduroys and thick wool sweaters, sometimes a blazer and tie, but ever since we'd moved to California he'd traded in his tweeds and woolens for madras shirts and blue jeans, flip-flops and sandals. He wore sunglasses now, even inside the house, and his skin seemed perpetually tan. At that time, he was probably only about thirty-five years old (an age I still consider young), but he likely could have passed for someone in their early twenties. He was the only person on our block, above the age of sixteen, who owned a pair of Vans.

In the evenings, once they'd made friends, my parents would have people over often—colleagues of my father's from the college or coworkers of my mother's from the hospital where she'd just started working as a nurse's aide—and I'd be asked to go to my room and do my homework, though I usually just lay there by the open window that looked out on the back patio and the pool, listening to my parents as they argued and laughed and got drunk with their friends. These dinners often went late into the night, usually long after I'd fallen asleep myself, but I do remember that at a certain point in the evening they'd always quiet down a bit, especially if certain people were over—the Havelins, for example, or the Bruenells—and I'd start to smell what had then become the familiar scent of cannabis floating up to my window from the pool. I'd peek out the window and see them, sitting down there with their friends, passing the joint back and forth and talking quietly, stifling their laughter with coughs. The blue-lit pool would be glowing from within and my parents and their friends would be cast in silhouette, a group of bobbing heads, swaying uneasily underneath the palms.

Once in a while, if they'd imbibed too much, or if they'd smoked a little too much pot, my father would walk up the small path to the house and knock on my door. He'd always stand there for a moment, kind of sheepishly, staring at me, then he'd step forward and ask me if there was any chance I might be willing to ride my bike down the street to the 7-Eleven and pick them up a pint of rocky road, or a bag of chips or Doritos, or some other such junk food—the type of food my mother would have never normally allowed inside our house, but which she seemed to consume with the same alacrity as all of her friends when she was stoned. As I'd make my way out to the garage, my father would start fumbling with his wallet, pulling out bills, adding more and more items to his list ("You know what, why don't you throw in a couple of those Devil Dog things, okay?") and I'd nod along, knowing that it never really mattered what I brought him anyway, that as long as there was enough of it, he rarely even remembered what he'd asked for in the first place, and then I'd hop on my bike and head out into the street, which was always quiet and empty that time of night, and start pedaling toward the main road and the 7-Eleven.

Sometimes, when I got home, my father would have his movie projector set up in the backyard. He had an old 16mm Bell & Howell projector from the 1960s, which he'd inherited from an old friend and colleague at F&M College in Pennsylvania and which he used to send up old movies onto the side wall of our cabana house, a cracked and bumpy surface that he had painted ivory white for this very purpose years before. At the time, his films of choice tended to be old black-and-white films from the 1930s and '40s—he had a whole collection of them sitting down in our basement, everything from Carol Reed's *The Third Man* to Howard Hawks's *The Big Sleep*. He had an affinity for any movie with a femme fatale, a morally ambiguous narrator, and a fatalistic sensibility, and of course he was especially fond of the films of Nicholas Ray and Fritz Lang and anything starring Robert Mitchum or Lauren Bacall.

When I'd turn the corner onto our street on my way home from the 7-Eleven, I'd see the silver glow of the cabana house in the distance, the palm trees in our backyard illuminated by the ghostly light of the screen, and as I pedaled faster and pulled in closer to our house I'd hear the rhythmic whir of the film projector, and then, above that, the hardboiled dialogue of Humphrey Bogart or Edward G. Robinson or Raymond Burr spilling out from our backyard. Dropping my bike in the driveway, I'd head in through the kitchen and then out to the backyard, the cartons of ice cream already melting, and find my parents and their friends, lying supine in the pool, floating on rafts in their underwear, passing a joint back and forth between them or sipping on tropical cocktails, above them the twenty-foot visages of these glorious icons from Hollywood's golden age, perfectly preserved in their celluloid brilliance, utterly beautiful, like strange deities from another time.

These are the images that I always think about now when I think about my parents' dinner parties—those vertiginous, alcohol-soaked evenings in the backyard of our house, the black-and-white flicker of my father's makeshift theater, the verdant splendor of my mother's garden, the flowing laughter of their guests, all at a time when my father was just beginning to establish himself as an important and well-respected young professor in the English Department at St. Agnes College. Years later, I'd find it ironic, or perhaps somewhat fitting, that it was at one of these famous backyard parties of my father's that everything in his life began to change, though of course he didn't know that then. In a letter that he wrote to my mother years later, he'd refer to the party I'm thinking of now as both the best and the worst party he'd ever thrown. I remember it as being a little larger than most of my parents' parties—it was a tenure celebration in honor of my father's good friend, David Havelin—and I remember it being a warm night, almost unseasonably so, and very clear. My mother had decorated the entire backyard in accents of white—white tablecloths on every table, white paper lanterns in the trees, white tulips in the garden, and she had even bought a special silver pitcher earlier that day to hold the sangria that my father had recently become famous for making, but other than this—other than these small touches—the party itself was fairly normal.

Earlier that night I'd had a swim meet at the Yorba Linda High School pool. It was the first meet of the summer season, and I'd come in fourth in both the 100-meter breaststroke and the 50-meter fly. It was a respectable showing, considering I'd just moved up from the 10 & under division to the 12 & under division, but still disappointing. On the ride home from the pool that night, as I sat beside my best friend Chau in the backseat of his mother's car, I found myself wondering what I'd done wrong and considering how I might do better the next time. By the time we'd pulled into my parents' driveway, I was convinced that I'd need to shave at least a second and a half off both of my times if I ever hoped to move up within the ranks of the team.

Closing the door behind me, I said goodbye to Chau, and then thanked his mother and started up the driveway toward our house. It was still early—maybe seven or seven-thirty—but I could tell that the party had started. From the edge of our front lawn, I could already hear the velvety voice of Frank Sinatra coming out from our living room, and beyond that the laughter and occasional shrieks of my parents' guests in the back. I headed in through the front door and then started down the side hallway, avoiding the eager smiles of my parents' friends, ducking and dodging before they could grab me by the arm and ask me how my school year had been or mess up my hair and tell me how handsome I'd become. By the time I'd made it to my parents' room, I was out of breath and dizzy from all the cigarette smoke in the air—it seemed that all of my parents' friends smoked back then—and quickly jumped in the shower and began to scrub off all the chlorine.

Through the slatted bathroom window, I could see a group of people in the backyard, huddled around a man who was talking dramatically about something or other, waving his hands above his head and smiling every time he told a joke, or every time he said something funny, luxuriating in the apparent hilarity of the moment. I'd never seen this man before, but I could tell that he was important, or at least popular, that there was something about him that seemed to attract other people. The longer he stood out there talking, the larger the circle around him grew, until my father finally had to break in and steal the stage, clinking on his wineglass and proposing a toast to David Havelin, the man of the hour. A few moments later, David emerged sheepishly from the back of the yard, holding his wife's hand and teetering slightly. In a loud voice, my father asked him how it felt to now be "unfireable," and David smiled and shook his head, and then raised his glass to the guests and winked. "Never say never," he said and everyone laughed. A half hour later, after everyone in the English Department had offered their own congratulations and laudatory remarks, the crowd began to disperse and I went into my parents' bedroom and lay down on their bed, my hair still wet from the shower.

Outside, I could hear the party still going full blast. The music had resumed now, and I could tell that people were starting to dance—it was late enough and dark enough for this to happen—and as I lay there, I began to picture them moving through the shadows, their faces warmly lit in the ethereal glow of the Japanese lanterns, their bodies swaying hypnotically to the sounds of Louis Prima or Doris Day or Rosemary Clooney. My parents owned more contemporary music at the time—they'd grown up in the late 1960s, after all—but when it came to these parties, they almost always reverted to the songs of their youth, or to the songs of their parents' generation, almost as if they were paying a kind of homage to that time. My mother was typically the first one out on the dance floor, the first one to start dancing, dragging her friends up onto the flagstone deck beside the pool, and shortly after that my father would usually follow, coaxing his colleagues to come up and "cut a rug" with him, as he liked to put it, but that night, for some reason, I could sense that something was different. The energy in the air was different. The music was louder and more frenetic, and I could hear people singing, not to the words of the song that was playing, but to something else, something I couldn't quite decipher. At a certain point I heard the sound of someone laughing in the front hall, and then a moment later my mother entered the room with a small plate of food and a diet soda. She sat down on the edge of the bed and handed me the plate of food.

"I thought you might be hungry," she said and smiled, and then she mussed my wet hair, and stood back up to close the door.

I looked at the plate of food. It wasn't much—a few crackers, some pimento cheese, a couple of cold cuts—and then back at my mother, who was now standing up at her bureau going through her drawers.

"I'm afraid your dear mother spilled wine on her slacks," she said, and then she turned around and laughed, as she held up a new pair before me. "So, are you planning to hide out here all night?" she said.

"That's the plan."

"Don't you want to watch TV or something? I could bring in the little black-and-white set."

"I'm fine."

"You sure?"

I nodded.

"Oh, Steven," she said. "Always the stoic." Then she came over and embraced me. "What am I going to do with you?"

I let her hold me for a brief moment, and then she smiled again and disappeared into the bathroom to change.

"I finished second," I shouted to her after a moment, "in both of my events today."

"Oh, honey," she shouted back from the bathroom, "that's wonderful."

I shrugged. "I don't think I like the coach though."

"Why not?"

"I don't know," I said. "I think he has it in for me."

This wasn't really true. The coach—Mr. Ortega—had only just started the week before, and I'd barely even spoken to him. I wasn't really sure why I'd said this. As far as I could tell, Mr. Ortega was a perfectly nice man and had been nothing but supportive.

"Well, if he gives you any trouble," my mother said, but then her voice was drowned out by the sound of the faucet running, and I couldn't make out what she was saying. I heard her opening some drawers in there, turning on the blow dryer, and then a few minutes later she emerged completely refreshed—a new outfit, new hairstyle, new makeup. She'd even put on perfume.

"How do I look?" she asked, walking back across the room now, and I told her what I always told her, which was that I thought she looked beautiful.

"I'll be back in to check on you in about an hour, okay?" she said, and then she gave me a wink, and closed the door behind her.

For the rest of the night, I lay in bed, reading a book that I'd borrowed from my father's library, a book about the films of Billy Wilder. My father was an Americanist, and for a long time the only books in his library were books about authors like Henry James or Edith Wharton, but recently he'd begun to become more interested in film, particularly American film, and his personal library had begun to reflect this change. Whereas there had once been books by William Dean Howells and Stephen Crane, there were now volumes on Jean-Luc Godard and Alfred Hitchcock. As an eleven-year-old, my ability to comprehend what I was reading was somewhat limited, but I remember liking very much the idea of reading what my father was reading, of sharing his interests and cares and of running my fingers over the same pages that he had run his fingers over. Occasionally, I'd find a small marking in the margins, a little note or query ("But what about *Last Year at Marienbad?*") and I'd study this scribble as if it contained some secret insight into my father's mind, some clue about his thought process. Most of the time, though, I just enjoyed looking at the pictures in these books—there were always wonderful depictions of classic shots—usually accompanied by a diagram or a short paragraph explaining the camera angle, the lighting, and so on. In the book that I was reading that night there were several long chapters devoted exclusively to *Sunset Boulevard*—a film that my father had made me watch several times—and I remember spending a lot of time staring at the different shots of the various actors, Gloria Swanson and William Holden especially, and then trying to make sense of what my father had written in the margins. I suppose I could have always asked my father what his cryptic scribblings meant, but somehow it seemed more fun, or at least more exciting, to try to decipher them myself, to think of them as a kind of puzzle or game I had to unravel.

The scribblings that I was looking at that night, though, didn't make a lot of sense to me, and they didn't seem to have anything to do with *Sunset Boulevard* either. One of them seemed to refer to my father's brother, Julian; another to the beach house down in Rehoboth that they used to rent before I was born. There were also several drawings—most of them fairly abstract in nature—and a series of numbers written under one of the photographs of Eric von Stroheim. Years later, I'd wonder if there was something to these scribblings, if they were an early indication of my father's mind unraveling, a forecast of things to come, but at the time, I simply saw them as interesting, just as I saw everything about my father as interesting, and I didn't think much about them except when I was actually looking at them, in which case I tended to attribute their strangeness to something beyond my comprehension, a clear-cut sign of my father's brilliance and erudition.

By the time I'd made my way through the second of the three chapters on *Sunset Boulevard,* I could tell that the party outside was beginning to die down a bit. The chatter outside in the hallway had started to soften, and off on the other side of the house I could tell that people were leaving, that the older members of my father's department, whom my mother referred to as the "old guard," were beginning to say their goodbyes, and even outside on the patio deck I could tell that the dancing had stopped and that the music had begun to slow down and grow fainter, and I imagined that people were probably easing into the pool now or pulling up their chaise lounge chairs and topping off their drinks. Whenever my parents threw a larger party like this, there were typically two phases to it, and I could tell that we had now entered the second phase, the phase in which the younger and less established members of the English Department began to finally relax and let down their guard. With the tenured members gone, the younger and less established could finally reach for that second drink or strip down to their bathing suits and get in the pool. Someone would turn down the lights in the backyard, maybe bring out some candles; someone else would turn down the music, and then after a while my father would get out his projector and set it up. A new bottle of wine would be opened, a joint would be lit, and pretty soon everybody would be gathered around the pool in the backyard, staring up at the cabana house wall, waiting for the opening credits of whatever film my father had chosen to show.

I walked over to the window beside my mother's bureau and

looked out. I could see that the film my father had chosen that night was *Double Indemnity,* a favorite of his and a film that I'd recently been reading about, and I could also see that a few of my father's friends and colleagues had made their way into the pool water now, several of them floating around on big blue rafts beneath the black-and-white images of Fred MacMurray and Barbara Stanwyck, and that my father himself was now sitting with a group of men at the far end of the pool, all of them drinking and laughing, stripped down to their boxer shorts and staring up at the cabana house wall, making comments about the film, dangling their feet in the water, passing a bottle back and forth.

Two of these men I actually recognized—Joseph Alors and Edward Bindley. Both Alors and Bindley had come in during the same year as my father, and both of them were a regular presence at my parents' parties, but the man sitting just beside them, or just to their left, I'd never seen before, or rather I didn't recognize him at first, and then, as he moved in closer to my father, out of the shadows, I could see that he was actually the man I'd seen earlier, standing at the edge of my parents' back lawn, holding court and speaking dramatically to a group of eager listeners. Now, without his clothes on, he looked a little different than he'd looked on the lawn, less impressive perhaps, less imposing. He was actually a fairly gaunt man, and I could see that he had a large scar across his chest and another one across his stomach, but other than these small blemishes, it was clear that he was handsome, almost boyishly so, and it was also clear that he was very much at ease among the other people at the party—so at ease, in fact, that I simply assumed he was one of my father's colleagues in English or perhaps another professor from another department. I watched him as he put his arm around my father's shoulder, and then watched my father as he did the same, and then watched all of the men as they all put their arms around each others' shoulders and then began to sway back and forth, gently, like a drunken chorus line, at the far end of the pool.

On the other side of the yard, I could see a small group of people gathered around the food table, and then just beyond them another group of three women chatting, but otherwise almost everyone else at the party had made their way across the lawn to the pool now and were either lounging there in the water or sitting down just beside it, watching my father and his colleagues as they sat at the far end of the deck, acting foolish. I could tell that people were laughing *with* them, but still, a part of me couldn't quite bear to watch. I'd seen my father embarrass himself at parties many times before and I knew the toll it always took on him, knew that he'd probably spend the next few days worried about the way he'd come off or how his behavior might affect his tenure case. There was always the burning off of steam and then the inevitable worrying that tended to follow. Who had seen him do such and such and what had they thought? I tried to look for my mother then, but couldn't find her, so eventually I just closed the curtains and went back to the bed.

It was dark in the room now—I had turned off all of the lights earlier—but I could still hear the sounds of the party outside, and for a while there I just lay in the dark, tossing and turning in the sheets, drifting in and out of a semiconscious state, a state in which I was aware of the sounds of the party, but not aware that I was in my parents' bedroom anymore, or inside of a house for that matter, or inside of anything, really. I remember waking up at one point and then looking at my parents' clock and taking note of the fact that it was just after midnight and that people were still outside, laughing and talking, and that the party itself might have perhaps entered another phase, and then closing my eyes again and falling back into an even deeper sleep, a sleep so deep that when the screaming finally started it almost didn't sound like screaming at first. It sounded more like the words of a song—a song by Rosemary Clooney or Doris Day—a song about longing and hope and despair, a song about being young and Italian, and then all of a sudden the lyrics of this song were shifting, becoming strident and harsh, and then, just like that, I was up in my parents' bed with a jolt, fumbling with the covers, trying to adjust to the darkness and catch my bearings, trying to figure out what was happening, and then finally pulling myself out of the bed and running over to the window and looking out.

I remember seeing a group of people standing around the pool, huddled there, and then one of them shouting, *get him out, get him out,* and then I remember hearing my mother make a sound that I had never heard her make before, a sound that seemed so guttural and deep it almost didn't seem real, and then seeing her fall to her knees, just out of sight from where I was standing, and then looking left and seeing my father's colleagues—David Havelin and Edward Bindley and Joseph Alors—all looking down at the pool and then wondering for a moment where my father was. I looked for him everywhere but couldn't find him. For a long time, in fact, I couldn't see anything at all—the crowd around the pool was so thick—but then eventually the crowd began to part, and I heard the sound of some weak laughter and some even weaker applause. Finally, I saw the sight of my father's back, as he emerged from the pool, still in his boxer shorts, clearly embarrassed, dripping all over the deck, and then the sight of another man—it was that same man from earlier, the gaunt, handsome man with the scar on his chest—as he swam over to my father and helped him out. Once he was on the deck, my father leaned over and coughed violently into his hands and then the man stood behind him and pounded on his back a few times, until he finally stopped coughing, and then for a while there everyone just kind of stood there, silently, as if stunned by what had happened.

After a moment, my father sat down in one of the chaise lounge chairs by the side of the pool, and my mother walked over to the projector, which was still playing *Double Indemnity,* and turned it off. Shortly after that, the men in the pool began to get out slowly, and I could tell that the party was over. A hush had fallen over the crowd, and it was clear that something had happened. I watched David Havelin as he came over to my father and handed him one of the beach towels from the cabana house, and then watched my mother as she turned around and headed back to the house by herself, not saying a word to anyone. Within a few minutes, everyone was standing up and getting dressed, their heads bowed down in a kind of communal acknowledgment that they had done something wrong, or that they had allowed something wrong to happen, or at least that they had allowed the party itself to get out of hand.

I looked over again at my father then, and I could see that he was distressed, that he was hunched over in the posture of someone who had just disgraced himself, staring down at his hands, shaking his head, avoiding eye contact with everyone around him. After a while, a few people walked over to him and patted his back, touched his shoulder gently, mussed his hair, and my father nodded at them shyly, though I could tell that it was difficult for him to even look at these people, that it was hard for him to even make eye contact with them. Before long, a few of the remaining guests began to pack up their bags at the edge of the pool, and a few others came over to join them. It was clear that everyone wanted to go home now, that they wanted to get as far away from the party, and this situation, as possible.

I watched them as they made their way back toward the house in a small group, then listened as they entered the kitchen and spoke to my mother in soft voices, assuring her that no, they didn't need coffee and that yes, they were okay to drive. It was amazing how quickly the party had ended and how suddenly everyone there had sobered up. From the edge of my parents' doorway I could hear my mother apologizing now, telling everyone that my father must have had a little too much sangria or that he must have made his latest batch a little strong and then insisting that she hadn't even realized he'd been drinking earlier in the pool with the others. There was a brief moment of silence, and then a few of the younger professors began to chime in, assuring my mother that it had been a wonderful party anyway and that in the morning nobody would even remember what had happened. One of the younger professors had even joked that this was part of what they got paid to do—to persist in the face of conflict—and a few of the other young professors had laughed at this, though it was clear that nobody there had found what had happened funny at all.

After almost all of the guests had left, my mother walked into the living room and turned off the music, then sat down on the couch by herself and lit a cigarette. I was watching this all from the hallway, out of my mother's view. I saw her put her head in her hands and then I saw her hugging herself, almost like she was bracing herself for my father, who was probably still outside, talking to David Havelin. A few minutes later, I heard the back door open, and then I heard the sound of someone entering the kitchen and then a moment after that I saw Mrs. Havelin walking into our living room and sitting down next to my mother on the couch and taking her hand. My mother said something to her in a hushed voice, and then Mrs. Havelin smiled and stood up and headed back outside to the lawn.

As soon as she left, I turned around and went back down the hallway to my parents' room where I stood at the window and watched Mrs. Havelin as she made her way back across the lawn toward the pool. I watched her as she said hello to my father and her husband and then studied her as she stood at the edge of the pool, talking to them. Everyone else was gone now, even the man who had helped my father earlier in the pool. At one point, David Havelin pulled out a pack of cigarettes and passed a few around, and then for a long time after that the three of them just stood there, smoking cigarettes and looking out at the pool water, and it seemed to me then that something significant had happened. I just couldn't say what.

As it would turn out, the events of that night—many of which I wouldn't learn about until years later—had already begun to change the course of my father's life, and by the end of the following week it would be clear to me that this would be the last of my father's great parties, the last of his famous soirees. From here on out everything about our lives in Fullerton would be different, though of course I didn't know that then. What I did know, or at least what I sensed, was that something had shifted and that this thing, whatever it was, didn't just have to do with whatever had happened that night in the pool, it had to do with something else, something I couldn't quite name or pinpoint, but nevertheless felt. I looked over at my parents' bureau then, where I noticed that the book on Billy Wilder was now missing, and then I closed the wood-slat blinds and started down the hallway to find my mother.

I could hear the sound of music coming from the kitchen and figured that this might be her, but when I entered the kitchen she was gone. I looked over at the side patio then, and noticed she was there, sitting by herself. I walked out to join her and she seemed surprised to see me still awake. She motioned for me to sit down beside her, and when I did, she put her hand in mine and squeezed it. She said she'd had a long night. In the distance, I could see my

father and David Havelin and Mrs. Havelin, standing in the moon-
light beside the pool, an image that struck me as both beautiful
and sad.

I asked my mother then what had happened—what all the
commotion had been about—and she just sighed. "You didn't see?"

"No," I said.

"Well, it's not important," she said. "It's not something for you
to worry about right now."

"Is Dad in trouble?"

"What makes you say that?"

"I don't know," I said.

"Nobody's in trouble," she said, though the way she said it,
dropping her eyes, wasn't convincing. She mentioned something
then about my father quitting smoking and how this had been
very hard for him, how he hadn't been himself lately, and then she
said something else about the alcohol they'd all consumed and
how that had probably been a bad idea, in retrospect, but then her
voice began to trail off and her eyes became distant, and I couldn't
really tell what she was thinking.

"We can talk about this some more in the morning, okay?" she
said. "It's pretty late."

I told her okay, but in the morning we wouldn't talk about it,
and we wouldn't talk about it again, not really, for many years.

After a while, my mother poured out the wine she'd been drinking onto the lawn and then leaned back in her chair, and I asked
her then who the man was—I described the scar on his chest and
his stomach, how he'd been sitting with my father earlier in the
pool, and so on—and she just shrugged and said that he wasn't that
important, that he was just a new professor in my father's department, a visiting professor whose name was Deryck Evanson.

I asked her if this Deryck Evanson had saved my father's life
and she just sighed and said that she wouldn't know about that,

that she wasn't exactly sure what had happened. Then she tried to change the subject again, and I could see that she was lying.

I can tell you this now because my mother is no longer alive and I am now several years older than she was then, at that moment, and so I can understand to some degree how she might have wanted to protect me in that instant, how she might have even sensed intuitively what was happening to my father and wanted to protect herself as well. But still, I can also remember how lovingly she had looked at him that night—this man who she had met when she was twenty-two, this man who she had followed across the country and back several times and who she had raised a son with and built a home with, this man who had finally delivered her to California, to what he promised would be their final destination and who was now quite possibly squandering the very thing he had always promised her.

She was staring at him with both compassion and pity, and if I had to guess what she was feeling at that moment, I'd guess she was feeling scared, but as I said I can't be sure, and in any event it doesn't matter. What matters to me now is only how she looked at him that night and the way that he eventually looked back, once he'd noticed us, the way that he stood there in the shadows at the edge of the yard and waved to us, kindly, like a man who loved us, like a man who would never hurt us, and the way that he kept standing there long after my mother had stopped looking, waving his arms in the air, beckoning us to join him.

2

Years later, when my father was no longer living in Fullerton, he would claim that the party that night had been the turning point in his time at St. Agnes College, that, after that night, things would never be the same for him in the English Department or on the campus at large. But when I asked David Havelin about this recently, he claimed that this hadn't been the case at all, that certain members of the English Department had turned on my father long before that.

I had tracked David down through the Human Resources Department at St. Agnes, and he had agreed to meet with me out at his apartment in Yorba Linda, a few miles south of where he'd lived when I'd known him. He had retired from the college several years earlier, had separated from his wife, Linda, and was now working part-time for the UCLA Extension Program, teaching courses in English as a Second Language (not because he needed the money, he claimed, but because he missed the classroom). His wife, Linda, was now living in Palos Verdes with another man, but he didn't seem to want to talk about that. He said that he'd been enjoying his retirement more or less, keeping busy by working on his research and scholarship, taking the occasional trip up to Santa

Barbara to see his godchildren, reconnecting with old friends. He and Linda had never had children themselves, he said, and that had probably been a blessing. He claimed that there was truly no animosity between them. No bitterness. They had simply grown apart.

The apartment that David was living in at that time was fairly small, a glorified one-bedroom that reminded me a lot of the types of apartments that Alison and I used to live in in Tucson right after college. The ceilings were low and the floors were uneven, but the apartment itself was very clean and the main common area was filled with lots of warm natural light and the balcony attached to the kitchen had a beautiful view of the Chino Hills State Park in the distance. I remembered the house that David had owned when I was growing up, a dank and musty ranch house, filled with old books, walls and walls of them, like some antiquated library that time had forgotten. I thought of asking him where all of those books were now, but figured it might be a sensitive subject, so instead I just followed him out to the balcony next to the kitchen where he had set up a small lunch for us: pita bread and various cheeses, a light salad, wine.

"I don't know if I'll be able to give you what you're looking for," he said after we'd sat down and started eating, and I'd told him a little bit about what I was doing, how I was trying to reconstruct my father's life in Fullerton, and at St. Agnes, so that I could have a better sense of what had happened to him. David had smiled and sipped his wine as I spoke. He looked the same: handsome and dignified, his long, thin nose and high cheekbones, his tiny glasses. He'd put on a little weight and his hair had thinned, but generally speaking time had been kind to him.

"Whatever you can tell me would be helpful," I said and shrugged. "Even stuff that might not seem that relevant."

He nodded again. "Well," he said after a moment, putting

down his glass. "I can tell you one thing. What they did to your father back then—what they put him through and what he had to endure." He shook his head then, as if the memory still pained him.

"I know," I said.

"They have regulations in place now to prevent that type of thing from happening—a formal protocol for tenure and all that—but back then, you know, it was like the Wild West. If you crossed the wrong person or if you said the wrong thing—" He shook his head again and shrugged.

"And my father crossed the wrong people."

"Oh yes," David smiled. "He definitely did." He looked out at the hills then and sipped his wine.

"Well, I know he always appreciated your support," I said. "I know it meant a lot to him."

David shrugged. "It was different for me, Steve. I had tenure, you know. I had a lot less to lose."

"Still," I said. "I know it couldn't have been easy."

"No," he said. "I guess not. They definitely never let me forget it." He looked at me then and laughed.

According to my father, David Havelin had been the only member of the entire English Department to support him, the only one to stand on the side of ethics, as my father put it, and I know that David took a hit for this politically and that he never quite recovered from it professionally, but I also know that for David it was never about taking some grand stand politically or making some grand gesture of friendship toward my father. It was simply about doing the right thing. As he explained to me later that day, "What they were doing to your father back then was unconscionable, Steve. It really was. It was a stitch-up, and everyone in the department knew it. So what I had to do, I guess, was decide what type of person I wanted to be." He looked at me evenly. "It was really that simple."

We were now on our second bottle of wine, and I could see the sun beginning to set in the distance, just beyond the green hills of the Chino Hills State Park. We had spent the past two hours talking about all of the people I remembered from my father's department—Joseph Alors and Ed Bindley, Deryck Evanson and even the chair at the time, Albert Doyle. David had brought out an old photo album at one point, and we had spent about an hour paging through it, all of these incredible photographs from that era, many of them discolored and faded, photographs of faces I barely remembered but that somehow seemed familiar, like faces from a dream or from a movie I'd once seen but forgotten, and others so vivid and haunting I had to look away from them—photos of my father in his Ray-Bans, for instance, holding a cigarette and a margarita at one of his famous backyard parties, or photos of my mother and Linda Havelin sunning themselves at the side of our pool in their bikinis, their faces astonishingly young, even photos of Deryck Evanson, as he was at that time, handsome and sculpted, completely oblivious to the effect his good looks were having on everyone around him.

As we paged through the album, David talked in a measured tone about the various people and what had happened to them. He told me that Joseph Alors had left for another job at UC Santa Cruz shortly after my father's fall from grace—he had seen the writing on the wall, David claimed—and that Edward Bindley had sadly developed multiple sclerosis in his late forties and retired early. He was now living in the Bay Area—Petaluma, he thought. As for Albert Doyle, he had died that past spring from pancreatic cancer at the advanced age of eighty-three. According to David, there weren't a lot of people left in the department from my father's era. Maybe just a handful. He rattled off a few names that he thought I might remember, but none of these names sounded familiar. I had hoped that David might be able to shed some light on what had happened to my father specifically during his bid for tenure, what they had done to him behind the scenes, but he claimed that legally he wasn't allowed to divulge anything specific. What he could tell me was that what had happened to my father was a travesty of the worst order and that the people involved were not people he kept in touch with anymore.

I asked him if he could give me the names of those people, but he said he couldn't. He said that if I talked to enough people, though, I'd figure it out. Or I'd know them when I saw them.

"It's not the *who* that's important anyway," he said, "it's the *why*."

"So why did they do it?" I said.

"I never really knew for sure," he said, "but if I had to guess, I'd say it was because your father was probably the most popular professor in the department at that time and definitely the best scholar. Also, and perhaps more importantly, he wasn't afraid of them."

I nodded and sipped my wine.

"But you have to understand, Steve, your father wasn't well at this time. You know that, of course, but not everyone in the department did." He looked down at the album. "He deserved tenure. There's no question about that. On paper, I don't know that I've ever seen a stronger case. But it wasn't all about that for some people. The discussions turned into something else. And that's what I'm afraid I can't talk about."

He leaned over then and picked up the photo album again and opened it to a page that showed a picture of my father and Deryck Evanson standing by the side of a pool in their bathing suits.

"This is probably the person you want to talk to," he said, pointing to Deryck Evanson.

"I've tried," I said. "I can't get a response."

"He teaches at Williams now, right?"

I nodded. "I've written him a dozen emails, some letters. I even called his office a couple of times."

"He's married now," David said. "A couple kids, right?"

"Three," I said. "I think."

David nodded again, as if considering the complications. Then he shrugged and put down his glass. "Well, it's maybe best just to leave it alone."

He stood up then and began to clear the dishes, and I could see that he was done talking about my father for the night. I helped him carry what was left of our late lunch into the kitchen, and then, as we stood at the sink, running the glasses under water, he asked me a little bit about my own family—about Alison and our son, Finn—who I'd avoided talking about for most of the night. Had they come down with me to Los Angeles? he wanted to know. Or were they still back in Berkeley? And how old was Finn now?

I couldn't bring myself to tell him the truth, that I hadn't seen Alison or Finn in close to three weeks, that I was no longer living in our apartment, or living in the Bay Area, for that matter, that I'd quit my job at the University of San Francisco, where I'd run the Writing Center for ten years, that in many ways I was more lost now than I had been when he'd last known me as a teenager.

"Next time we do this, you'll have to tell me more about them," he said, as he opened the refrigerator door and put away the cheese we hadn't finished.

I grabbed both of the empty wine bottles from the counter and placed them in the recycling bin.

"So you'd be up for doing this again?"

"Of course," he said, and smiled. "We've barely touched the surface."

I nodded.

He leaned over then and placed the cutting board in the sink and ran some water over it.

"By the way, where are you headed next?" he said.

"Santa Barbara," I said. "Ojai specifically."

"Ojai?"

"Yeah."

He nodded but didn't ask me why I was going there or who I intended to see.

Later, as we stood at the door, he looked at me plaintively. I could tell he was tired.

"I was sorry to hear about your mother," he said. "I wanted to come to the funeral but I was out of town."

"It's okay."

"She was an amazing woman."

I nodded.

"And I meant to ask you," he said. "I wasn't quite sure how to put it, but have you seen him at all recently?"

"My father?"

"Yes."

"No," I said and picked up my bag. "Not in close to forty years."

3

After I left David Havelin's apartment that evening, I drove back to my motel room in Huntington Beach and looked over the notes that I'd taken during our lunch. Most of them were inscrutable and vague, fragments of thoughts, partially written sentences that trailed off into chicken scratch, names without context. There was only one name that I'd even bothered to highlight with a star, that I'd underlined twice.

Deryck Evanson.

When David mentioned his name I wasn't at all surprised. I'd been trying to contact Deryck for months—first by email, then by letter, and then finally by phone. He was about as removed from the public sphere as one could be. Though he held a teaching position at Williams, he only taught one class a semester and didn't seem to hold regular office hours. On the info box next to his name on the English Department webpage, it listed only his email address, his office phone number, his teaching interests (Romantic) and his office hours (by appointment). I'd tried his office phone numerous times without luck and had even tried the English Department secretary, who said she rarely saw Dr. Evanson in the office, that he came in only sporadically, and that she wasn't at liberty to hand

out his home number or personal email address. On a whim, I'd
even tried to look up his number in the Williamstown white pages,
but of course it wasn't listed.

So this was Deryck Evanson now. A distinguished professor who
only had to teach one class a semester. A reclusive scholar. An
enigma.

But the Deryck Evanson I'd known back in 1983, when I was
eleven, was a very different type of person. By far the youngest
member of the English Department, a recent hire straight out
of grad school, a Princeton PhD who specialized in Restoration
drama and contemporary film (like my father). A beautiful man
by any superficial measure. A beautiful and oddly athletic man.
Graceful in every sense of the word, a quality not frequently asso-
ciated with English professors. I remember him swimming laps in
my parents' pool, his broad tan shoulders and slim waist, his tight
swimming trunks. My mother used to say he reminded her of Burt
Lancaster in *From Here to Eternity,* or at least I'd overheard her saying that once to Linda Havelin when they were drinking. I think
both of them had secret crushes on Deryck Evanson back then.
I imagine most of the faculty wives did. So young and still single,
they'd chime at cocktail parties, as if they sensed in Deryck Evanson the fulfillment of a broken promise, a path not taken.

I remember the first time I met him myself was at one of my
father's backyard screenings. This would have been about a month
or so after I'd first seen him at David Havelin's tenure celebration,
that infamous party. I believe the movie that night had been *All
About Eve,* and I remember Deryck Evanson mainly because he
seemed to know almost every single line in the movie and because
he'd occasionally shout a few out (in a dramatic voice) to everyone's amusement. He struck me as very brazen and confident for a

new hire and also very funny. I could imagine, even then, that he'd be a very popular professor. That evening was a fairly warm one in early spring—this was during the end of my father's fifth year—and I remember at the end of the night, after most of the guests had left, my father and Deryck Evanson and David Havelin had all walked out to the little flagstone patio at the back of my mother's garden and opened up another bottle of wine and smoked cigarettes and laughed until almost three in the morning. I remember watching them from my bedroom window, through slatted blinds, as I listened to a replay of the top 40 countdown on my radio, and I remember at one point my father stood up and led both Deryck and David around the side of the house to the front yard where they stood for a long time, smoking more cigarettes and laughing more, until finally my father embraced both men, and then David and Deryck took off in their cars and my father came back to the house, shaking his head.

Shortly after that night—maybe a week or so later—I came home one afternoon and found my father and Deryck Evanson sitting out in the cabana house drinking beer. It wasn't unusual for my parents to host their friends out in the cabana house—after all, there was a small fridge and stereo system out there, a couple of cabinets filled with food, some board games, cards, an Atari console—but I'd never seen my father actually host anyone out there in the middle of the day, and especially not on a weekday. But that day, and I believe it was a Wednesday because my mother was off at her clinic that day, I came home and found my father sitting with Deryck Evanson in the cabana house, both of them clad in their bathing suits, drinking cold bottles of Miller Lite and listening to a band I'd later come to know as Fleetwood Mac and an album I'd later come to know as *Rumours*.

I remember standing there in the doorway for almost a full minute before they noticed me. When they did, eventually, they both raised their bottles of beer and smiled, and then motioned for me to come inside, laughing, as they went back to their own conversation. I walked over to one of the bean bag chairs in the corner and lay down, opening up my skateboarding magazine and flipping through the pages as I listened to the woman's voice on the record, lilting and rising, rippling like the dappled sunlight on the white stucco walls of the cabana house. I didn't know a lot about music at the time, but I could tell that this woman's voice was special: raspy and deep and strangely hypnotic. *Velvety* was the word I'd think of later, the way it seemed to calm me almost immediately, as if it were speaking to me from some old familiar space, a soft room, a cave. *And have you any dreams you'd like to sell, dreams of loneliness, like a heartbeat drives you mad.* Outside the window, the wind blew lightly in the trees, and I leaned back on the beanbag chair and closed my eyes, drifting off. When the record finally ended, Deryck Evanson stood up and turned it over to the other side and started it again. Then he looked over at me, and perhaps sensing my interest, smiled.

"You like this, Steven?" he said.

I told him I did.

Later, when I went back to the house, I found my mother standing in the kitchen, folding laundry at the kitchen table and smoking a cigarette. On the table beside her was an ashtray that was nearly full.

"Where have you been?" she asked.

I told her I'd been outside with my father and Deryck Evanson and she nodded.

"Do you need my help?" I asked.

She shook her head.

"I could take these to your bedroom," I said, nodding at the pile of neatly folded khakis that I knew belonged to my father.

She shook her head again. "How's Chau's mother?" she asked.

"Better," I said.

She put down her cigarette as she folded a white blouse at the other end of the table. My best friend Chau's mother had been undergoing cancer treatment at St. Jude's, two rounds of chemo in the past six months. I didn't know what this meant at the time, didn't understand that this treatment wouldn't automatically make her better, but I could tell from my mother's expression that she was concerned.

"I ran into her at the hospital last week," she said. Then she smiled. "She said you have a good appetite."

I shrugged, feeling suddenly embarrassed.

"I told her you hardly eat anything I make."

I looked out the window where I could see my father and Deryck Evanson emerging from the cabana house. My father was fully dressed now, and so was Deryck Evanson, which seemed strange.

"Do you like Stevie Nicks?" I said to my mother.

"The singer?"

"Yeah."

"I saw her in concert once. This was when we first got here."

"I don't remember that."

"Your father and I used to go to shows a lot back then. It was all new to us—being able to see so many of the bands we'd only ever heard on the radio."

"You should have taken me," I said.

My mother smiled then, and shook her head, but as soon as she saw my father coming up the path from the pool, her eyes darkened and her smile disappeared. I could see him with Deryck Evanson at the edge of the patio, and then the two of them talking.

"So what was she like?" I said to my mother.

"Who?" she said. She was staring out the window at my father and I could see she was distracted.

"Stevie Nicks."

"Oh," she said after a moment, still looking out the window. "Beautiful, of course."

"And what else?"

"What else?"

"Yes."

In the distance I could see my father putting his hand on Deryck Evanson's shoulder and Deryck Evanson nodding. And then the two of them started to laugh, laugh at something Deryck Evanson had said. My mother turned away from the window then and looked back at me, her eyes steady.

"Fearless," she said. "She was totally fearless."

That summer. 1983.

I can't explain what happened to me those afternoons I sat out in the cabana house with my father and Deryck Evanson, listening to Stevie Nicks sing "Landslide" and "Gold Dust Woman" and "Dreams." In a few years from then, I'd be deeply immersed in West Coast punk rock—Suicidal Tendencies, Dead Kennedys, Black Flag. I'd pretend I'd never heard of Fleetwood Mac or, other times, I'd laugh at kids who liked them. I'd disavow any allegiance I'd once felt toward them. But those afternoons when I was eleven and the weather was always nice, always eighty degrees and breezy, I felt there was nothing in the world as transcendent as Stevie Nicks's voice, and nothing more intoxicating than sitting out by the pool as the sun went down at the far end of our yard, behind the palm trees, the silver glint of sunlight on the water, and the sound of Stevie Nicks's voice in the distance rising, singing, *Rock on, Gold Dust Woman. Take your silver spoon, dig your grave.*

Later, I'd get into their other albums—*Tusk, Mirage,* even some of the early albums before Lindsey Buckingham and Stevie Nicks joined the band, but that summer was all about *Rumours,* and later the self-titled album, but mostly *Rumours.* I'd never encountered an album so perfect, and yet so strange and somehow incomplete. There seemed to be all sorts of hidden messages behind the words of the songs, almost as if you were reading someone's diary, and it reminded me of the messages my father wrote to himself in the margins of his books, the cryptic scribblings that I still didn't understand. Like my father's marginalia, *Rumours* proved to be an inscrutable text and that's one of the reasons I liked it so much. It seemed the more times I listened to it, the more I noticed and the less I understood.

Once I asked my father and Deryck Evanson about it, and they both just laughed.

"It's just a rock album," my father said, "albeit a very good rock album, but it's still just a rock album."

We were all sitting out by the pool, our feet dangling in the tepid water.

"There's actually a lot of subtext there," Deryck said, smiling, "but Steven might be a bit young for that." He winked.

"I know they were all *doing* it," I said. "Everybody does."

My father scrunched his eyebrows at me, and then laughed. "Since when do you talk that way?"

"I read about it in *Rolling Stone,*" I said, as if I were quoting the Bible.

"Where do you read *Rolling Stone* anyway?"

"In the library at St. Agnes. They have all of the back issues from like the last two years in the periodical room."

My father rubbed his chin, and scrunched his eyes again, as if he himself had never been inside the periodical room, which, for all I knew, he hadn't.

Then my father asked me what else I read in the periodical room, and I gave him the list: *Interview, Variety, The Village Voice, Spin, Billboard,* and of course *Thrasher.*

"What's *Thrasher*?" he said.

"It's a skateboard magazine," I said.

"They actually have a skateboarding magazine in the periodical room?"

I shrugged.

"What's the academy coming to?" my father laughed, turning to Deryck Evanson.

Deryck Evanson sipped his drink, a blue-colored drink that he'd been drinking all afternoon.

"To progress," he said, raising his glass.

Inside the house, my mother was making something Mediterranean, something with lots of garlic and basil, and I could smell it drifting out through the open window above the kitchen sink. From time to time you could see a small slice of my mother's face in the window or her eyes looking out at us skeptically, but otherwise there was no sign of her at all. As always, she was both there and not there.

"Deryck's staying for dinner," my father said. "And after that I'm having a few friends over. Would you like to ask Chau to spend the night?"

I shook my head.

In the distance, from inside the cabana house, I could hear Stevie Nicks singing something about rulers making bad lovers.

A moment later, my mother opened the back door and stuck her head out. "Dinner's almost ready," she said.

Deryck Evanson flashed his winning smile and put up his thumb.

"Smells great," he said.

.　.　.

That night at dinner, my father and Deryck Evanson talked about the films of Rainer Werner Fassbinder and Louis Malle and then later about department politics, how they were having a hard time introducing a new minor in Film Studies that they'd designed that spring, how there was a lot of resistance from the old guard in the department, many of whom felt that Film Studies was not a legitimate academic field. Both had been told by their chair, Albert Doyle, that they were hired primarily to teach literature, not film, and that they were welcome to offer the occasional seminar or summer elective, but an entire minor in film was simply out of the question.

I can't remember too much about the conversation, only that the more they drank, the more outraged they became, even Deryck, who was typically mild and diplomatic, and that eventually my mother made a signal for me to come help her in the kitchen. As my father and Deryck Evanson complained in the other room, I helped my mother stack the dishwasher and wipe down the counters. She'd said almost nothing the entire meal and now looked weary.

When we'd finished, she leaned down and kissed me on top of the head. "It's Friday night," she said. "You can watch TV with me in our room if you'd like."

"Can we watch *Love Boat?*"

"Sure."

"And make popcorn?"

"We'll see."

"How about *Fantasy Island?*"

"Don't push it," she said and pinched me on my side.

Most of the time my parents entertained together, but every once in a while my father would have a group of just his friends, mostly other male professors from St. Agnes, and my mother and I would hang out in my parents' room watching TV or playing cards.

The guys that came over were usually the same group of familiar faces: David Havelin, Joseph Alors, Ed Bindley, Russell Briggs, and so on (all humanists and all big drinkers), but that night a group of men I didn't recognize showed up. All very young. These were friends of Deryck Evanson's, I assumed, and they didn't seem like academics at all. Instead of sitting around the outside table, drinking wine and debating the great mysteries of the world, these guys immediately stripped down to their bathing suits and jumped in the pool and then later disappeared into the cabana house where they proceeded to blast music on my parents' stereo and laugh uproariously.

At one point, after my mother had fallen asleep, I went out to the kitchen and watched them through the big window above the sink. They were all wearing tight swimming suits and dancing on the flagstone patio beside the pool, even my father and Deryck Evanson, who seemed suddenly youthful, as young as the college students they both taught. There must have been about eight or nine of them out there that night, all of them very drunk and clearly enjoying themselves, dancing to music from the recent past—early David Bowie, Elton John, ELO—slip-sliding on the concrete deck, pantomiming to the lyrics. At one point I remember one of the men sliding down his bathing suit and diving naked into the pool, and shortly after that several of the other men, including my father, following. Before long, everyone was naked in the water, laughing and splashing and pushing each other around. I'm surprised not one of our neighbors woke up and complained, that no one even seemed to notice.

As an adult, of course, the image of that night would hold a very different type of meaning for me, but at the time I simply chalked it up to another one of my father's wild nights, a version of many other nights that had preceded it, nights that had simply gotten a little out of hand, and after a while I went back to my mother's room and fell asleep in the bed beside her, pulling the covers up to my chin, listening to the shouting and splashing outside the window until eventually it stopped.

When I woke up the next morning, my father and Deryck Evanson were already gone. They'd slept in the cabana house, my mother explained over breakfast, and had left to take an early run at the track on campus. Still, she said, Deryck had left me something, a gift. She slid a small bag across the table to me. Inside was a cassette tape of *Rumours* and attached to it was a little note written in Deryck's elegant hand:

> *From one Stevie fan to another.*
> *Thought you might like this.*
> *—D*

I speared one of my Eggo waffles with a fork and dipped it in the syrup on the side of my plate. Then I opened up the cassette case to see if there was anything else inside, maybe a secret note, but there wasn't.

"What is it?" my mother said.

I showed her the tape. "*Rumours,*" I said.

She nodded and then smiled weakly. In the morning light, she looked suddenly much older.

"Can I go to the beach?" I said.

"With who?"

"With no one," I said. "Just me."

"Finish your waffles first," she said, and then she stood up and walked over to the sink, and it was only then, as she stood there in the bright morning light, that I realized she'd been crying.

. . .

It took about forty minutes to get to the beach from our house on the express bus, but that day the bus was moving at a slightly faster clip than usual, skipping some of the regular stops, the sun-drenched streets of Fullerton passing by in a silent blur, the few other passengers behind me looking down at their paperbacks or newspapers, their magazines, everything quiet as we sped down Harbor Boulevard, and then later down Euclid, sailing at a fast speed until eventually we pulled up close to Huntington Beach and the coastal roadway, and I could see the waves of the Pacific Ocean in the distance, glinting in the sun.

There were about ten to twelve surfers out there in the water that day, and as I got off the bus I could see them bobbing in silhouette, waving their arms at some people on the beach. I stopped at the edge of the esplanade and watched them. To my left was the parking lot where all the surfers parked their vans, and to the right there was a sandwich shop that was famous for its BLTs and its milkshakes, and farther down the esplanade there was a little break in the fence where you could find the sandy path down to the beach. This was the path that all the surfers used and it was the path I always used whenever I came to the beach. I put on my sunglasses, pulled out my hat, and started down the narrow path, the sage bushes scratching my arms and legs as I pushed downward, the surfers in the distance finally taking a wave, or at least some of them, and the kids from the high school coming into view, a whole group of them huddled under a beach umbrella that they'd just put up. Someone was playing an acoustic guitar, an older kid, and I could hear a few of the kids singing "Give a Little Bit" by Supertramp.

I opened up my backpack and took out my Walkman and slid in *Rumours*. Then I walked over to an empty patch of beach and sat down in the sand, leaning back on my elbows and looking out at the Pacific Ocean, rough and raging under a clear summer sky.

I thought about my father and Deryck Evanson and the scene from the night before, all of those men's bodies, tanned and naked and glistening from the pool water. If I had known the word *erotic* at the time, that's the word I would have used.

And, as I sat there that morning on the beach, looking out at the surfers, listening to Stevie singing the opening lines to "Dreams," I thought again about the first time I'd heard her voice and the way that Deryck Evanson had smiled at me and said, "You like this, Steven?"

And I remember later asking him what her name was.

"The singer?" he'd said.

"Yes."

"She actually has the same name as you."

"Steven?"

"Stevie."

"That's a boy's name," I said.

He smiled again and shrugged and then held up the photo on the back of the album of the entire group, a black-and-white photo with Stevie standing in the middle in a silky dress with her beautiful mane of feathered hair, her big eyes, her full lips. She was easily the most beautiful woman I'd ever seen. Deryck pointed at her face and smiled.

"Does she look like a boy to you?" he'd laughed.

Then he turned to my father, who had opened up the blinds and was now looking out the window absently, staring vacantly at the pool.

"Boys," my father said without turning around, "girls. What do those words even mean anymore?"

Deryck turned to me then and held up his hands, as if in apology, or embarrassment, for my father's strangeness.

"We've been drinking beer in here for a long time, Steven," he said, looking down at his watch, then shrugging.

"That's true," my father said, turning around. "Why don't we switch to wine?"

That day, when I got home from the beach, I found my mother sitting at the kitchen table, flipping through a magazine and smoking. If it was possible, she looked even more run-down than she'd looked that morning and again I noticed the puffiness around her eyes, the redness at the edges.

I poured myself a glass of water and sat down across from her.

I asked her where my father was and she motioned toward the cabana house.

"He's going to be staying out there for a while," she said.

"What do you mean?"

"He needs to focus on his scholarship this summer," she said, "his articles. It's important for his job."

Even at eleven, I understood the phrase *publish or perish*—it had been a recurring theme at the dinner table ever since my father had taken his first position in Pennsylvania—but something in my mother's tone, or perhaps her eyes, told me that this was different. She said a little bit more about how he needed to concentrate for long stretches of time this summer and how he wasn't able to do that when we were around, but all I could think about was the image of him dancing half-naked on the flagstone patio the night before. Was this the way he concentrated?

I stood up and walked over to the window and peeked out. I could see a light on in the cabana house now and two shadows dancing along the walls inside.

"Who's in there with him?" I said.

But my mother didn't answer. She just went back to her magazine and sighed.

4

In a letter my father sent to my mother in November 1971, he
wrote the following:

Dear Maya,

I know that what I wrote to you in my last letter must
have seemed insane. I hope you just tore it up. Truly.
I have no defense for any of it. What I'm coming to
understand is just how little I understand about anything
anymore. I read Proust's journals again this morning and
they seemed so profound but also so desperate. Different
from the last time. What's strange is this. If you actually
look at photos of the original pages, his handwriting is
so fluid but also almost illegible, as if he were writing
only for himself. You get the sense he wrote very easily,
though. And interspersed with the writing are these
surrealistic portraits that seem queerly delicate. I think I
love these the most for some reason. I'm not sure why.

I was thinking about this letter the next morning, the morning after I visited David Havelin, as I drove up the Pacific Coast Highway toward Santa Barbara.

This letter was one of a small group of letters I'd found in my mother's apartment just before she died three years earlier. My father had been consumed by Proust for most of his life, though he never wrote on him and, as far as I know, never taught any of his books in his classes. It was a private obsession, not unlike his private obsession with the films of Howard Hawks and Douglas Sirk.

He always liked to talk about the fact that *Swann's Way* had been self-published—how Proust paid out of pocket for all of it—as if this were some type of evidence of Proust's private belief in his own genius or importance. He also loved the fact that Proust was in love with an Italian chauffeur named Alfredo for many years, though I only found out about this later when I read my father's journals. He never said anything about this when I was growing up. From my perspective, as a young person, my father's obsession with Proust was purely intellectual. He often talked about how *Remembrance of Things Past* was the single greatest piece of literature ever created and how it could be read, in all seven volumes, over the course of one's lifetime and be appreciated in completely different ways at different ages.

At the time he wrote this letter to my mother, though, his mind was not well, at least according to her. He was in his second year of graduate school at Berkeley and had just had what she called his first breakdown. He would have several other breakdowns after that. One in Pennsylvania, one the year after the collapse of his career, and one that fall after I'd first met Deryck Evanson, the fall I was eleven. But this one was his first.

My mother had been living in New Hampshire at the time, in Hanover, which was where she'd met my father when he was an undergrad at Dartmouth and she was a recent dropout from

UNH, working at a restaurant near campus. They had met during the spring of my father's senior year and then dated throughout that summer, all the way until August when my father had to leave for Berkeley. Eventually, in my father's third year, my mother would move out to Berkeley and join him, but those first two years they'd lived apart, on opposite sides of the country, my father in a small apartment on Derby Street, just off Telegraph Avenue, and my mother in her childhood bedroom in her parents' house in Hanover, where she continued to work in the restaurant, much to her parents' chagrin. During the school year, they'd correspond and talk on the phone, and in the summers my father would move back to Hanover for July and August, renting a small apartment not far from the campus, but for the most part, at least during the school year, they lived apart.

According to my mother, my father had seemed troubled during that long summer between his first and second year at Berkeley, overwhelmed by the competitive atmosphere there, and when he eventually returned in late August she could tell he wasn't well. *Erratic* was the word she used when she described him to me later. His breakdown had happened at the beginning of the fall semester his second year, almost immediately after he'd returned, and she'd learned about it initially from his brother, Julian, who had called her in late September to say that my father had been admitted to a hospital in Berkeley. He'd end up spending two weeks in this hospital before eventually checking himself out, and during that whole time he'd continue to write letters to my mother, long, nonsensical letters that frightened her.

Eventually, over time, my father's letters would become more ordinary, more everyday, and by the time my mother finally saw him again, at Christmas, he was basically back to normal, back to his old self, at least according to her. Later, she would tell me that in some ways the fact that she hadn't been there when it happened, the fact she'd only heard about it, rather than seen it, had allowed her to diminish its significance in her mind. It had simply been a momentary setback, she'd told herself, not a worrisome sign of things to come. Not a harbinger or a warning. Not a red flag. It had simply been a case of too much pressure, she'd thought, too much stress. It was something that could have happened to anyone.

Still, all through that fall and winter, my father had written to her about Proust, and over time I think she began to make an association in her mind between my father's obsession with Proust and his mental instability, so much so that whenever my father made reference to *Remembrance of Things Past* when I was growing up, my mother's eyes would dim, her jaw tighten, and I could sense her mind beginning to work.

I remember this happening one evening in late July that summer I was eleven, the summer that Deryck Evanson was over all the time. We had all been sitting around the kitchen table—the three of us and Deryck Evanson—talking about my latest swim meet, and somehow the conversation had shifted from my poor swim times in the 50-meter fly to the concept of time in general, which naturally led to a discussion of Proust and a quoting of passages from *Remembrance of Things Past*. At one point, my father had stood up to get a copy of one of his old editions of *Swann's Way,* and my mother's eyes had dimmed. She'd glared at Deryck Evanson, as if this were somehow all his fault, as if he, and not my father, had brought up Proust; then she'd stood up and walked into the kitchen. When my father returned a short time later, his mind had shifted to something else, to Coleridge, and he was now reading from a long, obscure poem that even Deryck hadn't heard of before. I glanced out toward the sliding glass patio doors in the kitchen, where I could now see Chau sitting on the stucco wall by our flagstone deck, holding his skateboard. My parents always invited Chau to join us for dinner, but he never would, and he'd never come inside either. He said it was something his mother insisted on, though it was never clear why. I waved to him, and he waved back, and then I took the opportunity to excuse myself and head out to see him, passing my mother on the way, my mother, who was not preparing dessert, as she usually would, but sitting at the kitchen table, smoking a cigarette and talking to a friend on the phone.

Outside, Chau winked at me and patted his pocket, then made a smoking motion with his fingers, which meant he'd managed to lift a pack of his older sister's cigarettes. Then he nodded toward the cabana house, which was where we'd usually smoke, out behind it, at least, in a little clearing between two manzanita bushes.

"Tic Tacs," he'd said, patting his pocket, which was our code word for cigarettes, the word we used when we talked about them on the phone. *Do you have any of your sister's Tic Tacs?*

In the clearing, Chau sat down on one of the two metal chairs we'd brought out from our garage earlier that summer. If my parents had ever come back here, they would have surely discovered the piles of cigarette butts we'd kicked under the bushes and ground into the dirt, but they never did. This was our private space. A space where we'd both tried a sip of one of my father's beers earlier that year, where we'd pulled down our bathing suits just to show each other, where we'd kissed innocently one night for no apparent reason then never mentioned it again. And it's where we smoked whenever Chau came over, whenever he'd been successful in lifting one of his sister's packs of cigarettes.

Tonight Chau had managed to steal a full pack, which was rare, and after he'd pulled two out, and we'd both lit them, he looked out over my shoulder at a thin sliver of sky in the distance, a thin sliver of sky you could see through a hole in the manzanita bushes.

Lately, he'd been quieter, more removed, and I knew this was partly related to his mother, who was getting worse, and partly related to his father, who frightened everyone, including me. He rarely mentioned either of his parents, though, not unless I really pressed, which I rarely did.

"Your father still living out here?" he said after a moment, glancing toward the cabana house.

I nodded. "Just till the end of the summer."

Chau drew on his cigarette and squinted.

"Just till he gets his tenure file done," I said.

He tapped the edge of his cigarette and nodded then rubbed his chin as if he was thinking about something. "And then he can't be fired, right? If he gets it?"

"That's what he says."

"Even if he says *fuck you* to his boss."

I shrugged. "I don't think he'd do that. But yeah, I guess."

Chau thinned his lips then, as if he sensed something unjust about this. I knew that his own father had been laid off twice since they'd moved here from Vietnam, that his mother had had trouble keeping work too, that he'd grown up never feeling totally secure about anything.

"Think I can stay here tonight?" he said after a long moment, his head now turned again toward the sky, and I knew he wouldn't be asking me this if he wasn't desperate, if there wasn't something at home he was trying to avoid.

"Yeah, man, totally," I said, and then reached over and patted his arm. "No problem."

My mother was sometimes reluctant to let Chau spend the night because he'd wet the bed in the past, but that night she didn't protest. She seemed too tired to protest anything that night. Instead, she'd made up my trundle for Chau and then brought in the black-and-white TV from my parents' room and made us a snack, peanut butter and apple slices and a small bowl of potato chips. After she left, Chau and I lay in the dark, staring at the soft glow of the TV set, a rerun of *Hogan's Heroes,* neither of us talking. All summer there'd been the looming cloud of middle school hanging over us. Earlier that summer a boy from our class had died in a car accident, his older brother at the wheel, and somehow this had cast a shadow over everything before us. We would be going on to middle school, and he would not. He would always be eleven. I don't know why this occupied our thoughts so much that summer, why we talked about it so incessantly, only that somehow this boy had become intertwined with everything else before us, like an augury, or a shadow life, a path we'd been fortunate to avoid.

That night, though, we didn't talk about the boy or the tragic accident that had taken his life. Instead we just lay there in the darkness, the light from the TV illuminating our faces, our bodies still, our arms just barely touching, our breathing in unison but quiet. I could sense Chau drifting in and out of a light sleep, his eyelids heavy now, his mouth slightly open, but then suddenly he'd look up, as if from a dream, and his eyes would gradually refocus again on the TV, his body readjusting to a more comfortable position, his shoulders relaxing. He did this for a half hour or so and then finally he turned over on his side, away from me, and closed his eyes, drifting off to sleep.

At some point not long after that—I can't remember how late it was—I decided to head out to the kitchen to get a glass of water. The house was quiet that night, my mother asleep down the hall, and in the distance, outside the sliding glass doors, I could see my father sitting on the flagstone deck, sipping a beer and paging through a book, no sign of Deryck Evanson anywhere.

I stood there for a while, watching him, then slid open the sliding glass door and waved. He smiled when he noticed me and then beckoned me over.

"*La Prisonnière,*" he said, patting the cover of his book, as I sat down on one of the small metal chairs beside him. "Volume five. The Captive." He grinned then knowingly, as if he were making an inside joke, and I realized he was reading Proust.

He lay the book down on the patio table and closed the cover. "What are you doing up so late?" he said, reaching for his cigarettes.

"Can't sleep," I said.

He nodded. "Me neither. We're alike in that way." He leaned forward to light his cigarette with his lighter. "And I hate to tell you, it doesn't get any better as you get older."

I nodded.

"The insomnia."

"Right."

"But one of the nice things about it," he said, leaning back, "is that you get to enjoy this time of night when everyone else is asleep, you know? Most people miss this." He paused then to listen to the silence of the night then smiled at me. "It's nice, right?"

I looked up at the stars and nodded because he was right. It was nice. It was something I'd always felt but never heard another person articulate. There was a stillness in the air right now, the world on mute. In the distance, on the other side of the yard, I could see a faint glow coming from our neighbors' backyard, and before that, the bougainvillea my mother had planted a few years earlier, climbing along the white stucco wall that separated our two properties.

"We can call ourselves the Midnight Ramblers," my father said after a moment. "Okay? You and me." He smiled. "Do you know that song?"

I told him I didn't.

"The Rolling Stones?"

"No."

"Well, never mind, that'll be us, okay? Our own little club, and we won't tell anyone else." Again, he smiled, as if at some private joke, and I could tell he was a little tipsy from the beer. *"Le désir fleurit, la possession flétrit toutes choses."* He was speaking now as if to someone else, but again he raised both eyebrows and grinned widely at me. "Right?"

I nodded.

"You're going to win one of those swim meets by the end of the summer," he said. "And I'm going to get tenure, okay? That's the plan. Don't you think those things are going to happen?"

I nodded.

"Me too," he said and leaned back in his chair. "And then we'll celebrate, okay? We'll go out to Catalina maybe. Just you, me, and your mother."

I smiled, though I knew very little about Catalina Island, only that this was where the actress Natalie Wood had drowned a few years earlier. It seemed like a haunted place, ruined by the residue of that tragedy, not a place to celebrate anything.

"How does she seem to you anyway?" he said after a long pause, "lately?"

"Mom?"

"Yeah."

"I don't know."

"Tired?"

"Yeah," I said. "I guess so."

"Yeah." He nodded again and furrowed his brows.

I looked down at my feet then and he reached out and took my hand and squeezed it, smiled, and just then, over his right shoulder, I noticed a light go on in the cabana house behind us and it startled me. I hadn't realized anyone was back there. I almost said something to my father then, but instead I just sat there, confused, and a moment later I saw the curtain part and Deryck Evanson's worried face looking out. Deryck's chest was bare, his shoulders sunburnt. He looked confused.

He stared at me for an instant, our eyes locked, and then he waved vaguely and closed the curtain.

When I looked back at my father, he was still staring right at me. Had he known what I'd seen?

He smiled at me. "It's going to be a great year, buddy," he said. "Don't you think?"

I nodded.

"Yeah," he said and looked up at the main house again strangely, "me too."

5

On the outskirts of Ojai, just as you're pulling into town on Route 33, there's an unmarked turnoff that leads down into a secluded residential area, hidden among the trees, and it's near the end of this road that my uncle Julian has lived with his wife, Grace, since the late 1980s, long before Ojai became a trendy weekend destination for Hollywood celebrities and wealthy Angelenos. Earlier that day, as I drove along the PCH, the Pacific Ocean vast and choppy to my left, I'd felt a pang of loneliness and regret, a fear that I'd maybe made a mistake by contacting Julian after all these years, but later, pulling into his driveway and parking beneath a canopy of trees, the dappled sunlight reflecting off the glass wall of his large, modern house, a sort of timeless architectural wonder, just as modern-looking now as it had been when I'd first seen it as a teenager, I felt a sudden sense of relief, a realization I was home.

Julian had been out when I arrived. He still owned a bakery in town, a popular hole-in-the-wall that specialized in bread and pastries and that he'd recently expanded to include a wine bar and deli. The wine bar was mostly a labor of love, Grace explained to me later, after she'd greeted me at the door and led me into their kitchen, poured me a large glass of water. He'd opened it primarily to support and showcase the wines of his friends, several of whom were local winemakers in the Santa Ynez Valley, but the cost of the liquor license and the additional staff was canceling out any profits he might have made.

It's just like Julian, she'd said, and I knew what she meant. My uncle had never been practical, had always been one to put others' needs first. A lean, beautiful man, he was selfless to a fault. And yet, he'd still landed here, in this elegant modern home in the charming town of Ojai, a daughter happily married and practicing medicine in Palo Alto, a wife who supported him unconditionally, a solvent business that he loved.

It always seemed to me that Julian had wanted for nothing. Even when he was younger and had actually had nothing, even then it had always seemed like something, the way beautiful people always seem to have more.

Now, at seventy-two, Julian was settling into retirement, or semiretirement, according to Grace.

"Albeit reluctantly," she added with a smile.

She was younger than him by almost a decade, though she might have easily passed for a woman in her late forties. It was amazing how little she'd changed. Her smooth, olive skin, her dark hair pulled back in a bun, everything about her sun-kissed and radiant. Her peasant blouse, a throwback from her hippie youth, a look she still cultivated now. Her wrists still heavy with turquoise bracelets, her fingers lightly calloused from her years as a sculptor. As a teenager, my friends had always teased me about my hot aunt, about my uncle's good fortune, had always asked when she'd be visiting again. Now, in her mid-sixties, she seemed like only a slight variation of the person I'd known in my youth. She still had the same calm, the same warm, benevolent smile. The same placidity.

"They're going to have to pry the bakery away from him," she said. "I don't think he'll ever sell."

I nodded.

The skylight above filled the kitchen with a hazy light. We sat at opposite ends of the dark stone island in the middle of the room, a bowl of oranges between us. There was the promise of dinner a few hours off. Earlier, she'd asked about Alison and Finn, about my job, and I'd been evasive about both. Now it seemed like a subject we were trying to tactfully avoid. As always, Grace knew when and when not to push.

"Why don't you go take a shower," she said, reaching across to touch my hand. "Get some rest. I'll start dinner in about an hour."

Behind her, I could see the trees that surrounded their house, thick with foliage, through the high-windowed walls of their living room. Everything about the house seemed pristine, purposeful. The brown-leather couches, long and angular, the rustic side tables, the original paintings on the walls, Grace's sculptures strategically placed and highlighted, but not in an obvious way. Like everything else, the personal elements of the house were subtle and balanced.

"I could probably use a shower." I nodded. "Maybe a quick nap."

"You know where the guest room is," she said, pointing up the stairs.

"Yeah, next to Zoe's room, right?"

She smiled. "I left you some towels on the bed."

I ended up sleeping through dinner. A thick, dreamless sleep, a slumber that arrived without warning.

When I came downstairs around nine o'clock, contrite and embarrassed, Julian embraced me tightly and said not to worry, that they hadn't wanted to wake me, that I'd looked exhausted. He smelled like flour, and something else, citrus from the gin and tonic he'd left sitting on the island.

"Let me heat something up for you," he said, lifting the lid off a wide, shallow pan, revealing a beautiful paella that Grace must have made earlier.

I turned and apologized to her, but she just smiled and waved me off. "It was nothing," she said. "We would have waited if we'd known you were going to wake, but we weren't sure. What can I get you to drink?"

"Whatever you're having," I said, nodding at the glass of red wine on the island before her. "Whatever's open."

"Everything's open," Julian said, scooping a generous serving of the paella onto a plate, but by then Grace was already pouring the wine.

When she slid the glass across the island, I lifted it and smiled.

"It's so good to see you both," I said.

I clinked glasses with Grace, and then with Julian, who came around from behind, patting my shoulder firmly and then pulling me toward him again, tighter this time.

"It's been too fucking long," he said.

Over the next two hours, while I ate and Julian and Grace continued to drink, and then as we all sampled various treats from the bakery that Julian had brought home with him—olive bread, brioche, flaky mille-feuilles—Julian talked about my father, his brother, with a candor he'd never used before, almost like he'd been saving it up, collecting it, and was now ready, finally, to release it. I'd sensed an eagerness in his voice when I'd called him earlier that week and told him what I was up to, what I was doing, and now I could hear it again. At first, he talked mostly about their childhood, those idle years in Pennsylvania, their listless youth. I'd heard a lot of this before, from my father. Those long, lazy days out in the summer heat, the rural quiet of the small town where they'd grown up. Middlesex. A town not far from Lancaster, where we'd lived for a short time when I was young, when my father was teaching at Franklin & Marshall College, his first job. At that time, my father had talked about his youth in Pennsylvania nostalgically—or maybe it was later, in California, that he spoke that way—but that hadn't been Julian's recollection at all. *Those were very dark days,* he'd said, *and we were very poor. It's almost unimaginable now.* He spoke about their absent mother, my grandmother, who I'd never met, and their father who was often away for long stretches, disappearing on hunting trips with friends, leaving them alone in the house for days at a time. It had been my father who had made sure they got to school, who'd made their lunches. In many ways, it was my father who had raised him, Julian said. Even though he was only a few years older, he was like a father figure to him, the only source of stability in his life. His compass.

Later, of course, those roles would be reversed, with Julian caring for my father, checking up on him during his bouts of depression, during each of his breaks, moving out to California to be near my mother and me after my father disappeared. During their youth, though, it had been my father who'd kept Julian on course, who'd taught him multiplication, who'd picked him up each day at elementary school and walked him home. If not for my father, Julian doubted he would have made it through junior high, let alone high school or college. He certainly wouldn't be where he was now.

He paused then to sip his drink, and Grace stood up to get some more wine. It was hard for me to reconcile the image of my father that Julian described—this symbol of virtue and responsibility—with the man I remembered.

"He was driven too," Julian said. "His intellect, that he was born with, but he was also incredibly driven back then. And all through college too, even grad school, he was always working longer hours than everyone else, waking up earlier." He looked at me. "I know you don't remember him that way."

"I remember him working," I said. "I mean, on his tenure file, his articles, stuff like that."

"He was a first-rate scholar too," he said. "Not that I know anything about that, but I've been told. He won awards, big fellowships."

"I know."

"And he was railroaded, of course, but you know that." He looked at me. "Is that what you're after?"

Grace came back with the wine and refilled my glass, placing her hand gently on my shoulder as she did, then sitting back down.

"I don't know," I said. "I don't really know what I'm after."

Julian nodded, then smiled at me plaintively. "So what else can I tell you, Steve? What else would you like to know?"

"I don't know," I said. "Everything, I guess."

But Julian didn't tell me everything. It was late by then, and they were both tired, I could tell, so instead he talked mostly about the years after we'd moved to California, the years when my father was sickest.

He said he'd seen the first signs years earlier, when my father was still in college. A late night phone call during my father's senior year, my father weeping softly on the other end, then ranting nonsensically, an episode that my father would blame later on alcohol but that Julian saw differently.

It wasn't drunken ranting, he said. *It was paranoid. Your father was suspicious of someone on his hall, another student.* It was the type of thing that would play out later in different ways, a recurring theme. The idea of surveillance, his phone calls being monitored, intercepted, people listening outside the door. Then in Berkeley it grew worse. I knew some of this, too, from my mother, but Julian elaborated, saying there was much my mother didn't know. During his first year, for example, he'd been arrested twice, both times for shoplifting—first, a pack of cigarettes, then later a scholarly journal from a used bookstore on Telegraph Avenue. *Can you imagine getting arrested for shoplifting a scholarly journal?* Julian laughed. *A back issue no less. It would have cost him less than a dollar, probably less than fifty cents.* It wasn't about that though, obviously, the stealing, and Julian suspected it had been going on for years, maybe since high school.

There were other things too, subtle cracks in the polished veneer, things Julian would only realize later, that he mostly ignored at the time. An erratic decision to drop a class he'd needed to complete his PhD, a fight with his dissertation advisor, several periods when he'd almost dropped out. But still, his mind had always saved him, Julian said. His brilliance. People always forgave him, pushed him through. He'd managed to get a chapter from his dissertation published in one of the leading journals in his field and that had led to the job in Pennsylvania, at Franklin & Marshall. After that, he'd hunkered down and worked, building up his CV, eventually getting the job at St. Agnes.

Julian acknowledged that he was skipping over a lot, but I didn't stop him. I could tell he wanted to talk mostly about California, could sense his voice slowing down as he began to talk about that first year that we lived there, when I was just six. He asked me what I remembered, and I told him not much. Almost nothing from before California, almost nothing from Pennsylvania. All of that was just a blur. He asked me if I remembered the apartment we'd lived in in Huntington Beach when we first moved out here, and I told him I did but only vaguely. I remembered it had been a few blocks from the beach, very small and run-down, the white walls stained yellow in places. We had almost no furniture at the time, almost nothing to cover the stains on the walls, no pictures to hang, only my father's large bookshelf and a box of my toys, mostly Legos. I told him I remembered that the floor was always sandy, how there was often sand in my sheets, making it impossible to sleep, how my mother never cooked, how we always ate out at Carl's Jr. or one of the other hamburger places on our block.

Julian smiled and picked up his drink, dipped his finger in, and stirred the ice cubes, then took a sip. The house felt darker now, the candle-lit table making everything feel intimate. Grace reached across and rubbed Julian's neck, an attempt to soothe him or perhaps to relieve stress. His expression had darkened.

"There was an incident there one night," Julian said. "Do you remember anything about that?"

I shook my head.

"Do you remember why you had to leave?"

I shook my head again.

He looked over at Grace then back at me.

"I don't know how much of this you need to know," he said, "but there was an incident with another tenant one night, an altercation, and your mom called me up in tears. I think she'd taken you to a motel. Anyway, I don't know if charges were filed formally, but that was the beginning. Or, at least, what I've come to think of as the beginning."

"The beginning?"

"Of when we really started to worry. When we really began to worry that he might be a danger to himself or someone else."

I nodded. I told him I had no memory of that at all, which was true, though I realized I might have blocked it out, suppressed it.

I told him that my father had never been violent. Unpredictable yes, but never violent. I'd never seen that.

Julian nodded and looked down, and then said, "I don't know."

"What do you mean?"

"I mean, he could be, growing up. He was with me, boys in his class."

"But never with my mother."

"No." Julian shrugged. "No, I don't think so, no. But there was an erratic aspect to it all that frightened her, I know. She used to talk to me about it."

"She thought he might hurt her?"

"No, no," he said, "but she thought he might hurt himself."

Julian looked over at Grace, and she smiled calmly, her benevolent ease, then sipped on her wine.

"Would you like more food?" she said.

"I'm fine," I said.

Downstairs, I could hear their dog barking, a black and white collie named Sherman, and after a moment Grace stood up to check on him, leaving us alone.

"So what else made you worry?"

"What else?" Julian smiled. "Why everything."

He motioned for me to stand up and follow him out to the small outdoor deck beside the kitchen, telling me to bring along my glass and the bottle of wine.

Once we were outside, Julian lit a cigarette, which surprised me. "Once in a while," he said. "I try to hide it from Grace, but she knows." He opened the pack and handed it to me. It had been almost three years since I'd quit myself, but I found myself taking one without hesitation, leaning forward as Julian lit it.

It was a cool night, the sky clear and filled with stars, a light breeze, the trees surrounding their property swaying lightly. Down below us, I could see their driveway and carport, Grace taking the dog off its leash, disappearing in the darkness without noticing us.

"There's a lot of stuff I haven't told you," Julian said, "and some of it I should probably write down. But it was really that second year when things got bad. Your father was calling me almost every night. You probably weren't aware of that. He had ideas that your mother was being unfaithful to him, which is ridiculous, and later about his colleagues forming secret cabals. He'd developed a paranoia about them early on, almost from the start."

I nodded.

"The thing is, he was right to feel that way. They *were* vicious and duplicitous. They *were* vindictive. At least a lot of them were."

I nodded.

"It just got worse and worse, and then the two things kind of fed off each other. The more paranoid he got, the more erratic he'd act. The more erratic he'd act, the more they'd conspire against him, which of course only fueled his paranoia."

I knew a lot of this, or at least had pieced a lot of it together from conversations I'd had with my mother, but I nodded anyway.

"And then he just stopped caring, I think."

"What do you mean?"

"I mean he fell in love, but you know that." He stared at me evenly.

Just then, Grace reemerged from the darkness, calling us out. "You know I can see you!" she shouted, though there was lightness in her voice, a subtle teasing. She looked up at us from the driveway and shook her finger.

We both stubbed out our cigarettes on the railing and then held up our hands for Grace to see, but she just shook her head and headed inside with the dog.

Julian took the bottle and poured what remained of it into my glass.

"Were there others?" I asked.

"Others?"

"Other men?"

"You mean, besides Deryck?"

"Yes."

"Of course."

"Before?"

"Before," he said, "and after. Yes. There were always men in your father's life. But I don't know that he'd ever been in love before. Not before Deryck."

"And since?"

Julian sighed. "Well, that's a longer conversation, Steve, but no, I don't think he's been in love with anyone since."

Later that night, as I lay in bed, still a little tipsy from the wine, I felt a strange and sudden longing for the past. All of those memories of coming up here in my youth, on summer holidays and long weekends, first with my mother and then later alone, Julian stepping in seamlessly for my father, assuming that role, filling the space that he'd left behind. Up until now I hadn't realized how lonely I was, how lost. The softness of these sheets, the familiarity of the guest room. Everything felt right, like returning to an old childhood haunt or discovering a book you'd once loved but forgotten. And it didn't hurt that Julian and Grace hadn't changed a bit, that they'd remained untouched by time, as if they'd been frozen here all along, while I'd been off getting married and raising a child and living my life.

Earlier, as we'd sat around their dining room table, Grace long since asleep, Julian had talked rhapsodically about my father, about his kindness and his gentleness, about his general goodness, as if wanting to make up for all of the things he'd said earlier, balance them out. He talked about how sweet he'd been to my mother during their early years, how generous and doting, how much he adored her; and how much he cherished me, how lucky he felt to have a son, how his biggest fear in life was that I'd one day end up like him, that I'd somehow inherit his affliction, his curse.

"You're right to resent him," he said. "You're more than justified. But I just want you to know there were other sides to him too."

The candles on the dining room table were flickering, the flames low. In the dark room, Julian suddenly seemed old.

"I don't hate him," I said, but that was all.

And Julian reached then for the wine bottle, our last of the night, but I waved him off.

"It's late," I said.

And Julian nodded and then placed the bottle back where it was. The room was quiet and very still. A silence fell between us.

"You're right," Julian said finally. "It's late." He looked over at the wall, then back at me. "We can talk about this some more in the morning."

6

At the beginning of August that summer—that summer I was eleven—I remember there being a series of very hot days, a kind of minor heat wave, including one day when the temperatures topped off in the triple digits, the heat refusing to burn off, even at night. We didn't have air-conditioning at the time—you rarely needed it in southern California—but I remember one day my father went out and came back with a trunk full of electric fans of various sizes and shapes. Large box fans, small oscillating fans, fans that you could adjust to different angles and heights. Standing at the kitchen sink, my mother and I watched him through the kitchen window as he carried several of these fans into the cabana house, where he was still living, and others into the main house, placing one in almost every room. I could tell from my mother's expression that this was an expense we couldn't afford, an impulsive extravagance, but she didn't say a word. She just thinned her lips and ran her hand along the edge of the counter, searching for her cigarettes, her eyes still set on my father.

Later that day, she took Chau and me to the movies, a momentary respite from the heat, and when we returned I remember finding my father floating on a raft in the middle of the pool, a cold can of Miller Lite balanced on his flat stomach, his eyes obscured behind his Ray-Bans. My mother shepherded Chau and me into the kitchen, as if wanting to protect us from seeing something, then went back out to the pool to talk to him, squatting down beside the edge and saying something to him as he continued to float there, motionless, obviously discouraged and disheartened.

Earlier that day, before he'd gone out to buy the fans, I'd overheard him talking to my mother about the fact that the university press that had promised to publish his first book was now beginning to get cold feet, or at least it seemed that way to him. The two of them were sitting in the kitchen, and I was lying in my bed down the hall, but I could hear the desperate lilt of my father's voice and could tell that this was serious. They were demanding rewrites, he said, when before they'd said everything looked fine. They also claimed that one of the reports from an outside reader, an anonymous professor at another university, had recommended against publication, so they would need to approach a third reader. For some reason, this last fact seemed to trouble my father the most. He seemed incredulous that someone could recommend against publication given the fact that most of the individual chapters in his book had already been published as separate articles in top journals in his field. I didn't know what any of this meant at the time, but I did understand the significance of this book, how it represented a kind of protective shield against the people my father believed were conspiring against him in his department. As long as he had this book, he believed, they couldn't touch him. They couldn't deny him tenure.

Later, he'd begun to speculate about why this might be happening and who might be trying to sabotage him. Had someone from his department called the editor at the press? Had David Havelin leaked it? Eventually, frustrated by the heat, he'd gone out to buy the fans, claiming that he'd just need to work harder now, though it was clear the fans hadn't helped, that a part of him had given in to the sweltering heat, the innumerable forces working against him.

Chau and I watched my parents for a bit and then headed down the hallway to my room. I could tell that Chau was disappointed by the fact that we wouldn't be able to use the pool now, something that I'd promised him on the way home. Instead, we sat on the floor of my bedroom, both of us sweating in front of the small fan that my father had brought in earlier that day, listening to "Crazy on You" by Heart and then later to the tape of *Rumours* that Deryck Evanson had given me. I had managed to convert Chau into a Fleetwood Mac fan too, though he wasn't as fanatical about Stevie Nicks as I was. He told me that he thought she was a little "witchy" and that his older sister had told him that she might actually be one. That day, though, we both sat hypnotized by her voice in the still heat of my bedroom, the hazy afternoon sunlight making us drowsy, saturating the room with warmth.

At one point Chau stood up and suggested we cool off in the shower down the hall. It wouldn't be as good as the pool, he said, but at least it would be better than this. We could wear our bathing suits, he said, turn the shower valve all the way to the coldest setting.

I was hesitant at first but eventually I stood up and followed him down the hallway to the bathroom. Once inside, he peeled off his T-shirt and then locked the door behind us. I watched him turn the water to the coldest setting then kick off his flip-flops. He was wearing a pair of Ocean Pacific surfer shorts, like me, and after a moment he stepped into the shower and let out a loud yelp, *too cold, too cold,* he shouted, and then he danced around a bit, as he adjusted the valve to the right level of coldness. *Come on,* he said, reaching out and grabbing my arm, pulling me into the narrow tub, the cool water like a shock to my skin, but a pleasant one, and then both of us laughing, jockeying for position, slipping on the slick surface of the tub, almost falling out, and then laughing again. And I have to admit, it felt good, better than good, the cold water on my skin, Chau's arms wrapped around my chest, both of us laughing, a kind of horseplay, and then later, working up a lather with the bar of Zest, placing the suds on each other's chins, making soapy beards, mustaches, talking like Obi-Wan Kenobi, *Use The Force, Luke,* then rinsing ourselves off and doing it again. At several points I remember feeling relieved that my parents weren't inside and that Chau had locked the door, though I couldn't say why, only that it somehow felt like something they shouldn't see or know about, and later, as we lay on the floor of my bedroom, both of us still wet from the shower, I remembered the way that Chau's hand had brushed against the front of my bathing suit several times and the jolt it had given me, the way I'd enjoyed it.

Now, lying supine on our backs, the late afternoon sunlight beginning to fade, the room growing darker, I felt an awkwardness settling in, forming between us, a mutual embarrassment about what had happened in the shower perhaps, but also, strangely, a closeness. I reached over and turned down the volume on the stereo, and when I looked back at Chau his eyes were closed. I lay back down next to him and closed my eyes as well. I thought about my father and Deryck Evanson dancing with those men on the flagstone patio deck and suddenly felt ashamed. Then I felt myself beginning to relax, my limbs growing heavy, drifting off slowly into sleep.

When I woke up several hours later, the room was dark and Chau was gone. I lay there for a while on the floor, trying to process where I was. It was still hot, the air thick with it, and I could feel a dampness in my hair at the back of my head. After a while, I wandered down the hallway to the kitchen to make myself some dinner. Earlier that day, my mother had stocked up the pantry with cereal, so I stood at the counter next to the sink, eating a bowl of Cap'n Crunch in the dark and watching my parents through the kitchen window, as they sat in lawn chairs down by the pool, watching a black-and-white movie that my father had projected up onto the side of the cabana house. The volume on the projector was low, too low to hear very much, but I could still tell from the visuals, from the close-ups of Ingrid Bergman and Cary Grant, that it was Alfred Hitchcock's *Notorious,* a favorite of my father's and a film that I'd watched with my parents several times before.

In earlier days, I would have probably gone down and joined them, snuggled in between them, but I was so pleased by the sight of them sitting together, my mother's head resting on my father's shoulder, their bodies pressed together, that I just stood there, watching them, not wanting to disturb them or jinx what was happening.

At one point, my father stood up to get them some more beers from the cabana house, and when he returned he leaned down slowly and kissed my mother on the lips, a soft, gentle kiss, placing the bottles down on the grass beside them, then cupping her face in his hands. Even now, years later, I can still picture that moment, the two of them frozen in silhouette, the bright silver light from the screen, my mother's hand reaching up and gripping my father's shoulder tightly, the images of Cary Grant and Ingrid Bergman hovering above.

Later that night, they'd ended up stumbling into the house drunkenly, knocking over a table lamp in the kitchen as they made their way clumsily toward their bedroom, laughing and shushing each other, telling the other to be quiet, that they didn't want to wake me, but then giggling again, finally finding the door to their room and pushing through.

In my younger years, I used to find moments like this frightening, moments when my parents seemed out of control, but that night it filled me with a strange warmth, a comfort. The knowledge that they were sleeping in the same bed together again, that Deryck Evanson was nowhere in sight. It was one of the last moments I could remember feeling hopeful about their marriage.

The next morning my father would wake and begin working feverishly on a new project, a new book proposal that he planned to submit to a new press. He'd be in a panic, the beginning of a lengthy manic phase, one that would last for several days, but for that evening, at least, he seemed back to his old self. Not depressed, but not manic-y either. My mother had managed to calm him down and reel him back in (a couple of beers and a film noir, that was it), and now I could hear them through the walls of my room, giggling like teenagers. My father saying something theatrical, my mother trying not to laugh, but ultimately losing it, falling into convulsions. The two of them rolling around on top of the sheets, knocking things over. That mirth. It wasn't always there, but when it was it was palpable. Contagious. And I remember lying there in my bed, not bothered by the noise at all, but actually enjoying it, wanting to fall into it, the way one wants to fall into a memory or a dream or a song, the way you want to believe this momentary feeling is a deeper truth, a path that you can choose, rather than a fleeting kind of bliss, a film that might end.

After a while, the laughter died down, and the hall became silent, the only sound coming from the numerous fans whirring in the distance, in every room in the house, a kind of mesmerizing hum, like the voices of a chorus or the communal buzz of a swarm.

I got up after a while and walked down the hallway to their room. I stood outside their door and listened—listening for what, I'm not sure, only that I know it made me happy to be there, standing in the darkness outside their room, listening for their voices, their laughter, any sign that they were still in there and that life as I'd once known it might one day return to normal.

7

When I woke the next morning, I had to take a moment to orient myself and remember where I was, to put together the simple facts of the case. That I'd come to Julian and Grace's house. That I was sleeping in their guest room. That I'd drunk way too much wine the night before. That I could now feel the beginnings of a hangover coming on, that subtle throbbing that would only increase if I didn't find a glass of water and some aspirin.

Downstairs I could hear the rumble of the coffee grinder, the faint sound of public radio, Julian's and Grace's voices. I could smell the sweet doughy scent of something baking, the buttery aroma of eggs. I sat up in bed and surveyed the room, adjusted my focus. I wondered if I could feign fatigue and pretend to sleep in, maybe let them take off for work, then slip away without notice, with a polite note or a generous thank-you.

All of my nostalgia from the night before had dissipated, replaced now by something else, a low-level dread.

After a while, I got up and went down the hall to take a shower. Like every other room in the house, the upstairs bathroom was elegant and modern, minimalist but not cold. A swath of sunlight from the skylight above touched the edge of the floor, tiny white hand towels sat folded in a woven basket to the left of the sink. In one of the cabinets below, I found a bottle of aspirin and shook a few out.

In the shower, I felt revitalized, the throbbing in my head beginning to subside, the alcoholic residue of the night before beginning to wash off, the fresh eucalyptus scent of the shampoo, the water falling down from above like a soft rain. I found myself recalling the events of the previous night, Julian's rhapsodic musings about my father and, before that, his darker memories of their early days and our first few years in California. All of it had seemed theatrical in retrospect, a staged performance that he'd been preparing for days, in advance of my arrival. Like David Havelin, he'd wanted to cast my father in a certain light, I realized now, a light that made him seem both perpetrator and victim, but that really provided no insight into who he truly was. Maybe, like me, Julian was too plagued by guilt to imagine my father accurately. He'd carried it his whole life, after all, that guilt, from the moment my father first became sick to the moment he abandoned us, and even now he still carried it, the way he'd insisted I stay a few more days, maybe even a week, the way he still insisted now, in memory, that he and Grace had moved out here at Grace's suggestion, not because my mother and I needed him, not because my father had abandoned us. Poor Julian. Sweet, generous Julian. Even at his most honest, his most well-meaning, he was still too burdened by the past to be of much help.

Later that morning, after I'd heard Grace step out the back door and take off in her car, I headed downstairs and found Julian sitting alone at the kitchen island. He was seated at the far end of the room, near the large windows, and when he saw me, he beckoned me over to the stool in front of him. He had set out a plate of brioche and freshly baked rolls; some poached eggs and strawberries. The eggs were cold, I could tell, but I took one of the brioches and placed it on my plate.

"I don't want to make you late for work," I said.

"I'm the boss," Julian said, smiling. "When you're the boss, lateness can be a relative thing."

He reached over then for the French press and poured me a tall cup.

From the windows that ran the length of the far side of the room, you could see small patches of blue sky through the tall, leafy trees surrounding the house, and then, below that, the edge of the dirt driveway that disappeared up into the woods. I had forgotten how beautiful and peaceful this house was, especially in the mornings. The entire downstairs was imbued with a cool, calming light; everything perfectly quiet. Julian sat up on his stool and adjusted his shirt.

"How are you feeling?" he said, smiling.

"Better now," I said, picking up my coffee and then taking a sip.

"Grace was sad to miss you," he said.

I nodded.

"I was thinking maybe we could meet up with her later in town. I was hoping to show you the new additions to the bakery."

I looked down then, avoiding his eyes, and sipped my coffee.

"Or if you need to get on the road," he added.

"I probably should," I said, still not meeting his eyes, and though I wasn't looking at him, I could sense his disappointment.

After a moment, he stood up to get some orange juice from the fridge, and when he returned we sat there for a while in awkward silence, Julian pouring us both a glass, then placing the container down in front of me. I looked out the window then back at Julian, who was now staring at me in a more concerned, expectant way.

"I don't want to pry," he said finally, picking up his glass, "and

I know it's none of my business, Steve, but I did notice that you didn't mention them once last night."

"Who?"

He stared at me knowingly, and I looked down at my brioche and broke off a piece.

"And Grace noticed that you weren't wearing your ring."

I looked at him, then back at my plate. "And you're wondering why."

"Yes."

I nodded and sipped my coffee. "We're taking a break," I said finally.

"What does that mean?"

"I don't know."

"You're getting a divorce?"

"No," I said. "I mean, yes, possibly."

At this, Julian sat up, more concerned. "When did this happen?"

I could feel his eyes on me and suddenly felt ashamed, embarrassed, as I had in my youth whenever I'd disappointed my father. There was a part of my father in Julian, a very small part, but it was there.

"A couple of months ago," I said finally.

Julian nodded and picked up his cup. "And where are you living now?"

"Right now," I said, "nowhere." I smiled at him and motioned around the room, trying to make light of it. "Nowhere and everywhere, as they say."

But Julian wasn't amused.

"I have a lead on an apartment in Oakland, though," I said in an effort to appease. "Rent-controlled."

Julian nodded again and ran his hand up and down his legs. "And your stuff?"

"Still at the old place mostly. Alison and Finn are still there."

He picked up his cup, and I could sense again the profound disappointment in his face, or maybe that was just my own projection. Either way, it was a stronger reaction than I'd expected, a graver concern. I often forgot how much Julian still thought of me as a son, himself as a surrogate for my father. It had been many years since I'd thought of him that way myself.

"It's all very undecided," I said vaguely, again wanting to appease him, assuage his concerns, but he just sat there quietly. "As I said, we're just taking a break."

Julian let out a breath and nodded. "It's just a lot," he said.

"I know."

"A lot to process."

"Yes."

I could tell he had wanted to say more, that he had more he wanted to ask me on the subject, but I held up my hand in anticipation of his next question. "We can talk about this some more another time, okay?"

He nodded and pushed his brioche around his plate. For a while, he sat there again in silence. I told him that I was going to go upstairs and get my stuff and that we could maybe then have one more cigarette before I left.

"A cigarette," he said, shaken from his daze, surprised. "Oh no, I really have corrupted you, haven't I?"

"No, no," I said. "We had one last night. Remember?"

"I know. It's just—"

And I realized then that he'd never known that I'd smoked, a thought that both touched and saddened me.

"It's okay," I said, smiling, "we don't have to. And for the record, you could never corrupt me, Uncle Jules. That would be impossible."

. . .

Upstairs in the guest room, I packed my bag and checked my messages, but there was nothing, as usual. No voicemails from Alison, no texts. Just a few unanswered emails from friends and former colleagues in the Bay Area, all of which I ignored. In the past two months, any attempt to contact me had felt like a personal affront, a violation of my privacy, though I knew that these emails were all well intended, their subject headings filled with sympathy and concern. *Just heard,* read one. *Worried about you, friend,* read another. I closed my phone and looked out the window where I already saw Julian in the driveway, talking to someone on the phone with concern—probably Grace—and pacing. I waved to him, trying to catch his eye, but I could tell from his agitated movements, his accelerated gait, that he was too distracted to even notice.

When I finally got downstairs a short time later, Julian was sitting on a bench near the carport and motioned me over. He was already smoking, his legs crossed, his timeless, beautiful face looking up.

"You decided to smoke," I said.

He nodded sheepishly. "You promise I'm not corrupting you."

"Never," I said and took the pack from his outstretched hand.

"I know you don't want to talk about it anymore," he said, "but I just wanted to say that you're always welcome to stay here, Steve, and you can always stay as long as you like. You know that, right?"

"I do."

"Good," he said, and patted my hand. "Then I won't say anything more about it."

I lit my cigarette and stood beside him for a while, a silence forming between us.

"There's one other thing I wanted to tell you," he said finally.

"Okay."

He adjusted his body on the bench, as if bracing himself, then drew on his cigarette and glanced around. He was oddly quiet for a moment and I worried that he might have something terrible to tell me, but after a while he just put out his cigarette on the ground and regarded me, his watchful eyes set on mine.

"He called me," he said softly. "It was probably about five years ago now, but he did call."

"My father."

"Yes."

I sat there for a moment, processing this.

"Did he say where he was living?"

"Nope," he said. "But I sensed it was out here. On the West Coast. He mentioned Oregon a couple times."

"Did you tell my mother?"

"No, no," he said, "he was very clear about not wanting me to do that. He didn't want either of you to know he'd called."

I nodded and then just sat there calmly, processing it. Prior to this, the last known contact anyone I knew had had with my father was ten years earlier, when he'd called my mother out of the blue during one of his manic states and suggested a confab between the two of them, a conversation that had rattled my mother so much that she hadn't mentioned it to me for months. She was finally beginning to date again by then, had moved on in certain ways in her life; I think a part of her had even convinced herself he was dead.

"I'm guessing you didn't get a number for him," I said.

"No." Julian shook his head. "He showed up on my phone as an unknown caller. When I tried to call back, I just got a tone."

I nodded.

"I'm sorry I didn't tell you earlier."

"It's okay."

"I think I thought I was protecting you or something, that you wouldn't want to know."

"I probably wouldn't have before," I said and looked up at the house, the massive windows reflecting the sunlight, the large trees, and the cloudless sky above. "Did he say why he was calling you?"

"No," Julian shook his head, "not really. And we didn't talk for very long. Maybe about ten or fifteen minutes. I think he was probably just lonely."

I nodded. "And he sounded okay?"

"He did," he said. "You know, he sounded like himself. Like he was in a good place." He adjusted his shirt. "It was kind of strange, though. He mostly wanted to talk about our childhood, our parents, stuff like that. I'm not really sure why." He reached for his cigarettes again but then stopped himself. I could tell he could see I wanted more. "And he said that he missed you, of course. Both you and your mother. I could tell he missed you both a great deal."

I nodded. "Just not enough to call us, though."

"Right." Julian shrugged, then his eyes slid to the ground, the old guilt returning.

Earlier that week, when I'd called him to tell him what I was doing, why I'd be visiting, he'd asked me very seriously why I'd never bothered to hire a private investigator to find my father, if I really wanted to find him, if I really wanted to understand what had happened to him, and I'd told him then what I'd told Alison and what I'd also told David Havelin: that if my father had gone to so much trouble to hide himself that I needed to hire a private investigator to find him, then he probably didn't want to be found. This trip, I'd told him, wasn't about that; it was about something else. I just didn't know what.

At the time, he hadn't pressed me on this issue, but now I could see his concern returning, and later, as he walked me to my car, then stood outside the driver's side door, looking down, reluctant to say goodbye, he asked me again what I was doing.

"What do you mean?"

"I mean, all of this," he said motioning at my car, the backseat stuffed with books and bags of clothing, the front seat covered with fast-food wrappers, greasy napkins. "What's this all about, Steve?"

Later, on the road, I'd find myself thinking a lot about the people in my life and the way they'd all seemed to know so clearly what they wanted—my father at the height of his academic promise, his steadfast devotion to his scholarship and his students, Alison and her commitment to the innumerable political causes she supported and championed, her public policy work and her advocacy for the underrepresented, even Julian and the way he'd devoted his life to bread and baking, the way he'd realized early on in life what he'd wanted to do and then followed that passion, studying first at a series of boulangeries in Paris and then returning home and working his way up through the ranks, paying his dues at a number of renowned bakeries in Philadelphia before moving out to California and starting his own. He'd never lost his love for it, he'd told me calmly the night before, the tactile nature of the work, the flavors and aromas. He'd never lost his love for any of it.

I'd always admired people like my father and Julian and Alison because I'd never had anything like that myself. I'd never had that kind of purpose. Instead, I'd always felt like I was hiding in a bunker, avoiding shrapnel, or chasing phantom memories and dreams. Half the time I hardly felt there at all, like I'd been hollowed out, abandoned. Like I had become the residue of another person's life.

These weren't things that I could explain to Julian, though, so instead I just started up my car and put on my sunglasses and smiled at him. I told him I'd be in touch soon. Then I said, "In answer to your question, though, I really don't know what any of this is about, Uncle Jules." Then I reached out and took his hand, squeezed it tightly. "I wish that I did."

Part
2

8

When I think back on that summer now, that summer I was eleven, it comes to me mostly in images. Little pieces of memory or random fragments. I see my father sitting out in the cabana house alone, working assiduously on the files for his tenure case; I see my mother crouched down in the garden, weeding beneath her hydrangea bushes, her sunglasses perched atop her head, a thin line of sweat sliding down her brow, and always in the background I see Deryck Evanson, showing up in the late afternoon with a six-pack of beer or a bottle of wine, sometimes a group of his friends, always younger men, always handsome and fit, their stomachs astonishingly flat. I see them shepherding my father back into the cabana house, putting on music, mixing drinks. I see my mother retreating into her bedroom, turning on the television, closing the door.

These are the things that I see, but what's harder for me to remember now is the exact sequence of these events, the precise chronology of them. All I know is that the blur of that summer gradually hit a crescendo in early August with the heat wave and my parents' brief reunion, and then eventually tapered off into a quietness and a soberness, the semester starting up for my father, and the school year starting up for me. I can still remember now the way that my father sequestered himself during that time, hiding inside the cabana house, not to be disturbed by anyone for any reason, not unless there was an emergency of some sort or a phone call from his publisher.

Most of the time, my mother and I took great measures to keep out of his way, staying inside the house, doing quiet things, like reading, or going out for meals by ourselves, taking walks along the beach in the early evenings, spending Saturday afternoons at the mall. I could tell that my mother was annoyed, that once again my father's career was taking center stage, but at the same time she was very patient about it all. I think on some level she understood that this was the home stretch, that, after this, things would eventually go back to normal.

I remember one afternoon in late September—this was shortly after the summer swim season had ended and my afternoons were once again free—my mother picked me up after school and drove us down to the beach. My father's tenure file was officially due in a few weeks and he had requested that we spend some time away from the house so that he could concentrate on finishing up and organizing everything. My father had an office at school, of course, but he chose not to use it, claiming that he could never be entirely sure who else might have access to it, who else might have a key. This was perhaps an early glimpse into the type of paranoid thinking that would only increase as the fall semester went on, but at the time I didn't think very much about it. For better or worse, that stucco cabana house had become my father's new home. It was where he worked on his tenure file; it was where he planned for his classes; and it was where he hung out in the late evenings with Deryck Evanson and whoever else Deryck Evanson had decided to bring along. As my mother put it that day, as we sat down at a small picnic table beside the beach, looking out at the

Pacific Ocean, that stucco cabana house had become my father's private sanctuary, his cave.

"Maybe when all of this is over, though," she said, "he'll come back home."

She winked at me and squeezed my arm.

It felt good to be close to her. Lately we'd been distant with each other. Even that afternoon, we'd argued over the fact that she hadn't bought me a Swatch watch, as she'd promised earlier that summer. Everyone at my middle school seemed to have a Swatch watch, even Chau's older sister had one, but my mother claimed it was too great an extravagance at such a precarious time in our lives. I didn't understand what the word *precarious* meant, but I understood that she was referring to my father and the uncertainty of his future at St. Agnes. She'd said that if all went well, she'd buy me three Swatch watches in the spring, but right now we had to be cautious. I'd finally nodded and relented because I could tell how much it pained her to have to say this, to deny me.

Now, though, squinting out at the late afternoon sunlight on the waves of the ocean, she seemed different, lost. She could be up or down lately, and it could come on suddenly, without warning. In the distance, at the far end of the beach, I could see a group of girls laying out large beach towels, their bodies silhouetted against the silver waves, dwarfed by the cliffs just behind them.

"I know this must all seem very strange to you," she said finally, "what your father's going through."

I shrugged and looked down at my feet.

"I'm sure it is," she continued. "But the thing is, if we get through it, if we come out clean on the other side, things will be much different for us. Our lives. Everything will be different."

I nodded. I'd heard versions of this type of promise for years, and it no longer rang true to me. I no longer believed that my father would be magically transformed by some arbitrary promotion, that job security for life would suddenly reshape him into the type of father who spent Saturday afternoons planning family outings or watching my swim meets. I no longer believed this particular myth, and something in my mother's voice that day told me she no longer believed it either.

She put her arm around me then and pulled me close to her. She was still wearing her medical scrubs from work and her hair smelled of cigarettes.

Earlier, she'd asked me what I thought of her new hairstyle. It was different—highlighted and feathered in the style of some of the older girls at the high school—and I'd told her it looked nice, though it made me sad in a way too. I could tell she'd done this for my father, made this change. An attempt to win back his attention perhaps, to make herself look younger. Now, up close, I could feel the chemical crispiness of her highlights against my cheek, and closed my eyes.

"If there's anything you want to ask me," she said softly, squeezing my shoulder, "you know that you can, right?"

I nodded.

"Is there anything?"

I paused, and then, without looking at her, keeping my eyes steady on the ocean, I surprised myself by asking her why Deryck Evanson was always over at our house, why he didn't ever seem to go home.

I'd expected her to be taken aback by my tone, my implication, but she wasn't. It was almost as if she'd been expecting me to ask this question for a while.

"Your father and Deryck are close friends," she began, "and Deryck is helping your father out." I could tell she was searching for a way to explain things. "You know, when two people have been together for a long time, like your father and I, they sometimes need to take breaks from each other, spend time with other friends."

I nodded.

"In any event, he's only here until the end of the spring. That's when his contract runs out."

"Then he'll be leaving?"

"Yes."

Somehow it comforted me to know this, to know that there would be an end date on Deryck Evanson's presence in our life.

"Do you not like him or something?"

I shrugged. "I don't know."

"He can be a little snobby, right?" She smiled at me in a con-spiratorial way, and it made me feel good to know that we were aligned against him.

"Yeah, totally."

"And long-winded."

"Yes."

We both laughed at this, and my mother pulled me close to her again.

"Well, like I said, he won't be with us forever." And maybe this was the story she'd been telling herself too, the way she'd managed to compartmentalize it. That he wouldn't be around forever. "You know, some people come into your life for a short time," she said, staring out at the ocean, the sunlight glinting on the water, "and then just like that—" She waved her hand above her head wildly. "Just like that, they're gone."

On the way home that day, I asked my mother if she could drop me off at Chau's place, a small apartment just north of our house, a seven- or eight-minute walk by foot. Chau's parents used to live closer to the water, in Huntington Beach, but they'd had to move inland when Chau's father lost his job and then they'd moved again to a smaller place when his mother got sick and had to stop work-ing. His father worked at the docks in Long Beach now, a company called Old Dominion Freight Line, and he was there in the mornings and usually in the evenings too, working two or three different shifts, and then sleeping in between for five or six hours. It was because of this that I knew he'd be gone by the time my mother dropped me off—I always went out of my way to avoid him—and that it would just be Chau and his sister, and of course his mother, his mother who usually stayed in her room these days, sleeping or watching TV, or sometimes reading. She'd gone into remission toward the end of the spring—there was a brief window of hope— but now the cancer was back and more aggressive this time. The last few times I'd been over she'd looked gaunt and very pale, her movements slow and labored as she tried to move around from one room to another. Chau and his sister mostly ignored her, their eyes locked on the TV screen as their mother shuffled around from one room to the next, their minds frozen in a kind of willful denial. Whenever their mother eventually passed, they knew it would be just the two of them and their father, and this was a reality they couldn't quite face.

That day, when Chau greeted me at the door, the apartment was darker than usual, quieter. There was a funereal mood in the room, his sister sitting with one of her friends on the couch, solemnly, Chau whispering for me to come in. At the far end of the living room I could see that the hallway leading to their mother's bedroom was dark, her bedroom door closed. On the radio there was a light Vietnamese song playing, something balmy and sweet. Sunlight came through a window in the kitchen and there was the smell of fish sauce and incense. When Chau led me in, he motioned for me to sit down on a small chair across from his sister and his sister's friend, and then he disappeared down the hallway to his room.

I had come over under the pretense of wanting to see his new skateboard—his father, in a rare splurge, had bought him one of the new Christian Hosoi Sims boards—but mostly I'd just wanted to see him. Ever since middle school had started, we'd been in separate orbits. Chau was in the gifted and talented program, which ran on a completely different schedule than the rest of us. I'd see him heading out for lunch, just as I was heading in. We'd wave to each other vaguely across the quad, and then I'd see him slip into a crowd of older boys, their hands slapping his shoulder and mussing his hair with a strange familiarity.

Meanwhile, I'd met no one new, kept mostly to myself, often ate alone. I'd see kids from my old elementary school and sometimes wave at them but they barely seemed to recognize me. They'd stare back at me with a kind of dreamy fascination, as if trying to remember who I was.

It was not unlike the way that Chau's sister, Mai, and her friend, Lien, were staring at me now. I had never met Lien before—Chau had simply introduced her briefly when I arrived—but I could tell that she was an older girl, like Mai, a junior probably, and also, like Mai, very beautiful. If I were a little older, I would have probably been intimidated by these girls, but I could tell they didn't take me seriously, that they regarded me as a child, harmless.

After a moment, Mai picked up a small bowl pipe from the table and lit it. I looked down the hallway where their mother was asleep, or lying in bed, behind closed doors, then back at Mai, but she didn't seem concerned. Her eyes were set on mine now, as she ran the lighter back and forth above the bowl, the tongue of the flame sliding down the dark sides, then passed it to Lien, who did the same. It was only then that I realized how stoned they both were. What I'd taken initially for a kind of quiet aloofness was actually just vacancy. Absence.

Lien stared at me flatly, then motioned for me to come over as she held out the pipe. I looked over at Mai, who nodded in approval, as if to say, *it's okay,* then slid in closer to Lien. I had never smoked pot before, but I'd seen my parents do it dozens of times and knew what to do. I crossed the room slowly, then crouched down in front of Lien, as she leaned forward on the couch and held the pipe to my lips, running the flame above it, as I inhaled deeply, and then started to cough, almost violently, a deep-throated cough that sent both the girls into hysterics.

"You need to let it out slowly," Lien said in an older sister type of way, and then she placed the pipe back on my lips, and this time it went better.

After I exhaled, I looked over at the hallway again, and now I could see Chau standing there, staring at us.

"What the fuck?" he said to Mai, and then he said something else, something scolding, in Vietnamese.

Mai said something back to him in Vietnamese, and then they both looked down the hall at their mother's room and sighed.

After a moment, Chau walked over to the window in the living room and opened it up, fanning the smoke outside; then he walked over to the pipe on the table and, to my surprise, picked it up and took a long hit, exhaling extravagantly, as if this were something he did every day.

"Come on," he beckoned, motioning for me to follow, and then he turned around and started down the hallway toward his bedroom, "there's something I want to show you."

The rest of that evening blurs together now in my mind.

I know that I ended up staying longer than I'd initially planned, that Mai and Lien ordered pizza at one point and brought it into us as we were lying on Chau's bed, listening to music, and that Chau and I later took turns trying out tricks on his new Christian Hosoi skateboard, doing kickflips and ollies and heelflips on the shag carpet of his bedroom. At some point after that, I remember Chau motioning for me to come join him on his bed and then the two of us lying there, flipping through a stack of his old *Thrasher* magazines, sharing insights, the world still feeling a little surreal, the afterburn of the pot still lingering, a heaviness that filled my entire body, a dullness. There was the sound of New Wave music coming from down the hall in Mai's bedroom, and then Chau was sitting up and peeling off his T-shirt, claiming to be hot, then nodding for me to do the same, reaching over to actually help me pull mine off. Then we were both lying side by side, our bare shoulders touching, still flipping through the magazines, though it was different now, I could feel the closeness of Chau's face to mine, could feel him breathing. And then at one point it seemed he'd closed his eyes, just slightly, as if he'd gone to sleep, and I could feel his head dip into my chest and then move up a bit higher, his face pressed now against my shoulder, his chin resting on my collarbone. I could sense the softness of his stomach against my own, could feel his pelvis pressing gently into mine. And then at one point I could feel his lips on my shoulder, just lightly, a kind of kiss, though his eyes were closed, as if he were asleep and this was all just an accident. I didn't move toward him, but I didn't move away from him either. Instead, I just lay there, staring up at his walls, his walls which were covered with posters of his skateboarding heroes: Christian Hosoi, Tony Alva, Stacy Peralta. I stared at these posters and tried to concentrate on my own breathing, tried not to think about what was happening or what his lips were doing, though it all felt good, better than I was willing to admit. Down the hallway I could hear the music getting softer now, almost inaudible, a slow, languid drumbeat that seemed to mix with the haziness of my thoughts and mirror the slow rhythm of our own breathing. At some point shortly after that, I heard Mai shout out, and then the music go off in her room, and then I must have drifted off because the next thing I remember is Chau shaking me awake, telling me to get up, to put on my shirt, his voice urgent and stern.

His bedroom was dark now, and I could see that it was dark

outside too. I stood up and put on my shirt and then followed him out to the main room, which was also dark now, lit only by a small table lamp and a few candles, and then I turned and looked down the hallway where I noticed Mai sitting outside her mother's door, holding her knees close to her chest and weeping, saying *ma, please ma,* imploring her mother to open the door, but there was no sound from inside the room. I stood there for a moment, just watching her, her voice getting quieter.

"She's really stoned," Chau whispered, and then he put his hand on my shoulder and led me to the door. "You should go now."

I looked at him for a long moment. "What about—" I began, but then I stopped myself because I realized I had no idea what I wanted to say.

"I'll see you in school," he continued, patting my shoulder once more.

"Okay," I finally nodded, and then I started down the staircase to the parking lot and out into the night.

It was a warm night, the sky a deep navy, the streetlights illuminating the quiet backstreets, casting the palm trees in silhouette. I still felt drowsy from the pot, the world a little off-kilter, my movements thick and slow. Everything around me seemed to be moving at half-speed, dreamlike, and I wondered how much of what had happened that evening had really happened, how much I'd remember the next day.

Later, as I turned onto our street, I noticed that all of the lights in our living room were off, that ours was the only house on the street that wasn't lit up, that it almost looked abandoned, and I remember having a premonition then, a sense that something was off, and later still, as I approached our front lawn and started up the front walk, noticing that the front door was slightly ajar, that no one had bothered to close it, I remember feeling a growing dread, or perhaps it was fear.

As I passed through the doorway, I could hear the sound of Frank Sinatra in the kitchen, a staticky crooning, the radio dial set to the oldies station, and I knew that my mother was in there. I paused for a moment outside the kitchen entrance, and then I went in, ready with my excuses, though I really couldn't remember how late it was or how long I'd been over at Chau's. In the end, though, it didn't matter anyway, as my mother just looked up at me absently and drew on her cigarette, her face sallow in the dim light of the kitchen, her skin blotchy, her eyes puffy from crying, and I could tell that something was wrong, that something serious had happened. I stood there for a while longer, just looking at her, waiting for her to speak, but she didn't.

"I'm sorry I'm late," I said finally, wanting to break the silence, but she just shrugged and waved me away. Then she drew on her cigarette again and put it out in the small plastic ashtray. She seemed like she wanted me to leave. After a short time, she looked back at me.

"Your father's gone," she said quietly.

"What do you mean?"

"I mean, he's been asked to leave."

I stared at her. "By who?"

She sat up in her chair then and rubbed her arm. "By me," she said and reached for her cigarettes again, though she didn't open them.

"What happened?" I said, but I think I knew already what had happened, or what must have happened, that my mother must have seen something she wasn't supposed to see, something that could no longer be ignored or denied by either of them. My father must have been careless or must not have been expecting her when she came home.

"When's he coming back?"

But my mother didn't answer. She was shut off now, something that only happened to her when she was truly angry. She thinned her lips, and I suddenly wanted to do something for her, comfort her.

I walked up closer to her then and sat down at the table.

"Can I sleep with you tonight?" I asked, and it came out naturally, instinctually, though it must have seemed strange to her then, as I hadn't asked to sleep in my parents' bed since I was eight, maybe younger.

Still, she didn't miss a beat, didn't hesitate for a second. She just nodded and took my hand and then squeezed my fingers so hard it almost hurt.

"Of course," she said, and then she pulled me in closer to her and smoothed my hair. "And you don't have to worry," she said after a while, smiling.

"What do you mean?"

"I mean, you don't have to worry," she said again, touching my arm. "You're not going to be anything like him, Steven. You're nothing like him at all."

9

In the weeks that followed that night, not a whole lot about our lives really changed. My mother and I continued to live at home, following our regular routine, and my father continued to live wherever it was he was living, doing whatever it was he was doing. I assumed at the time that he was living with Deryck Evanson—I'd sensed, even then, that that's what this was about—but I'd find out later on that he'd actually moved into a motel room by the beach and that he was living there alone.

From what my mother had told me, my father had somehow managed to turn in his tenure file on time and he was also somehow continuing to meet his responsibilities at St. Agnes: teaching his classes, serving on committees, meeting with his students during office hours. Lying in bed at night, I'd sometimes imagine him living this secret life, this phantom life, away from us, sitting over cheeseburgers in his motel room, planning his classes in his car, coming home at night and sitting by himself at the motel pool, smoking cigarettes and drinking beer. For all I knew, his life was nothing like this, but that's what I imagined, and it made me feel bad for him, as much as I resented him. It made me feel bad for him, and it made me miss him.

I never mentioned any of this to my mother, though, and she said very little about my father herself, only that he was doing well, that I shouldn't worry about him, and that they were just taking a little time on their own to work some things out. The way my mother explained it to me felt very open-ended. There was no set timeline involved. No fixed date when my father might return. But at the same time, it was clear that the door on their marriage wasn't completely closed. They were simply in a state of limbo, a trial separation. Once or twice, I'd overheard my mother talking to my father late at night on the phone, her voice stern and admonishing, as she sat at the kitchen table in the dark, smoking cigarettes and drinking iced tea. Later, I'd hear her go down the hallway to her room and turn on her little black-and-white TV, a practiced ritual meant to stave off loneliness, to fill the absence my father had left in our lives. At the time, I don't think she realized that I could hear her crying behind the muffled laughter of *The Tonight Show,* and from what I remember she cried almost every night.

Sometimes, when it was really bad, I'd creep down the hallway and knock quietly on her door, ask to come in, feigning insomnia or pretending I'd had a bad dream. I'd ask if I could sleep with her, and she'd always let me, my presence immediately calming her. Other times, though, when I didn't have the emotional resolve to do this, I'd turn on my stereo—I was heavily into *Mirage* at this point—and listen to Stevie singing "Gypsy," or my new favorite song, "That's Alright"—her voice sliding into a country-ish twang as she sang, *I don't know why I always trusted, Sometimes I think I must have, I must have been crazy.* Leaning back on my mattress, I'd close my eyes or turn off the lights, sometimes just lying there in my bed watching the red LED on my stereo pulsing in the dark to Mick Fleetwood's drum beat, the blue light from the swimming pool outside slipping through my slatted blinds, the ethereal warmth of Stevie's rich harmonies filling up the room.

Later, if I really couldn't sleep, I'd sometimes wander down the hall to the other end, to my father's study, which was still filled with books, marked-up manuscript pages strewn across his desk, tattered notebooks filled with his cryptic scribblings. I'd recall what he'd said about our common affliction—insomnia—and how it didn't get any better over time. Then I'd turn, as always, to his books, pulling random ones off the shelves and searching through their pages for revealing marginalia, little notes that might provide me some insight into my father's inner world, little clues that might explain why someone like my father, someone who seemingly had everything, would go to such lengths to destroy those things he had and to hurt the people who loved him. I'd often sit there for an hour or longer, just glancing through those random books, or sifting through his journals, but rarely did I find more than an occasional reference to my mother or me, a mention of dinner plans perhaps, or a small reminder about the start time of my upcoming swim meet, little cues and prompts that were meant to remind him of us, but that quickly got swept up and abandoned among the more serious ideas of his scholarship, like tiny flickers in a vast universe, beacons from another life that were there and then forgotten.

It was sometime shortly after this—I'm not sure of the exact day, maybe sometime in mid-October—that my father showed up at our door one morning in blue jeans and a madras shirt and announced that he wanted to take me out for the day. I was sitting in the family room at the time, watching Saturday morning cartoons and eating cereal, but I could hear his voice in the distance, as he spoke to my mother at the front door, pleading his case. I hadn't heard his voice in a long time, and it was both strange and comforting to hear it. My mother was resistant at first. I heard her saying something about how he couldn't just show up like this, out of the blue, how he needed to call first, but then their voices lowered, and a short time after that I heard my mother calling my name, telling me to go get my shoes on, that my father was here to see me.

I slid on my Vans and turned off the TV, and then I ran out to the hallway where I saw my father standing in the entrance to our house wearing his Ray-Bans and holding two cherry Slurpees from 7-Eleven.

"Hey," he said, grinning. "How would you like to go down to Newport Beach?"

I glanced at my mother, who gave me a nod of approval, then turned back to my father and smiled. I told him I'd love that.

In my memory of my childhood, I have few memories of days like this, days when my father set aside the entire morning and afternoon just for me. Days when it was just the two of us doing something special. Even now, I'm not entirely sure what prompted it. Maybe a sense of guilt. Or maybe it came at the suggestion of my mother. Maybe this was one of the things he needed to do to gain back her trust, to earn her forgiveness. Whatever the reason, I still remember that day now with a genuine fondness. Cruising down the 405 in the early morning sunlight, listening to The Eagles and Tom Petty as we pulled into Newport Beach, the sky a perfect cloudless blue, the air crisp but still warm, a light breeze. I remember my father driving us down past Costa Mesa then out to the Balboa Peninsula, where he parked in a random parking lot then led me up toward the boardwalk and the low-tech amusement park, the classic Ferris wheel and the penny arcade. It was busy that day, crowds of teenagers and families spilling out into the restaurants and cheap souvenir shops, their shoulders sunburnt, their eyes hidden behind mirrored sunglasses, their bodies glistening and slick with coconut-scented suntan lotion. To the east was the water and farther off, just beyond that, Balboa Island, a short ferry trip across the channel, but that day the crowds were all on the boardwalk, young children begging their parents for paper tickets for the rides, teenagers jockeying for position at the funnel cake stands, everything lively and fun, as if this were suddenly the middle of summer, and not just a random Saturday in October.

As for my father, he seemed to regard it all with a quiet bemusement, a faint smile on his face. This was not his natural habitat, after all, but dressed in his flip-flops and Ray-Bans, he didn't look out of place. At times, he even seemed to be enjoying himself, glancing around as if waiting to be amazed. At one point I remember him reaching down and putting his arm around me, pulling me close to him, and throughout the day I remember him being gentle with me, squeezing my shoulder, mussing my hair. It seemed as if he was trying to reassert himself in some way, to reclaim a closeness that had never really existed. Still, I was at a point in my life when I still looked up to my father, when I enjoyed being seen with him in public, when I luxuriated in the idea of us being together, and I didn't mind these subtle overtures of warmth. If anything, I saw them as a hopeful sign of things to come. My allegiance would always be with my mother, of course, but there was something that happened in my father's presence, especially when he was being affectionate with me, that was hard to describe. It was like he had this power to suddenly make me forget everything that had happened before, everything but the moment we were in, and it was intoxicating in a way that made me feel guilty and traitorous, especially when I thought of my mother, waiting for us at home.

And that day, of course, my father was particularly generous and loving. There was nothing I wanted I couldn't have. No ride that I couldn't go on; no treat he wouldn't buy me. He had brought along a thick wallet of bills, and he handed them out to me liberally, almost without thinking, never asking for change. At one point we ended up in the penny arcade where they still had all of the traditional favorites—air hockey and Skee-Ball and bowling machines—but where they also now had full-size video game machines—Galaga and Asteroids and Donkey Kong—and I remember my father standing there that day, feeding five-dollar bills into the change machine and bringing me quarters, watching over my shoulder as I went for the high score on Asteroids and later, my new personal favorite, Tron.

We must have spent an hour or more in the penny arcade that day, but my father didn't show the slightest impatience. He simply stood there, patting my shoulder, egging me on, bringing me fresh stacks of quarters, and holding my Coke. Later, after I'd finally exhausted myself, we took the ferry across the channel to Balboa Island, where we walked around for a while, dipping in and out of souvenir shops, then finally stopping for lunch at a pizza place on the main street. My father had been unusually quiet that day, mostly just smiling and making light jokes, but over lunch he talked more earnestly about missing my mother and me, not going into detail but simply saying he'd like to come home. I told him I'd like him to come home too, and he smiled then and reached across the table and squeezed my hand.

Later, on the ferry ride back to the peninsula, he asked me to close my eyes, and then I felt his hand on my wrist, squeezing it slightly and tightening something around it.

"Don't open them yet," he said, and squeezed my wrist again, and I started laughing then.

"I'm serious," he said, "no peeking."

"I'm not," I said, and laughed again. And then I finally did open them, unable to wait any longer, and when I did, I saw the Swatch watch I'd been begging my mother for all summer, the exact color and style, red straps with a black lug, a white face and black hands, exactly like the one I'd pointed out to her in the store in the mall, and I wondered then how he'd known this, how he'd figured it out.

"I heard you wanted one of these," he said, his hair blowing in the wind, both of us bouncing up and down in our seats as the ferry pushed across the channel.

I could have hugged him then, could have kissed him right on the lips, but instead I just nodded and smiled.

"How did you know I wanted this one?" I said, though I was already thinking about my mother and how hurt she'd be when I got home, when she saw what my father had bought me. Already just wearing it felt like a betrayal.

"Who knows?" my father said. "Just a lucky guess, I suppose." Then he lowered his Ray-Bans and winked at me mysteriously.

"Aren't they expensive?" I said. "I mean, I thought they were too much."

But my father was turned away from me now, looking out at the choppy waves, the shore of the peninsula as it approached. "They're not too bad," he said. "And besides I don't want you worrying about that stuff anymore. From now on, we're not going to be worrying about money. Okay?"

He turned to me then and lowered his Ray-Bans again, and I felt strangely comforted.

I nodded.

"And I don't think we need to say anything about this to your mother. Do you?"

I shook my head no. Then I looked out at the peninsula myself, the late afternoon sunlight glinting off the water, the Ferris wheel and the boardwalk coming into sharper focus, the sounds of the amusement park reasserting itself, everything on that side of the channel, on the mainland, getting bigger.

10

For the rest of that month, and part of the next, I kept my promise to my father and didn't say a word about the watch to my mother. I did this partly out of a sense of loyalty to him and partly out of a sense of guilt. Just the thought of wearing that watch around the house felt like a betrayal of some sort, a breach of some kind of tacit understanding between my mother and me, an unspoken agreement that we were both aligned in solidarity against my father, that we were on the same team.

In the late afternoons, when I got home from school, I'd immediately go into my room and hide the watch underneath my pillow, or in between the mattresses of my bed, then I'd head out to the kitchen and begin making myself dinner. My mother was working double shifts at the hospital at that point—usually a shift in the morning, and then another in the late afternoon—and by the time she got home from work she was usually too tired to do much more than sit on the couch and watch TV, sometimes nursing a whiskey sour or sipping on a glass of wine. I'd often sit down beside her and try to talk to her, but she rarely wanted to talk. Mostly she just wanted to be still, it seemed, to be still and do nothing. Later, long after she'd gone to bed, I'd sometimes call up Chau, and we'd commiserate about our mothers, about how they both seemed to be slipping away from us, about how we were both powerless to do anything about this. These weren't the exact words that we used, of course, but that seemed to be the subtext of those conversations. Chau would complain about his father and Mai and how they never seemed to be home anymore, and I'd complain about the fact that my mother barely seemed to eat anymore, that she basically subsisted on a diet of black coffee and cigarettes.

Later, before we hung up, we'd always make plans to see each other soon, but somehow these plans never panned out. Something always came up. I knew that Chau was starting to spend a lot more time with his new friends in the gifted and talented program after school, and I also knew that he had to be home in the evenings to care for his mother, that his father had started working later at night, that Mai was now always over at her new boyfriend's. We never talked about that last time we'd seen each other either— that kiss that I thought he might have placed on my shoulder— but sometimes it still seemed to be there, floating between us, an unspoken intimacy that perhaps never happened.

One night, as I was sitting in the dim light of our kitchen, the phone cord wrapped around my arm, I remember him talking about being worried that Mai might run off with her new boyfriend and what this would do to their mother.

I reminded him that Mai was sixteen, a high school student, but he didn't seem reassured. He said that she'd been saying some crazy shit lately.

"She's too young to get married," I said.

"I know," he said, "but I'm not talking about married. I'm talking about vanishing."

"You really think she would?"

He was quiet for a while. Then he said, "I think she might."

Later, after we'd said good night, I wandered outside to the pool deck where I found my mother sitting beside the side of the pool reading. I hadn't noticed her slip outside earlier and realized she must have gone through the side door in my parents' bedroom, a door she almost never used. Suddenly it occurred to me that she might have overheard me on the phone earlier with Chau, the things I'd said about her.

It was a warm night that night, a warm night for early November, a little windy, the palm trees hitting against the side of the cabana house. When I approached, she looked up at me from behind her paperback and smiled flatly.

"So you think I'm depressed," she said, putting down her book. I walked up to her. "I didn't say that."

"It's okay," she said. "Sit down." She motioned toward the other chair in front of her. "You're probably right anyway."

I sat down at the patio table and looked at her.

"But it's okay to be sad sometimes," she said. "And it's okay to let yourself be sad when you're really sad, you know? You should never feel that you have to hide it, okay?"

I nodded.

"Have you been feeling sad?"

"A little," I said. "Sometimes."

She rubbed at her legs. "Well, of course you have," she said. "I'm sure you miss your father."

I looked up at the palm trees to avoid her eyes. "Do you think he'll be coming back?" I said.

She was quiet for a long time. Then she said, "It's possible." She straightened her back. "We've been talking a little."

I took it as a good sign that they'd been talking, though I wondered when this was. I hadn't seen my father since the day he'd taken me to Newport Beach and hadn't heard my mother talking to him on the phone for weeks. I wondered if they'd been meeting up somewhere, if he'd been stopping by her work.

"He might be coming by a few afternoons next week," she added. "Just to work in his study. I told him I thought that might be okay. I'll probably be gone when he does, but just so you know."

I nodded.

"Is that okay with you?"

I told her it was.

"Okay," she said. "Like I said, we'll just see what happens, all right? Take it slow."

I nodded again.

Later that night, as I lay in bed, I remember reaching under my pillow for my Swatch watch and finding it gone. It was a strange sensation, feeling the absence of it, and I remember growing panicked. Without turning on the lights, I lifted up the mattress and patted underneath, then searched around the bed covers, but it was nowhere. Later, as I sat on the floor of my room, trying to retrace my steps, I remembered that my bed had been neatly made when I first came in and realized that my mother must have found it while I was talking on the phone with Chau earlier, that she must have found it and then taken it, and now the only way to get it back from her would be for me to acknowledge my betrayal, which was never going to happen.

Years later, I'd recognize this as a brilliant move on my mother's part, a way of reminding me of whose team I was on, but at the time it simply felt crushing, crushing and devastating, a sobering disappointment that would follow me all the way through school the next day and all the way home from school, all the way until the moment I walked back into my bedroom the following afternoon and found sitting on my pillow a brand-new Swatch watch, the exact same model my father had bought me, only brand-new, just sitting there, locked in its clear plastic case.

I stood there for a long time, just staring at the watch, and then finally I picked it up and put it in my desk drawer and then I walked out to the kitchen and made myself dinner.

In the days that followed, my father stopped by the house several times in the late afternoon to work in his study, but I can't remember him ever staying very long, and I can't remember him talking to me very much during these visits. Mostly he'd just sit in his study, glancing through his books or jotting down notes, sometimes talking on the phone, the phone cord stretching across the hallway and under his door.

Later, when he came out, he'd sometimes stop by my room and peek in, ask me how my classes were going or inquire about my swim times, even though the summer swim season had ended months ago and the winter one had yet to begin. He'd just stand there, his shoulder pressed against the door frame, his eyes glancing around the room as if surveying a foreign territory. I could tell, even then, that he was different, that he was no longer the same carefree person who had taken me down to Newport Beach the month before, that he was distracted by something now, preoccupied.

I remember one afternoon, in particular, when he seemed especially bad. This was toward the end of November, right before Thanksgiving, and I remember him talking on the phone that day with David Havelin, complaining about a group of their mutual colleagues in English who he believed were conspiring against him—*ambushing* him was I think the word he used—his voice trailing down the hallway and into my room where I lay on the floor listening to Stevie Nicks. I couldn't make out everything he said that day, but I could tell that he was worried, and after a while his voice began to soften a bit and lower in volume until I could no longer hear it.

Later, when he got off the phone, he stopped by my room and peeked in, asked if I'd like to join him out on the back patio as he had a cigarette. He seemed a little calmer than he'd been earlier on the phone, more relaxed, and I of course always welcomed any opportunity to be alone with him. When I stood up and turned off my stereo, he nodded at me, and then he walked over and put his arm around me and led me outside.

It was a cool day, cool but not too cold, the wind blowing the palm trees at the far end of the yard, my father and I both wearing windbreakers and blue jeans. It was late afternoon, the sun setting just beyond the cabana house, everything on that side of the yard cast in silhouette, the golden hour, as everyone out here called it. My father was wearing sunglasses and had brought along a beer, which he sipped slowly as he talked, his other hand holding a cigarette. He seemed like he had a lot he wanted to say that day, a lot on his mind, though his thoughts were jumbled and scattered, almost stream of consciousness in nature, almost as if he were reciting an impromptu free-form speech to an audience of one.

At one point, I remember him talking about our lives out here in California a little. I remember him saying that California was a wonderful place, yes, but that there were other wonderful places too. St. Agnes was a wonderful school, yes, but there were other wonderful schools too. I didn't really know what he was getting at, but it worried me. I knew that switching schools at this point wasn't an option for my father, not unless he received tenure. And if he didn't receive tenure, all bets were off. There wouldn't be a school in the country that would touch him. That's what I'd overheard him saying to my mother, at least. That tenure denial was a kind of academic death for most professors. One might try to resurrect a career at a junior college or at a university overseas, but it was unlikely he'd ever be hired again as a professor in the States. These were the stakes, and I'd been aware of them for many months now, which was why it worried me that my father was suddenly bringing up the prospect of moving again, of switching schools.

Later, I'd find out from my mother that my father had already written some type of open letter to his colleagues at this point, the first of many open letters he'd write that year. The letter had something to do with the fact that he'd overheard a remark one of his colleagues had made to another colleague in the hallway about his book. I don't know the details, only that my father felt compelled to correct them, to set the record straight.

This is what I'd find out later, many months later, but at that moment I simply knew that my father was worried, that he perhaps sensed that he'd made a mistake of some sort and was already beginning to consider an escape plan. We were still a few months off from the department's official tenure review—their official decision—but already it seemed that things were unraveling.

There were tiny fissures in the foundation, cracks in the surface. At one point he'd made an allusion to the party he'd thrown for David Havelin that previous spring—the infamous tenure celebration at which he'd humiliated himself—saying that certain members of his department seemed to be unwilling to forgive certain moments of indiscretion and personal weakness, as if his own embarrassment weren't enough. It's possible he was referring to something else, but that's what I'd assumed he'd meant when he used the word "embarrassment" and when he'd later said, "There are things that happen in the classroom, right, and then there are things that happen in the privacy of your own backyard, and there's a difference, Steven."

I'd nodded, though I wasn't sure where this conversation was headed. It was getting darker now, and my father had already gone back inside once to get another beer. Usually he left before my mother got home, but that day he didn't seem to be in any particular hurry.

"I'm sure a lot of this must seem ridiculous to you, huh?"

I shrugged.

"Well, it is in a way," he said. "In a way, your father has chosen a pretty ridiculous career."

I looked at him.

"Not that what I teach is ridiculous," he said. "Or what I write on. It's just the formalities of it, you know, the procedures they put you through. The fact that they ask you to put your future in the hands of a few very opinionated and obstinate individuals." He sighed then and looked over at the cabana house wall. "I'm talking about people who really have no clue of who you are or what you're writing on, you know?" He picked up his beer and took a sip.

"But you have a book," I said. "Right? Isn't that all you need?"

I'd heard my father say this many times, that once he'd published his book, or had his book accepted for publication, he'd be essentially untouchable. They'd never be able to deny him. But that day the mention of his book seemed to deflate him.

He glanced over at the wall again. "I mean, yes, technically," he said. "Of course, we're still in negotiations, but that's typical." He tapped his wrist. "There's certainly strong interest." He glanced down then, as if I'd suddenly stumbled upon some shameful truth he didn't want to acknowledge.

And it worried me then because my mother had led me to believe that my father had worked all of that out already, before he'd submitted his file. Or maybe this was just a fiction I'd invented in my own mind. A lie I'd told myself.

My father picked up his beer and took a sip.

"Can I ask you something?" I said.

"Sure."

"What's your book called?"

My father smiled. "I could tell you, Steven, but I'm afraid you wouldn't understand. It's a very long title."

I nodded, a little disappointed. "What's it about then?"

Again, my father smiled. "Maybe when you're older," he said, "that's something you and I could talk about together." He shot me an amused look, and I nodded again and looked back at the house where everything was dark.

"And, for what it's worth," he continued, as if we were still in the earlier conversation, "it's more than just having a book, you know." He paused. "At least at St. Agnes. But yes, a book would certainly help." He seemed to be drifting a bit now, and I felt sorry for souring the mood. "It's going to work out, though," he said finally. "And I don't want you to worry about it, okay? Whatever happens we're going to be fine."

I looked back at the house again.

"I don't want to move again," I said quietly.

My father reached over then and patted my hand. "And you don't ever have to," he said, "okay? I promise."

When my mother got home a half hour later, my father was still outside, though he'd moved over to the deck area and was now shifting hamburgers on the grill. I'd been too hungry to wait, so I'd eaten a bowl of cereal earlier, in the kitchen, but now I was worried about my mother and what she might say when she saw my father out there on the back deck where he wasn't supposed to be.

She was still in her medical scrubs when she appeared at the back door, peering out. I'd expected her to be angry, but to my surprise, she just looked out at my father abstractedly, as if she'd been expecting him to be there, as if they'd planned this all out ahead of time.

"Who said you could make those hamburgers?" she said, feigning indignation, and my father turned around and smiled, and I could tell then that something was different, that they'd reconciled perhaps, an old familiarity settling in.

He held out his spatula at her dramatically and squinted his eyes. "Keep on riding me and they're going to be picking iron out of your liver," he said in his best hard-boiled detective voice, his best Sam Spade, and my mother laughed. I could tell it was a line from a movie.

"So you're a tough guy, huh?" she said, playing along.

"That's right," my father said, still in character. "And what would you know about tough? All you broads care about is money."

My mother laughed again.

"You like money," he said. "You've got a great big dollar sign there where most women have a heart."

"Is that right?"

"That's right," my father said. "And you're never going to win that way. That's not the way to win."

"Oh yeah? So there's a way to win?"

"Well no," my father said and smiled at her, and I could see then he was still in character, still reciting the lines from a famous scene. "But there's a way to lose more slowly."

At this, my mother grinned in playful recognition, delighted by the game, and walked over to my father and punched him lightly in the arm.

"You know, with my brains and your looks," my mother said, "we could go places."

My father laughed at this and pulled her in closer to him and then whispered something in my mother's ear I couldn't hear.

I'm not sure when my father officially moved back in. It wasn't all at once. It happened slowly, over the next few weeks. But in my memory that was the night I realized he would. That was the night I recognized my mother had let down her guard and let him back in. I remember her going back inside the house to change, while my father finished up the burgers, and then the two of them sitting out on the back patio eating and drinking beer, and then later calling up friends—the Havelins, the Alorses, the Bindleys—having a little impromptu party out in the backyard, like they used to, the previous year, and all of the years prior to that. It felt a little like things were getting back on track—the music from the 1940s, the sound of laughter and splashing in the pool, and later a joint being passed in the shadows—but there were also the things that my father had said to me earlier about his job, the references he'd made to moving, and before that, the things he'd said to David Havelin on the phone about being ambushed. Words that cast a shadow on all of the mirth outside. And there was also, later that night, a phone call from Deryck Evanson that came in just as I was getting ready to go to sleep.

I was back at my usual perch on the kitchen counter, looking out at the backyard, all of the commotion down there, and the sound of Deryck's voice on the other end surprised me, like a jolt from a dream. He said that he was looking for my father and wondered if he was in. I paused for a long time, wondering what to say, and then finally I said, "He's not living here right now."

"I know," Deryck said, "but I heard he was over there tonight. That people were over."

I looked out the window where I could see all of the grown-ups down in the pool, lounging in the shallow end, passing a joint back and forth, the sound of Frank Sinatra's "The Summer Wind" playing in the background. The heat from the pool water creating a light ethereal mist on the surface, everything surreal and strange.

I told him he was wrong about that.

"What do you mean?"

"Nobody's here," I said, and then I paused to see if he'd protest, but he didn't. "They all left," I said.

"They all left?"

"Yes," I said and then I looked down at the pool again where I could see my father with his arm around my mother in the shallow end, her head balanced on his shoulder. "They all left," I said again. "They all went home."

Then I walked over to the other side of the kitchen and said goodbye and hung up the phone.

11

Joseph Alors's office was located at the far end of a long hall on the second floor of the Department of Literature at UC Santa Cruz, a school where he'd taught since the mid-1980s when he left St. Agnes and where he still taught the occasional seminar on Chaucer each year and served as a dissertation advisor for a small handful of graduate students.

He was telling me this the morning after I'd arrived in Santa Cruz from Ojai, my body still a little exhausted from the long drive up the day before, my left arm sunburnt from resting out the car window the whole way, and my eyes only now beginning to adjust to the bright morning light of his enormous office. The entire Humanities building was modern, but Joseph Alors's office seemed especially so—the ceilings high, the long walls lined with hundreds of books organized neatly inside elegant built-in bookshelves, the opposite wall almost entirely glass, tinted windows that stretched up to the ceiling and that looked out upon the verdant campus grounds, the towering redwoods and Douglas firs, the quiet meadows and the long stretches of untouched field that stretched on for acres, accented in parts by futuristic classroom buildings or small patches of forest, giving the entire campus the feel of an untouched nature preserve or sanctuary, a kind of academic nirvana.

Earlier, Joseph Alors had been talking about how his time at St. Agnes had felt like part of another life, a life he rarely thought about anymore, how his academic career had only really started when he'd arrived here. He was older now, of course, and you could see it in his movements, and in his face, the way it seemed to pain him to lean forward at his desk, the way the hair on the top of his head had begun to lighten and gray, but he was also youthful in other ways, the way he'd greeted me at his office door in Birkenstocks and a T-shirt, his blue jeans speckled with paint, his arms tan from weekends at the beach. He'd offered me a coffee when I first came in, and as he sipped his own, reflecting on St. Agnes and those early years there, he seemed to be drifting off to another place, his eyes distant and soft. He said it was sad what had happened to the school, the financial strain it had been under in recent years and the way the campus had fallen into disrepair, the way they could no longer compete with those East Coast liberal arts schools, like Amherst, how they were now losing students left and right to places like Pepperdine and Chapman and Loyola Marymount.

I was surprised that he'd followed the demise of St. Agnes so closely, but when I'd asked him about this he'd simply shrugged and said, "Well, it was a special place in its own way, you know? I have fond memories there. And I still have a few friends on the faculty."

I nodded.

Earlier, when I'd called to tell him I was in town, I'd mentioned that I'd recently seen David Havelin, but he'd said very little to this, making me wonder if they'd had a falling-out of some sort. When I'd mentioned my father, though, his spirits had noticeably brightened, and later that morning, as we began to talk more about him, I could tell that a part of him still thought about my father often, that perhaps, like me, he'd never fully gotten over what had happened to him.

"In a way," he said at one point, leaning back in his chair, "you kind of have to admire him, you know? I mean that. In a way you kind of have to admire him because he never gave into them, Steven, never backed down. He may have made some bad decisions, some errors in judgment, but he never let them intimidate him. And for that, you kind of have to admire the guy."

I nodded and looked down at my hands. Earlier, I'd asked him if he'd had any contact with my father since he'd disappeared from our lives all those years ago, but he said he hadn't, though he admitted he often thought about him and often did searches for him on the internet. Every two or three months, he said, he'd type his name into Google and see if anything popped up, but nothing ever did. He'd wondered then if I thought my father was still alive, and I'd told him the truth, which was that I wasn't sure. He nodded and tapped his leg, but said nothing more about this.

"You know, when I was talking to David Havelin last week," I said after a moment, "I got the impression that they'd given my father a pretty hard time back then—at least, when he was going up for tenure."

Alors nodded. "Well, yes," he said. "I mean, they gave us all a pretty hard time back then."

"But my father especially."

"Yes." Alors glanced at me uncertainly. "It's possible. It was certainly a complicated case."

I stared at him, waiting for him to say more, but he didn't.

"David used the word 'stitch-up,'" I said.

"Stitch-up?" Alors raised his eyebrows skeptically. "I don't know if I'd go that far."

"What do you mean?"

"Well, it's not like your father didn't bring it partly on himself, Steven." He picked up his coffee and took a sip. "I mean, I was going up for tenure myself that year, so I wasn't in on any of the conversations, but I did hear things."

"Like what?"

Alors shifted uncomfortably in his chair and looked up at his bookcase, as if searching for a delicate way to say what he wanted to say.

"Well, look, Steven, this is your father here, and I know he's had his troubles, so I don't want to sound insensitive."

"You can say anything," I said. "Truly."

Alors met my gaze and pursed his lips. "Well, like I said, it was a complicated case. And there were politics involved, for sure. But it was also just a complicated case."

"You mean, because my father had burned so many bridges?"

"Well, yes, that." Alors paused. "That was definitely a part of it, but that wasn't really the sticking point." He looked at me evenly. "The sticking point," he said, "was that your father never ended up publishing that book of his." He picked up his coffee and took another sip. "And he could have, you know?"

"I thought the publisher rescinded the offer."

"Is that what he told you?" Alors shook his head. "No, no. Oxford wouldn't have done that. I mean, we're talking about the top press in the field, the holy grail of academic publishers. They're a class act there. They wouldn't have pulled something like that."

"So what happened then?"

"I don't know." Alors held up both hands and shrugged. "I mean, that's the great mystery, right? I wish I did." He looked out his window at the grassy stretch of field beyond the redwoods surrounding the building. The sun had shifted in the sky, and the light in his office was softer now. "All I know is from what I heard," he said. "And what I heard was only secondhand speculation, so you have to take it all with a grain of salt, okay, but what I heard was that your father had written a pretty brilliant book, right?" He looked at me. "Or at least the first eight chapters of a pretty brilliant book. And all of those chapters had already been published in some of the top academic journals in the field. And I'm talking about the top of the top. *American Literature, American Literary Realism,* places like that." He paused then to put down his cup. "But then there were these other two chapters apparently that he'd tagged onto the end. The ninth and tenth chapters. And these were unpublished chapters that he'd written the summer before. And again, I don't want to sound insensitive here, but from what I heard those chapters were just completely incoherent, a kind of stream of consciousness manifesto on time and Proust and a whole bunch of other stuff your father had been thinking about at the time." He looked at me. "They bore no relation at all to the rest of the book is what I'm saying."

"So why didn't they just tell him to cut them?"

Alors smiled. "Well, they did," he said. "Or at least that's what I heard. I mean, to their credit, they were still willing to honor their offer to publish the book, minus those two chapters, of course, though I'm sure the whole thing must have raised a few eyebrows."

"So he could have published it," I said, "if he'd been willing to cut those two chapters?"

"He could have published it."

"And he would have gotten tenure?"

"He would have gotten tenure. I mean, I don't see how they could have denied him."

I nodded and looked out the window where I could now see students walking along a path in the distance. "So why didn't he then?" I said, though the question wasn't really posed to Alors.

"I don't know," Alors said, as if it had been. "Like I said, that's the big mystery." He looked down at his phone for a moment then turned it over. "I mean, your father was a stubborn man, Steven. You must remember that. And I'm sure he must have thought he'd done enough without the book to get tenure; and maybe he was thinking some other publisher out there might publish it as he wanted it. I don't know. It was probably a bit of a calculated gamble, I think."

"Which he lost."

"Right." Alors shrugged and held up his hands again but said nothing.

I sat there for a moment, processing this information, though I wasn't entirely sure if I believed him. I knew that my father and Joseph Alors had always been close, that Alors had come over to our house all the time when I was growing up, but I also knew that there had always been a competitiveness there too, a jealousy, at least on Alors's end. They had come into St. Agnes the very same year, after all, had entered the exact same department at the exact same time, so naturally they'd been compared to each other from the start, had gone through the tenure process on the same schedule, had learned the verdicts of their cases at the same time, and so on. As David Havelin had said to me the week before, *Your father was a rock star, Steven, and Joseph Alors—well, Joseph Alors was not. A passable scholar, a mediocre teacher, but definitely not a rock star. And I think that always bothered him, you know?*

Now, though, it seemed that Joseph Alors had had a modestly successful career. He'd published a few books, had earned one of the larger offices in his department; he seemed comfortable in his life. I wondered if any of that old jealousy was still there, if any of it still lingered.

"My father also said some other things," I said after a moment. "Some things about certain people in the department—or at least he seemed to think that certain people in the department were conspiring against him." I put down my coffee. "And David Havelin kind of confirmed this last week, though he wouldn't say who."

Alors looked at me evenly. "And you're wondering if I will."

I shrugged.

"I could only speculate," Alors said finally. "And I'm not sure that I want to. I'm not sure what good it would do. Half of those people are dead now anyway."

"The old guard?"

"Yes." He laughed. "Is that what your father called them?"

"Among other choice names."

Alors smiled. "I don't know if this will be of any help to you, Steven, and I'm not sure how to put it exactly. But your father never seemed particularly concerned with making the right moves, you know? I mean, someone like him shouldn't have had any trouble getting tenure. But those fights he picked, all of those open letters to the department, the book thing. It always seemed to me that he was trying to sabotage himself in some way, you know—almost from the start."

I nodded. "And the parties."

"Yes, and the parties too. And don't get me wrong, I loved those parties, but he wasn't smart about who he invited over. He'd just invite everyone—professors, members of the administration, students, his male friends." Alors looked down then, as if he'd misspoken and now felt embarrassed.

"It's okay," I said, and I wanted to say something then about how I was very aware of my father's sexual past, how it didn't bother me in the least, how I'd made peace with it a long time ago, but instead I just sat there and crossed my arms, smiled.

Alors's eyes slid back down to the ground. "And your mother," he said. "She was like this incredible rock that kept him grounded, you know? I always felt so sad for her."

"Why?"

"Well, just what he put her through," he said.

I stared at him. "I think my mother knew what she was doing," I said. "I mean, nobody was forcing her to stay with him."

"Yes," Alors said, "but it was a lot different back then, you know? For one, it was a lot harder for women to ask for a divorce. It wasn't like it is now. There were still certain stigmas attached."

"I don't think she would have ever divorced him at that time," I said. "I mean, during the years we're talking about."

"Really?"

"No."

Alors glanced at his bookshelf again. "Well, like I said, your father was a complicated man. But an interesting one too. And we all know what happened at the end, but you still have to admire him for sticking up for himself." He paused. "Like I said, as bad as it got, he never backed down."

He looked down, and so did I, and just then I could hear a group of students outside his office door, talking, and a moment later, a knock.

"Office hours," he said and held up his hands, as if in apology.

"It's okay," I said. "No worries."

I had wanted to ask him more about the secret cabals my father had always alluded to, the people who'd been conspiring against him, but I could tell he probably wasn't going to budge on that. And I wondered too if he was perhaps a part of one of those cabals himself. David Havelin had told me the week before that I would know them when I saw them. Had it been Alors he was referring to?

Alors stood up and walked around his desk, and then he reached out and patted my shoulder, shook my hand. His body looked frail, but his handshake was firm.

"We were all just children back then, Steven," he said wistfully. "Children with PhDs wandering around the world in grown-up bodies. But we were still just children."

I nodded, and I could sense a sincerity in the way he said this, in the way he squeezed my hand.

"Are you in town much longer?" he continued.

"Just a day or so," I said, and looked down, and then I thanked him again for all of his help.

"I'm not sure how helpful any of this was," he said, "but I'm certainly happy to speak to you again."

"Okay," I said. "I'd appreciate that."

He stood there for a moment then and studied me, a faint smile on his face, almost as if he hadn't noticed something earlier. "You know," he said after a pause. "You look just like him, Steven. Does anyone ever tell you that?"

I smiled then and turned around. "All the time," I said and moved toward the door. "More than you'd imagine."

On the way back from Alors's office that day, I stopped by the beach on the other side of Santa Cruz and sat for a while and read. It was a warm day, the sun high in a cloudless sky, the beach mostly empty. At the far end, there was a pier that stretched out into the ocean, with a boardwalk attached, but I was on the quieter side of the beach, just a few surfers here, putting on wetsuits, laying out towels.

It felt good to let my shoulders sink into the sand, to rest my head on the pillow I'd made from my bundled-up sweatshirt. I'd been reading the second and third books of Proust's *In Search of Lost Time,* but that day I just read a mystery, a cheap paperback I'd picked up at a used bookstore in Berkeley before I'd left. Among the many things I'd left at my old apartment were my books, the boxes and boxes I'd accumulated over the years, like tiny keepsakes or mementos of periods in my life. My Flaubert period, my Baldwin period, my Annie Ernaux period. I'd had to separate them from Alison's before I left, place them into cardboard boxes, and it felt in a way like the untangling of two lives, or perhaps the erasing of two pasts.

. . .

I was thinking about this later, as I sat in an open-air bar near the beach, drinking a margarita and jotting down notes from my conversation with Joseph Alors. The bar was mostly empty, just me and the bartender and a woman at the far end who was drinking a tall blue drink and flipping through a magazine.

On the wall behind the bar there were Polaroids of people wearing sombreros, chugging beers, holding up their arms in victory. You could tell this was the type of place that drew crowds on the weekends, on Friday and Saturday nights, but on a random Thursday afternoon, like this, it was mostly quiet. On the awning out front, there were palm fronds hanging above the entrance, which opened up directly onto the beach, a perfect frame of the Pacific Ocean in the distance, the choppy waters of Monterey Bay.

I looked down at my notebook where I'd written almost a page and a half of notes, mostly things that only confirmed what I already believed—that my father had faced a lot of adversity in his department, that Joseph Alors had potentially conspired against him, that nobody really knew what had happened with my father's book—but there were also some new ideas too: the question of whether or not my father might have been able to publish his book had he wanted to, had he not acted so selfishly, and so stubbornly, had he not decided to put himself before us. Was it possible, as Joseph Alors suggested, that my father had been out to sabotage himself from the start? That it hadn't been about his colleagues, or his publishers, or anyone else. That it had simply been about him all along?

I closed my notebook and nodded at the bartender for another margarita, and then I sent a text to Alison, asking her if she had a moment to talk. We'd agreed that we'd talk at some point today, though I didn't have anything in particular to tell her. This was simply something we'd agreed upon—a regular check-in, a weekly, or sometimes biweekly, conversation to touch base about Finn and other things related to our separation. In the past, these conversations had felt very businesslike and formal, but that day, for whatever reason, when she eventually called back, her voice sounded different, more relaxed and casual, almost as if she'd already begun to let go of something. We talked for a while about our apartment, and the shared expenses that were building up, but then we moved on to other things: Alison's new interest in baking, her friend Allegra's new dog, a movie she'd seen recently on Joan Didion, a book she'd read about The Clash. I could almost sense her body loosening as she spoke, and then at one point, for the first time in many weeks, she asked me about myself, about my trip.

"Are you finding what you're looking for?" she said.

"I don't know," I said. "But it's been interesting."

"How so?"

"I don't know," I said. "I'll tell you when I see you." There was a long pause. "Can I see you?"

Alison said nothing to this at first. I could hear her breathing softly on the other end of the line. Finally she said, "It's been kind of a crazy time, you know?"

"Sure," I said. "Of course."

"I mean, it would be a little strange, I guess," she said quietly. "I'm not sure I'm quite ready."

"Sure," I said.

"When do you think you'll be in town again?"

"Pretty soon," I said. "Maybe a few days. I'm heading up to Petaluma to see Edward Bindley; then I'm going to check out that apartment in Oakland I was telling you about."

"The sublet?"

"Yeah, the rent-controlled one. By the lake."

She was quiet again.

"How's Finn?"

"Okay."

"Anything else happen with that teacher?"

Alison said nothing to this.

We'd had a few run-ins with Finn's third-grade teacher, who'd written him up a few times for causing a commotion in class and being disruptive during group activities. When we'd met with her, she'd suggested that we get him some outside counseling, and when Alison explained to her that we already had, she said nothing. *We're currently separating,* Alison had added then, *my husband and I,* as if this might somehow explain Finn's behavior, but the teacher again said nothing to this. She just looked at us blankly. Finally, she said, *Well, I think that might be a part of it, yes, but I think it could be other things too.* And when she'd said that phrase "other things," it encompassed all of my worst fears: that I had passed down to Finn what my father had passed down to me, that the genetic cycle had not been broken.

"He's doing better," she said finally, "but he had a fight with that kid James again last week."

"James?"

"The kid who was bullying him."

The incident didn't register, just as much from the past few months didn't register, but I didn't say this.

"Did his therapist say anything more about the possibility of getting him medicated?"

Alison hesitated for a moment, then said, "She wants to wait, I think. She wants to wait and observe him more. She said she doesn't like to rush into medicating with kids his age."

This was another area where Alison and I disagreed. She saw medication as a last resort, whereas I saw it as a pretty good option, as long as the therapist agreed. In Alison's mind, what Finn needed most was a sense of stability, a sense of calm. He was a boy who thrived on orderliness, neatness, logic, and what was happening now between Alison and me was anything but that. At the same time, she often reminded me of his sensitivity and perceptiveness, the fact that he understood so much more than we sometimes realized. And I agreed with this too, often felt unmoored by it. I'd sometimes tell her about the very adult-like things that Finn would say to me, how I sometimes felt that he could see through me, how I sometimes sensed that he could tell what I wanted even more clearly than I did, and she would say that this was because he was just like me, an introvert, sensitive, highly attuned to the pain of others. His acting out in school, she'd said to me that night we'd met with his teacher, it wasn't happening because he didn't feel anything for his classmates. It was happening because he felt too much.

I was thinking about this as I looked over at the other side of the bar where a woman who looked to be about my age—beach-weathered but pretty—was punching songs into the juke-box. Jimmy Buffett's "Margaritaville" came on and she started to sway lightly, her body silhouetted by the ocean behind her.

"Where are you?" Alison said when she heard the music.

"Just a place in Santa Cruz."

"A bar?"

"Yeah. I mean, a bar and grill, I guess."

I looked at the clock on the wall above the cash register and saw it was only one o'clock in the afternoon, and could feel Alison's silent disapproval. In the past, she might have asked me if I was drinking, but I could tell she was too exhausted to do that anymore.

"I really do want to see you," I said, finally. "Will you at least think about it?"

"Steven."

"Please."

"Okay," she said finally. "I'll think about it."

"I want to call and talk to Finn some night this week too, okay?"

She paused for a moment. Then she said, "Okay."

There was a tension now between us, and I worried that I'd pushed too hard, asked for too much. When Alison had suggested the separation months before, it was for several reasons, but the main one was simple: she felt that I'd pulled away from her and didn't love her anymore. She said she knew I loved her on some level, an emotional level, but not on a physical one, and she needed someone who loved her on both. *I want to be desired,* she said. *I know that sounds stupid but that's what I want at this point in my life. It's important to me.* I tried to tell her that I did desire her, that I'd always desired her, but she didn't want to hear it. Not then, and not later. She had been putting in a lot of long days at work, taking on a lot of new cases at her public policy job, and I knew that this was a part of it: she was burnt out. But I also knew a part of what she was saying was true. I had pulled away, and I couldn't say why.

Not long after that she suggested the separation in a more formal way, laying out the specifics, the parameters. And it was also around this time that she suggested that I take some time away to work out some things in my life. She asked me why I thought I was so unhappy lately and I told her I didn't know but that I thought it was rooted in my father and the lack of closure there, that it had always been that. No matter where my mind went, it always came back to that. *Then that's what you need to do,* she said finally, *but be careful.* And in this way she'd given me her uncertain blessing.

Now, though, listening to her silence on the other end of the line, I wondered if I'd done the right thing. I tried to think of something to say to her, something to pull her back in, but the buzz from the margarita and the mid-afternoon sun was making this hard. I looked out at the ocean again and felt suddenly drowsy. Finally, I said, "I'll call you tomorrow, okay?"

But by the time I said this, by the time I spoke again, I realized that there was nothing but a quiet drone on the other end of the line, that somehow I must have drifted off, and that in the meantime she'd already hung up.

12

At the start of January that year, my father came home one night with a VCR, a sort of late Christmas present to himself and to the family. At the time, only about half the kids I knew had a VCR in their house—it was still considered a bit of an extravagance—and it certainly wasn't something our family could afford at the time. Not according to my mother at least. Almost daily she lamented the fact that we were living way beyond our means, that the monthly maintenance of the pool alone was sinking us further and further into debt. What we really needed to do was move, she'd say often over dinner, but my father wouldn't hear of it. *I want to be buried in this house,* he'd always counter, leaning back in his chair. *They're going to have to drag me away.*

This was a far cry from the types of things he'd been saying before Christmas—all of his vague ponderings about other places we might live, or other schools where he might teach—and I found it comforting in a way, the fact that he seemed so confident and committed to staying here. As for the VCR, that was only further evidence that things were looking better with his tenure case, or at least that's how I'd decided to interpret it. Just as he'd splurged on Christmas that year—buying my mother a Chanel purse from

Neiman Marcus, me, a new skateboard just like Chau's (the new Christian Hosoi Sims board)—he'd been bringing home small extravagances all month—a new cassette player for the cabana house, bamboo nested tables for the living room, a Mr. Coffee coffeemaker for the kitchen.

The night he brought home the VCR, I'd been sitting with my mother in the family room, watching *Falcon Crest,* when my father appeared in the hallway, holding a large cardboard box. He was wearing a madras shirt and shorts, and he was sweating profusely.

"You're going to need to turn that off," he said and smiled, as he put down the box on the floor. "I have something better to watch."

My mother stared at the box for a moment, seemed to surmise what it was, and then stood up and walked into the kitchen for her cigarettes. Things had been better between them lately, but this latest purchase had put her over the edge, I could tell.

"How would you like to watch *The Philadelphia Story,*" my father said, pulling a plastic video case out of a small yellow bag, "right in the comfort of your own home? How about *Dial M for Murder* as many times as you want?"

By now, I'd surmised what it was myself and was standing up, eager to open it, but when I looked back at the kitchen my mother was gone, down the hallway to her bedroom perhaps or outside to the cabana house. I hadn't noticed her leave.

"Looks like it's just you and me," my father said, shrugging, clearly unfazed. "Ever seen *Fitzcarraldo*?"

That first night my father had not only brought home a VCR but also almost a dozen rented movies from the video store—more movies than we could possibly watch in the three allotted days before he had to return them—but this didn't seem to concern him. We started with *Fitzcarraldo*—a movie by Werner Herzog that had come out the year before—and then moved on to *The 400 Blows,* a movie he'd often talked to me about but never shown me. Later, I'd realize that he'd rented these movies in one of his manic states, just as he'd purchased the VCR in a manic state, but at the time I didn't care. I was simply happy to be sitting there beside him on our brown upholstered couch, our faces illuminated by the hazy glow of our old TV, the wind blowing the palm trees outside the window, as the black-and-white world of 1950s Paris flashed by us, the subtitles moving too fast for me to follow, but somehow none of this mattering. I remember simply being transfixed by the visual poetry of the film, the cinematic dream of it; and I remember looking up at one point and noticing my father's face, his eyes transfixed as well, and then nestling into him, leaning my head on his shoulder, which was something I hadn't done in years, and my father eventually putting his arm around me, pulling me closer, and then at one point reaching down for his cigarettes and laughing.

"These French films," he said, shaking his head, a, strange, bemused smile on his face. "They always make me want to smoke."

In the days that followed, my father would go on a movie-watching marathon. When he wasn't teaching or grading papers or preparing for class, he was sitting in front of the TV watching some obscure Scandinavian documentary or classic noir or French melodrama. I know that this was partly related to the stress he was under. He had turned in his tenure materials two months before and was now simply playing the waiting game, waiting as these materials were being evaluated, but I think another part of him was genuinely delighted by this new technology, the fact that he could now watch as many movies as he wanted to in the comfort of his own home, the pleasure of this somehow surpassing even the pleasure he felt during his backyard screenings on the cabana house wall.

If I'm being totally honest, though, a lot of the films my father watched during that time were too difficult for me, too challenging, too artistic and strange. Still, I enjoyed watching them with him, as did my mother after a while, and over time I also began to realize that eventually I'd be able to rent movies myself, or at least ask him to rent movies for me, and that's what happened the following week, when he asked me one night if I wanted him to pick up anything for me at the video store, maybe something for me and Chau to watch, and I suggested *Tron* and then later thought better of it and made a try for the one movie I'd been dying to see for months, *Fast Times at Ridgemont High,* the most popular movie among the other boys at my middle school, a movie that we all revered, even though very few of us had actually seen it.

It was a kind of strange phenomenon, in fact, being so intimately acquainted with a film you'd never actually seen. It was strange that we knew all the classic lines, that we knew that Phoebe Cates got naked, that we knew that Sean Penn had already been anointed as a comic genius for his role as Jeff Spicoli, all without any context at all. It was sort of like when I'd owned *Star Wars* figures long before I'd ever seen *Star Wars*. It was something that had simply been woven into the fabric of my young life whether I'd wanted it to be or not. And the fact that it was R-rated made it all the more exciting, the fact that it was something we had to be creative and cunning to actually see, that we had to trick our parents into letting us watch.

With my father, of course, it wasn't that hard. I knew he'd never check the rating on the box, that he'd be too oblivious to ever notice. And when he brought it home later that night, I remember the excitement I felt upon cracking open the plastic case and seeing the title, written in that shadowed script. I remember glancing over at my mother, standing on the other side of the kitchen, then tucking it under my shirt and racing into my bedroom to hide it. A short time later, I called up Chau and told him what I had, asked him if he felt like coming over the next night to watch it. I told him my mother would be out of the house—she worked the night shift on Saturdays—and that my father would be too, that he was going out with David Havelin and some of his other friends.

Chau was quiet on the other end for a while, and I had to bite my lip to contain my excitement.

Finally he said, "Yeah, man, that sounds cool, but I actually got a better plan. You think you'd be up for hanging out tomorrow night?"

I was quiet then myself, a little deflated. "Where?"

"I can't tell you right now, but it'll be rad. Trust me." He paused. "We can pick you up."

"Who?"

"Mai and me." He paused again. "You in?"

I looked down at the plastic video case in my hands, suddenly feeling foolish. "Sure," I said finally. "Sure. Just tell me when."

For most of the following day, I remember being distracted, curious about what Chau had in mind but also disappointed that he hadn't been as excited as I was about watching *Fast Times,* almost as if he'd already moved past that. Chau had turned twelve the previous summer, and I'd be turning twelve in a few weeks. Sometimes it felt like there was an eternity separating us, though it was probably closer to six months. He just always seemed much older, much more mature and confident. That day, as I watched my mother out in the garden—planting verbena, transplanting delphiniums—moving around the backyard in her sun hat, my father beside her, helping out, I remember feeling a strange sense of calm, a placidity I didn't quite trust. I remember the sun being high in the sky that day, the midwinter air crisp and cool, everything quiet. I remem-

ber standing at my familiar perch behind the kitchen sink, looking out at them through the kitchen window, watching the digital
numbers on the kitchen stove turn, waiting for Chau to call, the
sound of Stevie Nicks's voice drifting in from my bedroom: *She
is dancing away from you now, she was just a wish, she was just a wish.*
And in the distance, the quick flicker of sunlight on the pool
water, a kind of dance that pulled you in, the undulating ripples
and waves of refracted light moving in an unsteady rhythm, a kind
of harmony, a trance.

As it turned out, the destination Chau and Mai had in mind wasn't
as glamorous as I'd been expecting. We weren't driving into Bev-
erly Hills or out to Palos Verdes. We were simply driving over to
Mai's boyfriend's house in Sunny Hills, an upscale neighborhood
on the other side of Fullerton, a neighborhood with big properties
and long front lawns and large houses set back from the street.

Mai's boyfriend's house was on a corner lot. It was a large
Spanish-style home with a circular driveway out front and tall
palm trees rising up from a center island. On the drive over, Chau
had mentioned that Mai's boyfriend's parents were out of town for
the weekend and that Lien would be meeting us over there also
with her boyfriend, Bao. I had never met Bao before, but I knew
that he was Vietnamese, a boy she'd met in church, whereas Mai's
boyfriend, Brody, was white, a fact that Chau often liked to mention, as it was a major point of contention between Mai and their
father. Their father who didn't trust white boys, especially the
type that wanted to date his daughter.

As we got out of the car that night and moved closer to the
house, Chau said something about this again—something about
Mai's *white* boyfriend—and Mai gave him the finger over her left
shoulder, without even looking at him, and then walked straight

to the front door and pushed through, pushed through with the confidence of someone who had done this many times before, and then Chau and I followed her into the large front foyer, this enormous tiled room with high ceilings and arched doorways and these beautiful decorative sconces along the stucco walls. On the other side of the house—in the kitchen, I assumed—I could hear the sound of the new Van Halen album playing and the sound of Lien and the others laughing. We followed Mai as she weaved through the dark living room toward the light of the kitchen and then straight to Brody, who was standing with Bao at the edge of the long wraparound counter, attempting to emulate David Lee Roth's high kicks. Brody was handsome, a tall California surfer boy with floppy blond curls, and he immediately embraced Mai and gave her a kiss. Then he walked over to Chau and gave him a little pat on the arm, smiling, telling us both to make ourselves at home.

On the other side of the large kitchen, you could see a blue-lit swimming pool through the sliding glass doors—not the type of pool like my parents had, but the type you saw in brochures for pools, the type with large boulders and a strategically lit waterfall and a separate Jacuzzi set off from the rest of the pool. Chau mentioned something about the pool being nice and Brody nodded in approval.

"Yeah, man. If you guys want to take a dip, be my guest. Bathing suits are optional here." He gave us a wink and then he looked over at Bao, who shook his head. "Also," he continued, "we got pizza for you guys." He motioned over to the kitchen counter where there was a stack of pizza boxes, some of them already open, and some two-liter bottles of Coke. "We got beer in the fridge. Some vodka and stuff out at the pool bar. And we got other stuff too," he said, motioning toward a bong that was sitting on the other side of the kitchen, by the pizza boxes, "if you choose to partake."

"I choose to partake," Mai said before Chau and I could even speak and then she walked over to the other side of the kitchen and picked up the bong, pulled out her lighter, and took a hit.

When she finished, she exhaled slowly, passed the bong to Lien, and then Lien did the same and passed the bong to Bao. When Bao finished, he packed the bowl again, and passed the bong to Brody, who shook his head, saying he was fine. "I'm all good, man. All good." Then he nodded to us. "You guys?" he said.

I looked at Chau but he was already walking over to take the bong from Brody, reaching for the lighter on the counter as he did. After he'd taken a hit, he looked over at me and nodded and then showed me how to put my finger over the hole on the side of the pipe and inhale as he ran the lighter above the bowl. At the very end, he took my finger off the hole and released it, and I pulled the last of the smoke into my lungs, a sudden rush, and then started coughing as soon as I did.

"Easy there," Brody said.

And then I bent over and Chau hit me several times on the back and then everyone started laughing.

"First time?" Brody said, once I'd finally stopped coughing.

"No, no," I said. "Just my first time with one of these." I nodded at the bong.

Brody narrowed his eyes skeptically. "How old are you guys again?"

I looked over at Mai and she just crossed her arms.

"Old enough," Chau said.

"Old enough," Brody said, laughing, shaking his head. "All right, man. I like it. I like it."

At some point later that night, after we'd all partaken many times from Brody's bong, after we'd spent about an hour watching music videos on Brody's parents' large-screen TV, after we'd finished almost all of the pizza, Brody and the others went out to the pool to go swimming, and Chau and I started wandering around the house, moving through the unlit Spanish hallways, as if we were walking through the corridors of a famous museum. It had been a long time since I'd been alone with Chau, and it felt good to be near him.

"I feel like we're in that song 'Hotel California,'" Chau said at one point, as we moved through one of the second-floor hallways in the dark, using Chau's lighter to guide us. "Like this house is that hotel."

"You're stoned," I said.

"I'm serious, man. Aren't you getting that vibe?" He shook his head. "Can you imagine living in a place this size?"

At the end of the corridor, there was a series of bedrooms, two that seemed to be guest rooms, and then one that was clearly Brody's, a messy room with surfer posters on the wall and a small shrine to Christie Brinkley above his bed. Chau shook his head. "I don't know what she's doing with this guy," he said. "Just trying to piss off my father, I think. Dude's a moron."

I looked at the corner of the room where there was an electric guitar and amp, a small microphone, a four-track recorder. I tried to imagine Brody starting a band, imagined what it would be called. Chau shook his head again and then turned off the lights.

"Let's go," he said.

At the very end of the hallway, tucked around the corner so you almost didn't see it, was another bedroom, a fourth bedroom, which we quickly surmised belonged to Brody's sister, his older sister, who was currently off at UCLA, according to Chau, and who Mai often talked about because she adored her. Chau told me once that he thought Mai loved Brody's sister almost as much as Brody. She's just apparently very cool, he'd said. And when he flipped on the lights to her room I could suddenly see why.

I'd never been inside a teenage girl's bedroom before, let alone a college-aged girl's, but I was pretty sure most of them didn't look like this. Taped along the far wall were over a dozen different paintings of various sizes and styles, all original paintings by Brody's sister, I assumed, all on pretty dark themes, haunting and strange. A crucifix, a flaming coffin, various vampire-like creatures. On the other walls, there were old mirrors, concert posters from various punk bands, a bouquet of black roses hung upside down. There were also little scraps of paper that seemed to contain poems, or perhaps quotes, simply thumbtacked to the wall in various places, and on the wall above her bed there was a giant poster of Siouxsie Sioux from Siouxsie and the Banshees, her face blanched beneath her mane of black hair, her name written in giant purple letters. The room itself was fairly dark, but warmly lit in places by accents of string lights that were draped in interesting patterns along the walls, illuminating certain things, like her desk, which was piled high with journals and paint supplies, her bookshelves, which were crammed with paperbacks and spray-painted silver, covered on the sides with stickers, and her bed, which was completely black in every way, from the bedsheets to the comforter to the pillows.

I walked over to the bed and lay down on it, and Chau moved over toward her closet.

"She's totally punk rock," he said, pulling out a pair of black platform combat boots and holding them up, then reaching back in for something else, a pair of fishnet stockings that he dangled on a finger. "Look at this stuff." He disappeared again inside the closet and then came out a moment later shaking his head.

I felt very high at that point and somehow the room was making me feel higher. I couldn't explain why, but I felt more at home in this room than I'd felt in almost any room I could remember. It was just so atmospheric and artistic and strange. I could smell the residue of incense on the bedsheets and pillows, and on the table next to the bed I saw a pack of clove cigarettes unopened on top of a deck of tarot cards. There was also a Polaroid of someone giving the middle finger to the camera, their face obscured by their hand.

I looked over at Chau, who was now sitting cross-legged on the floor, going through Brody's sister's record collection, holding up album covers for me to see. I could tell he recognized some of these bands but I had never heard of most of them before. The Misfits, The Dead Kennedys, The Damned. At one point he held up an album by a band called Agent Orange and smiled. He said that Mai had seen this band before, that they were from right here in Fullerton. A surf punk band. Then he pulled out another album from a band he claimed he loved, a band called The Cure. He slid the record out of the sleeve and flipped on the stereo, the red LED lights flashing from across the room.

"You're going to like them," he said, putting on the record, and then a moment later I heard the sound of a syncopated drum beat, and a distorted guitar, and the soft, plaintive vocals of a man with a thick British accent, singing things I couldn't quite decipher. It was dark and haunting music, atmospheric like the room, and somehow it just worked.

Chau walked over to the window on the other side of the room and peeked through the blinds, reporting that they were all still down there, swimming in their underwear. He said something under his breath then about Mai and started to take off his shirt.

"Aren't you hot?" he said, pulling his shirt over his head, and I just looked at him because it wasn't hot at all in the room. If anything, it was cold. I thought about the last time he'd taken off his shirt, that day in his room, and how confused I'd been by it then too.

A moment later he walked over to the bed and motioned for me to slide over. I did.

"I'm so fucking stoned," he said and lay down beside me.

I remember noticing how low his swim trunks were, the white

flash of skin beneath his tan line, his flat stomach. I know now that what I felt at that moment was attraction but I didn't have a name for it then. I closed my eyes and tried to think of other things. In the distance, on the other side of the room, I could hear the slow, hypnotic beat of the music increasing, could feel my own heartbeat speeding up too. I shifted in the bed just slightly and then lay still again. I kept my eyes closed. There was a feeling of weightlessness in my body now, a sort of floating sensation. I bit my lip.

After a while, I felt the brush of his fingers on my arm, then his hand tugging on my T-shirt, the loose material on the sleeve. "You should really take this off," he whispered, "it's so hot."

I tensed for a moment, and then I did as I was told, pulling off my T-shirt and then dropping it on the floor beside the bed.

Chau eased in next to me so that our arms were touching just lightly. Then I felt him press his shoulder against mine. I closed my eyes again and for a moment we just lay there, though I remember being very aware of his breathing and the way our chests were rising and falling in unison, in rhythm.

On the stereo, the music was getting softer, slower, and after a while I felt his fingertips on mine, taking my hand and interweaving his fingers with my fingers, though not doing it forcefully, just sliding them in tentatively as if testing to see if I'd resist. But I didn't. It felt good. And it happened so naturally and so slowly that it almost didn't seem that it was happening at all.

"Sucks that we don't see each other in school anymore," he said after a while, softly.

He gave my hand a squeeze then, and I felt a jolt, an electrical current moving through me.

I said nothing.

"I miss that," he said.

"Me too," I said finally.

Then we were both quiet for a while, the sound of The Cure

playing quietly in the background, the occasional shrieks and splashes from downstairs. At one point I remember wondering if something else was going to happen, if he was going to try to kiss me, and I remember hoping he would, but then he seemed to drift off for a moment, and so did I, both of us falling asleep, though our arms remained entwined, our fingers interlocked, our bare shoulders touching.

In the years that have passed since then, since that night, I've often wondered if we'd secretly wanted to be discovered, if it was something we'd subconsciously intended. It had been a risky thing to do, after all, to lie there in bed like that, only half-clothed, knowing that we might fall asleep and that someone might stumble upon us by accident and reveal us. It's possible also that we were simply too stoned to know what we were doing, or what we wanted, even subconsciously. All I know is that later that night when we finally were discovered, it was terrifying, maybe the most terrifying moment in my life to date, the sound of Mai's voice, and then the sensation of her waking us, shaking our arms, slapping our legs, practically screaming, *what the fuck!, what the fuck!,* and then screaming something at Chau in Vietnamese, and then Chau screaming back, but also shielding his eyes, looking down, lowering his head in shame.

We dressed quickly and followed Mai along the long upstairs corridor in the dark, then down the steep winding staircase to the front foyer, the two of us trailing her like scorned children, Mai moving quickly, practically ignoring Brody as he stood there at the front door, perplexed. *Hey babe!* he'd shouted but Mai was already walking to the car by then, opening the driver's side door and shouting that she'd call him tomorrow.

Tomorrow?

Yes.

On the drive home, Mai blasted the radio and didn't look at us, and Chau sat silently in the front seat, staring out the window. A few times Mai turned to him and said something again in Vietnamese, but Chau didn't respond to her. He just kept looking out the window, silently. Outside, the streets of Fullerton were empty and quiet, and I remember feeling as if I'd somehow undone my life, as if I'd somehow revealed myself as something I'd always secretly been and that now everyone would know. And I worried too about what Chau was thinking because I couldn't get a read on him at all. He was simply sitting there in the front seat, stone-faced, like he'd passed over into another reality and would not be returning anytime soon. Meanwhile, Mai was speeding along the dark streets of Fullerton, her expression flat, her fingers gripping the steering wheel so intensely I thought she might break it, and I worried then about what she might do, what she might say about us, whether she might reveal us to our families, or our classmates, or our friends.

But when we finally pulled up to my house later that night, I could sense a subtle shift in her expression, a calmness now, and I realized that she wasn't going to say anything, that our secret was safe with her. *I'm not going to say anything about this, Steven,* her expression seemed to say, *but you owe me, okay,* and then she smiled at me just slightly, as if in forgiveness.

"Good night, Steven," she said, and then she looked back at the road and waited for me to get out.

I was still pretty stoned at that point, as I made my way clumsily up the front walk and through the front door. It was probably close to one or two in the morning by then, and I remember feeling grateful that my mother would still be at the hospital, working the late shift.

As for my father, I wasn't sure where he'd be, but as I walked into the front foyer that night I remember being surprised by the sound of the television down the hall and the smell of freshly made buttered popcorn. I tried to make my way slowly toward my bedroom, but my father heard me and called me over.

I could tell right away that he'd been drinking—there was that familiar flush in his cheeks—and that he'd had a fun night out with his friends. He had his feet up on the table and was holding a cigarette in one hand and a drink in the other. On the table in front of him was a large bowl of popcorn, which he'd barely touched. Then I noticed on the screen in the distance the movie he was watching, and it wasn't a classic noir or a seminal work of the French New Wave, but rather the one film I thought I'd hidden from him, *Fast Times at Ridgemont High,* which I realized just then he must have found on my desk, where I'd stupidly left it.

He looked over at me and then smiled and beckoned me over. He patted the spot on the couch next to him and told me to sit down. Then he said something about how hilarious this film was, how I really had to sit and watch a little bit with him. I sat down next to him and stared at the screen and thought about how I was probably the only kid at my middle school who would actually watch this film with one of their parents, with their blessing, in fact. Then I looked back at my father and leaned my head on his shoulder and closed my eyes just briefly as he put his arm around me and pulled me closer. I was still thinking about Chau, still wondering if what had happened back at Brody's house would be irreparable, but I was also feeling in that moment a sense of peace, a sense of security, just being there in my father's presence, comforted by our closeness and by the fact he'd put his arm around me.

In a few days from then, my father would learn about his tenure denial. It would be on a Wednesday night, the following week, and from that moment on our lives would forever change, but at that moment, sitting there beside him, I couldn't remember him being happier, and I couldn't remember feeling closer to him, the way the light from the TV was catching his eyes, illuminating his smile, the way his handsome face kept cringing and laughing, as he shook his head. There was a hopefulness there and an optimism I rarely saw these days, and would never see again, but it was there that night, as we sat there on the couch, and I remember feeling a sense of loneliness then for no reason, the way you might begin to sense that something is vanishing right before it does or the way you might begin to miss someone, or something, long before it's gone.

I looked up at him at one point, wanting to catch his eyes, wanting to say something to him about the film, but when I did I realized his eyes were shut now, that he'd leaned his head back on the couch and closed them, that somehow, in the midst of one of the funniest scenes in the film, one of the most iconic moments, my father had fallen asleep.

13

In a journal entry my father wrote a few days before he learned he would not get tenure—would never get tenure—he quoted a passage from Proust about grief. It was a long passage, but I remember one line in particular that he underlined: "It is often hard to bear the tears that we ourselves have caused." Later, he quoted another line: "We are healed of a suffering only by experiencing it to the full." In between these various quotes from Proust were vague reflections about different things, most of them too esoteric for me to follow, but I remember feeling at the time I read them— and this was many years later—as if there was something eerily prescient about these quotes and passages, almost as if he might have known already on some level what was going to happen.

The date of that last entry was January 23, 1984, a few days before he learned of his tenure denial and the Monday after the party at Brody's house. There would be no other entries after that. Not in that journal at least. In fact, there would be very little personal writing at all in the weeks that followed—or, if there was, I never came across it. I only came across this particular entry by chance, in fact, home one weekend from graduate school, visiting my mother at her new apartment in Newport Beach. She'd been organizing and trying to get rid of old things, putting various books and notebooks into boxes, and she'd come across this journal by accident and mistaken it for mine. *Your handwriting is so similar to his,* she'd said, surprised. *I would have never known.* She hadn't actually read the content.

I asked her then if she wanted to keep it, and she paused for a long time and then said no.

"Are you sure?"

"Yes." She nodded.

"Would you like to read it, at least?"

Again, she shook her head.

It was late afternoon. The sunlight forming patterns on the Saltillo tile of her new apartment, piles of unpacked boxes lined around the room. She'd been trying to downsize lately, moving from a small casita in Costa Mesa to this apartment, and she would have to downsize again by the end of the year when she could no longer afford this place.

I asked her then if she thought it would be okay if I read it, if I kept it, and she said, yes, of course, though she asked me not to tell her if I came across anything upsetting.

I told her I wouldn't.

Later that night, as I lay on a futon in the one guest room in the apartment, surrounded by cardboard boxes, I read through the journal from start to finish, though much of it was illegible and hard to comprehend, discourses about various texts and films. When I came across the quotes from Proust, however, at the end, in that final entry, I remember feeling a sense of disorientation and confusion, especially after reading the date.

I knew when that date was, of course, knew when it was in relation to his denial, and it just seemed strange to me that he'd be writing about enduring "suffering" and "grief" days before the suffering would actually begin. It seemed almost as if he was anticipating it in a way. And when I reread that first quote again, it almost seemed to directly reference the verdict of his tenure case and the effect it would have on my mother and me. *It is often hard to bear the tears that we ourselves have caused.* This seemed to be a direct acknowledgment of his own culpability and failure to us.

It was only later, when I was rereading other parts of the journal, entries that seemed to be referring specifically to Deryck Evanson, that I realized that those quotes might have been referring to Deryck and not us. That the suffering was the heartbreak my father was feeling then, that the tears were not tears that he had caused us but that Deryck had caused him, that the grief was not our grief, but his.

Later that night, when I came out of the bedroom to join my mother out on the back balcony for a glass of wine, I told her a little bit about the journal entries and the strangeness of them, though not much, as I knew she didn't like to talk about my father very often, not unless I pressed. She paused for a moment and shook her head, then agreed that they sounded strange, though she also added that I wasn't likely to find many answers by trying to decipher my father's thoughts, that this was why she never reread his journals or letters.

It was close to ten o'clock at night by then, the streets around my mother's apartment mostly empty, illuminated by streetlamps, the occasional car passing by below us. The apartment itself was only a few blocks from the beach, and though you couldn't see the ocean from the balcony you could smell it and occasionally hear the waves if it was quiet enough.

All day long my mother had been hounding me about Alison, asking me when I was finally going to propose to her, and I could tell that she probably wanted to get back to that subject now. But something about those quotes was still bothering me. I wanted to know more, more about my father.

I sat up in my chair and sipped my wine, and then I asked my mother what she remembered about the immediate aftermath of my father's tenure denial, and she sighed then and shook her head and said not much, that she thought she'd blocked most of it out. She looked over at me plaintively and shrugged.

"Nothing?"

"Well, not much. Like I said."

I stared at her.

"I mean, I remember that he was just beside himself at first, just hysterical. You must remember that, right?"

And I did. A part of me would probably never forget that night, the image of my father racing around the house in a frenzy, knocking over lamps, pushing books off the bookshelf in his study, smashing a plate in the kitchen sink, a rage that seemed to have no end, that only increased in intensity as the night went on, until finally my mother had to pack up a bag for the two of us and drive us to a small motel on the other side of Fullerton, a motel where we spent half the night just lying there in bed, in silence, unable to sleep.

"And I think he was just incredulous, you know, incredulous that it had happened." She looked at me. "And so angry that Alors had gotten it without a book, while he hadn't. He couldn't believe that part. That Alors got tenure." She looked at me again and sipped her wine. "And neither could I for what it's worth."

Down below us on the street I could hear a group of high school kids, walking back up from the beach, probably returning from a bonfire party, shouting at each other and laughing.

My mother waited for them to pass, and then said, "And then that following week he showed up at that department meeting and confronted them all. Do you remember that?"

I told her I didn't.

"Oh, it was terrible," she said. "So embarrassing."

She looked out at the palms trees and shook her head, as if trying to forget the memory.

"And what else?" I said.

"What else?" She shrugged. "I don't know." She looked down the street. It was empty now and her mind seemed to drift. "Well, you remember the letters, don't you?"

"The letters?"

"The letters that he wrote to everyone."

I stared at her.

"The department, the administration, the trustees. The members of the tenure committee."

"Oh yeah," I said and nodded.

Of course I remembered the letters.

One of the reasons I remembered the letters was because my father had written the first one on my birthday the following week, had spent the entire day writing it up, then revising it.

This was on a Monday, and I had woken that morning to an empty house and then had ridden to school, as usual, on my bike. When I got home later that day, I had expected to find some presents, maybe some light decorations, a cake; but instead what I found was just my father, sitting at the kitchen table, surrounded by a sea of loose-leaf paper, documents from his tenure box, a pile of notebooks and legal pads. He was so preoccupied when I walked into the kitchen that he didn't seem to notice me, didn't even seem to hear me. The kitchen itself smelled of cigarette smoke and coffee, and I noticed that the ashtray beside my father's hand was piled high with tiny butts, that there were actually two cigarettes burning at the same time, as if he'd somehow forgotten that he'd already lit one cigarette before lighting the other.

I stood there for a while, waiting to see if he'd notice me, and then finally turned around and walked down the hallway to my bedroom and turned on some music. Lately, I'd been revisiting the songs on *Tusk,* especially the songs by Stevie Nicks. There was a beautiful, melancholic song she sang called "Sara," but my favorite was a song called "Storms." There was one line in particular that always haunted me: *But never have I been a blue calm sea, I have always been a storm.* I thought about Stevie's tempestuous relationship with Lindsey Buckingham and other men, about the fact she'd never married. She seemed to me a true artist, unwilling to sacrifice her art for romance, even though her songs were often laments about this very thing, about the unbearable pain she felt in the wake of unsuccessful relationships.

On the wall above my bed, I had recently taped a poster of the entire band, all five of them standing in front of a barn at some point in the mid-1970s. Stevie is standing off to the far right but is somehow still the central focus of the picture, her blond hair perfectly feathered in a seventies shag, a floral-print peasant blouse and skirt, a pair of red suede platform boots running all the way up to her knees, and of course that angelic smile, those eyes.

Lying on my floor, staring up at Stevie, I often found myself wondering whether I was in love with her or whether I simply wanted to *be* her. Already at that age I was beginning to identify more and more with girls, was noticing that I tended to like the things that girls liked more, that I tended to be drawn more toward groups of girls than I was toward groups of guys. With the exception of Chau, I didn't really have a lot of guy friends. Even though I hung out with them at school, even though I'd begun to sit down at their tables during lunch, to emulate their styles and interests, it all felt like a bit of a charade, which was one of the reasons I'd told my mother not to bother throwing a party for me that year, that there was no one I really wanted to invite.

She'd stared at me plaintively and then suggested a few boys from my swim team, some friends of mine from elementary school, Chau, of course, but I just shook my head and said I wanted to keep it simple.

"It's your twelfth birthday," she'd said. "That's an important one." But I just shook my head and said no.

Now, though, lying on the floor of my room, I was beginning to wonder whether I should have maybe taken my mother up on her offer. It had been a difficult week, after all, a chaotic week, my father vacillating between bouts of rage and despondency, between incredulity and anger. I had spent a lot of time in my bedroom, lying on the floor, listening to music, trying to drown out his shouting. It was terrifying to consider what might lie ahead for us now: that we might have to move, sell the house, that we might have to leave California.

On the other side of the house I could hear my father talking on the phone now, pacing around the kitchen, going over the various people from the English Department who might have betrayed him, voted against him. He'd done this almost daily with David Havelin, since he'd found out the verdict. *It was Harris,* I heard him saying at one point. *I fucking know it was Harris.* And later: *They're dead to me. Every single one of them is fucking dead to me.* Sometimes I'd imagine David Havelin on the other end of the line, listening patiently with a cigarette in his hand, trying to console my father. I'd imagine him trying to reason with him, though my father was not a man who could be reasoned with at that point.

It was actually David who had first suggested to my father that he write a letter expressing his concern and confusion about the tenure committee's final decision. What I don't think he could have imagined at the time was what my father ultimately wrote: a twenty-page counterargument going over all of the committee's and the department's missteps and oversights, explaining in great detail how they'd all made a grave mistake.

At the end of the call I heard him asking David if he'd come over later that night to look at the letter and give him some feedback—he said his plan was to have it typed up and photocopied by noon the next day—and David must have agreed because my father's voice became suddenly animated then, excited.

"You're not going to believe what I wrote," he said. "Just wait till you see this, Dave. And I really think it's going to work. I do. Trust me on this, okay?"

When David Havelin finally arrived later that night, I was already in bed, listening to *Tusk* on my stereo with the lights off, but I heard him come in through the side gate, heard the creak of it, and then heard my father walking out to the back deck to greet him. Earlier that night, my mother had come home from work with a pepperoni pizza, a birthday cake from Ralphs, and a bag of modest presents: a few video game cartridges I'd asked for, a new pair of Vans. Over dinner, my father had talked more about his letter and about his general strategy to appeal the committee's decision; and later, after we'd finished the cake, he'd talked optimistically about his chances. My mother had stared down at her plate the whole time he spoke, pushing her food around with a fork, and after we'd cleared the table, she'd come up behind me and put her arms around me, held me tight. She said she couldn't believe how quickly I was growing up.

Now I could hear my father and David Havelin outside by the pool, talking in a conspiratorial way as they moved toward the cabana house to work. I turned over on my back and looked up at the ceiling, then closed my eyes. A moment later, I heard my door creak open, and when I opened my eyes I saw my mother standing in the doorway, silhouetted by the bright light behind her. She walked over to the stereo and turned down the music and then walked over to my bed and flipped on my bedside lamp. She sat down then on the edge of the bed and put her hand on my shoulder, ran the other one through my hair. She smelled like white wine and cigarettes.

"Did you have a nice birthday?" she said.

I looked at her. I told her I did.

"You don't have to say that, you know?"

"I know," I said. "But it was nice." I thought then about how I'd gone through the entire day at school without anyone knowing it was my birthday, how I hadn't even seen Chau, how the only thing anyone was talking about that day was how Michael Jackson's hair had caught on fire while filming a Pepsi commercial that weekend.

I looked back at my mother and took her hand.

"Did you like your presents?" she asked.

I nodded.

"I wish I could have gotten you more. It's just such an uncertain time, you know?"

"I know," I said and nodded. "It's fine." I looked over at the window where I could see a thin sliver of moon through the slatted blinds. "Do you think Dad's letter's going to work?"

She stared at me then looked down at her hands. "I don't know," she said. "Maybe. It's possible." She ran her hand along the side of her leg and looked up. "But probably not, if I'm being honest. Not on its own, at least."

"Why not?"

"I don't know," she said. "That's just not really the way your father's world works, I guess."

"The world of colleges?"

"Yes."

I nodded.

"He does have a chance to appeal, though," she added, her voice softening, "and he has a pretty good argument to make, you know?" She steadied her gaze. "What they did to him was pretty terrible."

I looked at her, nodded.

Outside, I could hear music going on in the cabana house, something light and acoustic.

"Why did they do it?" I said.

"I don't know," she said. "That's a good question. It's hard to know what motivates people sometimes."

I could sense the distance in her voice as she said this, and she seemed to drift off for a moment, then return.

"How have you been doing?" she said, her voice plaintive now. "I know this has been a crazy week."

"I'm okay," I said.

"You'd tell me if something was wrong, right?"

"Yes."

"Have you been worried about things?"

"A little." I nodded and looked away from her then. "Do you think we're going to have to move again?" I said, my eyes on the wall, my head still turned away from her.

"I hope not," she said, touching my cheek and turning my head back to face her. "I really like it here. Don't you?"

I nodded. A long silence passed between us and my mother just sat there rubbing my arm gently.

"Is there anything you're worried about?" I said finally.

"Me?"

"Yes."

"Oh, I worry all the time, honey."

"About what?"

"Oh, about everything. About your father, about you, about our house." She looked over at the window again and then returned her gaze to mine. "Mostly I worry that when you're older you'll look back on this time and resent me for not doing things differently."

"What do you mean?"

"Just what I said."

"I'd never resent you," I said.

"I know," she said. "I mean, I know you believe that now, but I still worry about how things might be when you're older. How you might look at things, how you might look at me." She smiled slightly. "It's natural to worry, though, right? We all do."

I nodded.

"Do you want to come sleep with me tonight?" she said, squeezing my hand.

"No," I said. "I'm okay."

"You sure?"

"Yes."

She smiled. "I forgot," she said. "You're twelve years old now, right?" She mussed my hair. Then she just sat there on the bed for a long moment, as if lost in thought or perhaps not wanting to leave quite yet. She seemed like she might cry, but then she composed herself. "I keep thinking about when you were first born," she said softly, shaking her head, but then stopped herself, as if putting away the thought, rubbing at her eyes gently. "I don't know why I keep thinking about that." She sighed.

Finally she turned back to me and patted my hand.

"We're going to be all right, sweetie, okay?"

"Okay," I said.

And then my mother stood up slowly and walked out of the room.

When I woke up the next morning, my father was busy at work in his study, typing up the final draft of his letter, all twenty pages of it. I could hear him from my bedroom, the steady staccato of the keys, the hypnotic rhythm of it. Later that day, he'd go into campus and have one of the secretaries in the English Department photocopy seventeen copies of it, one for each of the tenured members of the department as well as a copy for the provost, the head of the college's tenure committee, and the college's president, Roger Lynn. He'd drop these letters off personally, signing each one at the end, and then he'd come home from campus, having canceled classes for the day, and await the response.

By the time I got home from school, around four or five o'clock, my father was already fairly drunk, having spent the afternoon out in the backyard holding court in front of a group of his friends. He'd invited over all of the usual suspects—Russell Briggs, Edward Bindley, David Havelin—as well as a few I didn't recognize, or only vaguely recognized, and he'd pushed together the long outdoor patio tables—the ones my parents usually used for parties—so that they made one larger table, and then he'd situated himself at the far end, where he sat on a stool, his back to my mother's forsythia bushes, leaning forward and reading his letter, or at least passages from it, rocking back and forth. Later, I'd come to understand this for what it was—a sympathy party, a party of commiseration, his best pals getting together to show their support, but at the time I didn't understand what it was, or what it meant, only that it seemed inappropriate, out of place, given the circumstances.

My mother was working a double shift at the hospital that night and wouldn't be home till almost ten, so after standing at the back door for a few minutes, watching, I turned around and headed back inside to make myself dinner. The kitchen was still a mess from the day before—my father's papers still strewn across the counters and the table, the remnants of my birthday cake sitting out on the island, uncovered. There was also now the residual smell of alcohol—a watery strawberry daiquiri, sitting out on the counter, a few half-finished liquor bottles, empty beer cans. I peered outside the kitchen window above the sink and noticed my father was growing more animated in the fading light of the day and that a few other people had arrived, everybody talking and smoking heavily, occasionally applauding or cheering my father on, encouraging him as he read his letter.

. . .

I realize now that he was in the midst of a grieving then, that that's what this was. That despite the festive atmosphere, he was grieving the end of his career. Saying goodbye to it. Even if he was in a state of denial, a part of him understood that it was over. And when I've tried to explain this to other people in other careers they've never fully understood the significance of it, that this was the end of everything he'd spent his entire adult life working toward, that there would be no second act after this, that this was it. It was the equivalent of a kind of excommunication from a religious institution, only in this case the religious institution was the world of academia, the only world he'd ever known and understood, the only world that had ever valued him. Later, there would be the embarrassment and the disgrace to contend with, but at that moment it was all about the loss. It was all about the fact that he'd not be able to stay at this particular party forever, that eventually he'd have to leave.

And that evening, as he sat there on his stool, holding court, reading his letter as the sun went down behind him, I think he was grieving inside. Even as he was laughing and making jokes, voicing his indignation, inwardly he was devastated; inwardly he was frightened and unmoored. And I remember at one point watching him stand up and excuse himself, walk over to the cabana house, and disappear inside for a few minutes, almost as if everything that was happening right now was just too much for him. And then a short time after that, the people at the table began to stand up and move around to other parts of the yard, get themselves fresh beers from the ice chest by the grill, turn on the radio by the pool.

I walked down the hallway to my room and unpacked my bag, looked at the homework I wasn't going to do—the worksheets and the problem sets—and then put on my sweatpants and a new T-shirt and walked back out to the kitchen.

When I did, I noticed Edward Bindley and David Havelin were now standing at the blender, eyeing the strawberry daiquiri that someone had made there earlier.

"I don't know if I'd drink that," Edward said, staring at the daiquiri skeptically. "Who knows how long it's been there?"

Edward Bindley was a tall, slender man, almost completely bald, but very youthful in appearance. He always wore bright-colored shirts and white capri pants and tan espadrilles. That day he was smoking a very long cigarette and wearing a fedora. I could tell both men were drunk.

"I think I'm gonna stick with beer," David agreed and then walked over to the refrigerator to get one.

Neither man had noticed me standing in the doorway, watching them, and I remained there quietly until David finally turned and caught sight of me.

"Hey, Steven!" he said, shaking his head. "Didn't see you there." He walked over and mussed my hair. "How long have you been standing there, buddy?"

I told him not long.

"It's amazing," Bindley said, turning then. "Just like his mother, right? Doesn't he look just exactly like her?"

He looked me up and down then in a way that made me feel uncomfortable, exposed.

"Everybody tells me I look like my father," I said.

"No, no," Bindley said, winking, "definitely your mother."

"You looking for something, Steven?" David asked. "Your mother home?"

I told him she wasn't. Outside I could hear that more people had arrived, that the party was growing. I thought of what my mother was going to do when she got home from work.

"Well, I think your dad's outside in the cabana house," David said. "Would you like me to get him?"

"No, that's okay," I said.

"Would you like to join *us*?" Edward said. "We're going to brave the pool."

"*You're* going to brave the pool," David said. "It's way too cold to swim."

He turned then to Bindley and Bindley smirked.

"It's heated," I said quietly but both men were already moving toward the patio door, laughing.

"Good to see you, Steven," David said, turning around, and then both men looked back at me briefly, the way you might look at someone at a wake, or a funeral, someone whose parent had just died.

The party went on for a few hours after that. I'm not sure how long. At a certain point I began to lose track of time. More people arrived; more alcohol was served. A few people started to dance out by the pool. Younger faculty, people I didn't know. All of them here in solidarity against the tenure committee's decision, it seemed, all of them here to support my father. At one point I remember my mother calling up to check on us, to see how things were going. I remember her saying that she'd probably be home a little later than usual that night, maybe closer to midnight, and I remember the guilt I felt in lying to her, telling her that everything was fine here, that my father was just hanging out with a few of his friends.

After we hung up, I went back to the kitchen door and looked out, watched as people walked up to my father and put their arm around him, commiserated with him, all of them realizing that he was perhaps living proof of their own greatest fears. I walked back to the refrigerator and got myself a Coke and then went over to the window and looked out at the party. I could see Edward Bindley in the pool with a few others, steam rising off the lit water, and in the trees the tiny lights my mother had strewn between the branches the week before, a sort of celebration of winter, of her winter garden. Everyone was laughing and talking, as if they'd forgotten why they were even here, and on the far side of the yard I could see my father back at the cabana house again, talking to a group of his colleagues, his arms moving wildly.

It was at some point shortly after this, I think—sometime shortly after I'd noticed my father out by the cabana house—that I looked into the middle of the crowd and noticed a group of people talking, two of whom I recognized—two women from other departments—and several others I didn't. They were all bunched together, so it was hard to make out everybody's faces, but when they eventually parted I realized with something like panic that one of the men standing in the group was Deryck Evanson. Even though his body was turned to me, so I couldn't see his face, I recognized the unmistakable shape of his back—his broad shoulders and close-clipped hair, his slim waist—and felt an immediate sense of dread. I hadn't noticed him come in, hadn't thought that he'd dare to show his face, and yet here he was, standing in the middle of the party, laughing, as if nothing had ever happened. I thought immediately of my mother, of course, thought immediately of calling her up and telling her what was happening, but I knew I could never do that. I knew that she could never know about any of this.

Still, I watched him as he moved through the party, watched him as he moved from group to group, gradually getting closer to my father, and I watched my father as he occasionally glanced over and regarded him then turned back to whoever he was talking to. At one point I noticed my father excuse himself from the conversation he was having and disappear inside the cabana house by himself. A short time after that, I noticed Deryck Evanson casually strolling over to the pool area, looking cautiously over both shoulders, then disappearing inside the cabana house himself.

Suddenly I understood that they were in there together, the

two of them, that there was no one there to stop them, and I felt that growing sense of panic again, a tightening in my chest—but also something else—a kind of sickness and shame that I couldn't quite explain.

I stood there for a while, watching the cabana house door, waiting to see if they'd emerge; but when a few minutes passed with no sign of them I eventually gave up and got down from my perch at the sink and walked over to the other side of the sticky kitchen floor and sat down at the table.

The table itself was covered with half-eaten watermelon wedges now (on top of my father's papers), a bag of Doritos, and a bunch of empty beer cans. Outside, the music was getting louder, and I felt a sudden desire just to leave my house, just to head out the front door and run.

A moment later, I found myself standing up and grabbing the phone off the wall, taking it down the hallway where it was quieter and calling up Chau. I hadn't talked to him once since that night at Brody's house, hadn't even seen him in school, but suddenly I had a desire to talk to him now, to see if he wanted to hang out, maybe smoke some cigarettes over at the park near his house.

The first time I called, though, nobody answered. And when I called back again, a few minutes later, I got Mai, not Chau, her voice sleepy and annoyed.

"He can't come to the phone right now," she said.

"Why not?"

"He's sleeping," she said.

"He never goes to sleep this early. It's only eight o'clock."

She was quiet on the other end of the line, waiting for me to hang up.

"Well, will you tell him to call me tomorrow then?"

Mai was quiet again. "Look, Steven," she said finally. "Our mother has been getting worse lately."

"Okay."

"So maybe don't call here for a while, okay?"

I said nothing to this at first, not knowing what to say, and then eventually I said, "Well, can you at least tell him I called?"

But Mai didn't respond to this. She just waited silently on the other end of the line, breathing. Finally, she said, "Look, Steven, he doesn't want to talk to you, all right?" And then hung up.

I stood there for a while, just staring at the receiver, feeling gutted and confused, but also ashamed, knowing what this was, what had happened, that this was all connected to what had happened at Brody's house.

I walked back to the kitchen and hung up the phone; and when I looked out the window again, I saw my father back at his spot by the cabana house, talking to Russell Briggs, and no sign of Deryck Evanson anywhere.

In the weeks that followed, there would be other letters. None of the people who had received the first letter would end up responding, and so my father would write another, and then another after that, each one growing more insistent and indignant, the silence on the other end driving him to tears.

It wasn't that the letters themselves were so crazy, David Havelin had explained to me that day we'd had lunch at his place. It was just the sheer number of them, and the length, the fact he kept writing them even though no one was responding. It gave the impression that he was becoming unhinged.

Which he was.

Over the next several weeks, my father would become increasingly unhinged, and the letters would be both a cause and a manifestation of this. But there would be other things too. Confrontations with the chair of his department, Albert Doyle, long meetings with the college's president, Roger Lynn, many conversations with many members of the college's administration and faculty, all about the injustice of what had happened, even some articles in the school paper, some organized protests by his students—protests, I should add, that he initiated and encouraged. As Joseph Alors himself had acknowledged, my father wasn't going to go down quietly, he wasn't going to go down without a fight.

But that night wasn't about any of that. If anything, it was about the opposite.

It was about the accepting of reality before the fight. It was about the lament before the protest. And I felt it myself that night, as I stood there at the kitchen sink, looking down at my father, as he sat there by the pool, saying goodbye to the last of his guests, shaking their hands and embracing them, wishing them well as they patted his back and told him to stay strong, to fight the good fight, encouraging him even as they were pitying him. I felt the sadness of this moment, for him and for everyone. And I remember at one point, as I was standing there at the window, seeing him look up at me and smile, as if just realizing I was there, and it was a strange moment, the way he looked up at me then, almost confused, and it was a strange smile that he gave me, a smile that seemed to be saying *I love you,* but also *I'm sorry,* just as he'd say this to my mother later that night behind the closed door of their bedroom, *I'm so sorry,* his smile seemed to be saying, as he sat there in the soft evening light, his back turned to the last of his guests, his shoulders hunched. *I'm so sorry, Steven. I'm so sorry, I'm so sorry.*

Part
3

15

On the west side of Petaluma, just a few miles south from the downtown area, there's a gorgeous regional park that stretches on for about two hundred acres, two hundred acres of untouched pastures and green rolling hills and long winding trails that weave up through the grassy hillsides and onto these incredible ridge-top vistas. From the tops of these vistas, you can see for many miles in all directions, almost all of Sonoma County, and to the east you can see a good bit of Petaluma as well.

When Finn was about six months old, I remember taking a day trip to this park with Alison and him, packing up a picnic and spending the day hiking along those long, looping trails, moving steadily toward the vistas, but taking our time, stopping every so often so that Alison could nurse Finn, eating a small lunch by a little pond near the peak of one of the hills. It was a perfect day, sunny with a light breeze, and I remember that the pastures were very green that day and that the California poppies were out in full bloom.

Later, on the drive home, we stopped at a microbrewery in southern Sonoma County and had a light dinner and some beer, talking quietly at an outdoor picnic table while Finn slept soundly in his carrier seat. I remember that the light was starting to fade by that point and that Alison was sleepy, and later, as we drove the rest of the way home to Berkeley, I remember Alison falling asleep in the passenger seat next to me, her head tilted against the window, a strange smile on her face, and I remember staring at her from time to time, just glancing over at her beautiful face, and thinking, this is it, right, this is what it's all about.

That was the last time I'd been to Petaluma, the only time I'd ever been here before now, but it felt like a lifetime ago. Another life. And I was thinking about this the next morning—the morning that I'd driven up from Santa Cruz—as I sat at a small outdoor coffee shop in the downtown area, drinking a coffee and trying to bide time until my lunchtime meeting with Edward Bindley.

I had arrived about two hours early for the meeting, having awoken that morning in a strange state, still thinking about my conversation with Joseph Alors the day before, the things he'd told me, and still feeling a pang of regret for the way my conversation with Alison had ended; now, though, I was feeling better, more relaxed, even peaceful, as I sat there in the mid-morning sun, the bright rays warming my neck, the distant chatter from inside the coffee shop doors, the sleepy streets of Petaluma mostly quiet.

Earlier, when I'd first arrived at the coffee shop, I'd called up Alison to apologize for drifting off at the end of our last phone call and to see if we could maybe set up a time to meet the following day in Oakland. I told her that I'd be stopping by to see the sublet around noon and suggested a tapas place near Lake Merritt that we used to go to in our early days. She was quiet on the other end of the line for a long time and then finally suggested we meet in Berkeley instead. Not at our apartment but somewhere else. She said she'd think about where and then text me the next day. I could tell she was nervous about the prospect of this meeting. I could hear it in her voice. There was a caginess there, a defensiveness. Maybe even a slight reluctance.

Later, before we hung up, I asked her if she could put Finn on, and he and I talked for a while, mostly about his teacher and his classmates at school, his academic and discipline issues, subjects I hadn't really wanted to get into but that just sort of came up naturally. Lately, he'd been distant with me, but that morning he seemed especially so. There was a coldness in his tone, an absence in the long silences that followed my questions. I knew that on some level Finn blamed me for the separation, even though it had been Alison's idea, and that he also saw me as the one who had abandoned the family, rather than the one who was trying to give his mother space, the one who was trying to work things out on his own so that we could all heal together.

I knew that's how he saw me, and there wasn't a whole lot I could do about it. He was nine years old, after all, and to a nine-year-old I knew how all of this looked: I had left, while his mother had stayed. It was that simple. In his eyes, there wasn't a whole lot left to say.

Toward the end of our conversation I tried to steer the discussion in a slightly different direction, focusing instead on something I knew that Finn loved: baking. The previous summer, Alison and I had enrolled him in a two-month-long intensive baking camp called The Art of Baking Artisanal Bread, and though Alison had rolled her eyes the day we dropped him off, saying, *only in the Bay Area, right?*, Finn had loved it. He had loved the tactile feel of making bread, and he had loved the many friends that he'd made there. Mostly, though, I think he'd loved the fact that he was good at it. I had joked with him that he must have inherited the baking bug from his old Uncle Julian, but it was true that it was there, and it was true that it seemed to calm him. Later that summer and throughout the early fall, he and I had baked together, spending whole days mixing and folding and proofing, following all of his teacher's directions to a T. I could tell that he loved the simplicity of it but also the precision, the scientific accuracy of the craft, and that morning, as I asked him more about his latest bakes, I could sense him relaxing, could feel him warming up to me again. We talked about the types of pre-ferments he was using, the types of temperatures and mixtures he was experimenting with, and toward the end of the conversation I mentioned that I'd really like to take him down to see his Uncle Julian in Ojai sometime soon, to see his bakery and his breads.

"Do you think you'd like to do that?" I'd said, pausing. "A little road trip perhaps? Just the two of us?"

He was quiet for a short time, and then finally he said, "Yes."

"Good," I said. "I'm glad."

He coughed, and I could hear Alison in the background saying something about wearing a coat.

"I miss you," I said.

"I miss you too, Dad."

"I think about you all the time," I said. "Do you think about me?"

"Yes."

We were both quiet then for a while, and I could see a group of kids on mountain bikes congregating across the street, packing up their gear, slapping each other on the back.

"When are you going to come home?" Finn said finally.

"Soon," I said. "I'm closer than you think."

"What do you mean?"

"I don't know," I said, pausing, realizing I might have misspoken. "I just mean that I want to come home soon, okay?"

"Okay."

"I love you, sweetie."

"I love you too, Dad."

After we hung up, I'd just sat there for a while, taking in the sun and the quietness of the day. I felt worn out, though I couldn't say why. Lately, I'd been thinking a lot about Alison and the way that things had changed between us recently and somehow being in this setting—this setting where I'd last been in better times— was bringing back a lot of those old feelings. In particular, I was thinking a lot about the weeks leading up to our separation and the way that I'd sensed that it was going to happen long before it did, the way that I'd *known*. At the time, Alison wasn't even using the word separation, of course—she was calling it a break— but I'd known what it was and what it meant. On the night that she'd first brought it up we'd just come back from an evening out with friends—a group of our old friends from the nonprofit public policy organization where Alison had worked for years—and it had been a fun night overall. Lots of good wine and laughter, lots of rich Italian food. We'd walked back to our small apartment in Berkeley feeling tipsy, and after we'd paid the sitter and checked on Finn, I'd opened up another bottle of wine and poured us both a glass. Alison usually sat down next to me on the couch, but that night she pulled up a chair across from me and that's when I'd first sensed that something was up. She walked over to the other side of the room and turned down the lights and then turned off the radio that the babysitter had left on and then came back to the chair and sat down. She stared at me for a long time, kind of strangely, and then finally she said, "We need to talk, Steven."

What she wanted to talk about, of course, wasn't a surprise. I'd been sensing the distance between us for months, had felt it growing. What did surprise me, though, was how definitive she was, how certain. She talked for a while about how removed I'd been lately, how both physically and emotionally I'd been checked out and how it didn't seem to be getting any better at all. What I needed to do, she felt, was figure out what was going on and then address it because the way things were going now wasn't good. It wasn't working.

I sat there quietly and said nothing, in part because I knew she was right and in part because I didn't know why I'd withdrawn from her lately, at least not then. Later, I'd come to recognize this as a pattern in my life and in all of my past romantic relationships, a tendency to pull away for no clear reason, a tendency to suddenly withdraw. It's possible that some of it was related to what Alison herself was going through, her struggles at work, her unhappiness in her current position. I know that this was something we'd talked about a lot and that after a while I'd begun to feel uneasy, even nervous, about these talks. There were perhaps echoes of my father's own unhappiness there, too, his own work struggles, or maybe of my mother in the years after my father disappeared, tiny glimpses of past traumas that frightened me. These were all things that I'd consider later, that I'd talk about with my therapist at length, but at that time I didn't know what was happening. I just knew that she was right.

And so I sat there quietly as she went on about what she saw as my unwillingness to engage emotionally and as she talked about the logistics of taking some time away from each other, of making some space. Her voice remained calm, steady, very matter of fact, though her eyes were looking down, and after we'd talked for a while about Finn and the best way to break all of this to him, she laid out a very clear plan. As I said, she wasn't using the word separation at this point, so none of this was seeming particularly dire. We were simply taking a break, she said. Maybe a week or two. Possibly a month if we needed. Maybe longer. However long we needed to get to the point where we were ready.

"Ready for what?" I'd asked.

"Ready to be together again," she'd said calmly, "as a family. If that's what we want."

The following week I moved out, taking only a small bag of clothes at first, then coming back for my books, more clothes, various personal items. For the first two weeks, I stayed at a motel in Walnut Creek, then I stayed with various friends in the East Bay, sleeping in guest rooms and crashing on couches until I'd outstayed my welcome. I wasn't working at the time—I'd stepped away from my position at the University of San Francisco several months earlier—so that made things easier in certain ways but harder in others—namely, in a financial sense. At one point, I remember calling up Alison and asking her if I could make a small withdrawal from our savings.

She asked me how much, and when I told her she paused.

"What's this for?" she said.

And that's when I mentioned the trip. I hadn't expected to bring it up right then but it had been on my mind for a while and I felt like I needed to give her a reason for the withdrawal. Also, the more I talked about it, the more it began to make sense. If I was ever going to do it, when would be a better time? I wasn't working, Alison and I were on a break. When would I have a better opportunity?

At the end of the conversation I also talked a little bit about the other reason for the trip, the real reason perhaps, which was that it was something I felt that I needed to do for us, for the family, and for Alison and me.

I talked about how Finn's troubles at school were undoubtedly related in some way to my own issues recently, that he was clearly internalizing my own struggles. And I talked about the fact that everything I'd been going through lately, everything I'd been doing—my emotional withdrawal, my physical withdrawal, my drinking—how all of it was rooted in my father to some degree, in the lack of closure there, the unresolved feelings. I told her that I wasn't out to find him, just to understand him and to understand what had happened to him. That was it. That's all this was about.

"And what if you don't get the answers you want?" she said. "What if you don't get any closure?"

"Then I don't," I said. "But at least I tried."

She was quiet for a while.

"And what if you don't like the answers you do find?" she said. "That's a possibility too, right?"

"Then I don't," I said, "and I'll have to live with that, I guess. Whatever that means."

She was quiet again for a while and then finally she said, "And you're sure about this?"

"I am," I said. "I'm sure."

"Okay," she said. "Then go ahead and make the withdrawal." And that was the last thing she said to me for several weeks.

16

The area of Petaluma where Edward Bindley lived was located on the east side of town. A charming enclave of quiet suburban streets lined with modest modern homes, everything in its place, everything uniform and well groomed. It wasn't the type of place I would have imagined him living, but then again I hadn't seen him in close to forty years and really knew very little about his life these days. Only that he'd married a man named Hadid, a radiologist who was currently at a conference in Portland, that he'd divorced his wife, Angela, in the late 1980s, shortly after coming out, and that he'd been happily retired for over twenty years, ever since he'd left St. Agnes. These were all things that I'd learned within the first ten minutes of arriving at his house—a cute Craftsman-style home set back from the street with a beautiful garden and a small swimming pool in the back.

He'd greeted me at the front door in a pair of khaki shorts and a white linen shirt and then he'd immediately shepherded me inside and down a long hallway toward the kitchen where I could see he'd made us a small lunch: a cold pesto dish, some gazpacho soup, a light Mediterranean salad.

He looked very much the same. Like David Havelin, time had

been kind to him, though he was now completely bald and the skin along the sides of his neck was sagging a bit. Still, he was slender, and I could tell he'd kept in shape, his arms and legs deeply tanned despite the season. *My tennis tan,* he'd remarked when I mentioned it, his bronze glow, and then he'd blushed a bit in a way that told me he might have been a little nervous about our meeting as well.

Later, after we'd both sat down and had a glass of wine, he'd talked a little more about his retirement from St. Agnes, which he described as the best decision he'd ever made. He said that he'd initially retired after being diagnosed with MS, but that even later, after his MS had ended up progressing at a much slower pace than he'd anticipated and he'd realized he could have stayed on much longer, he hadn't regretted it. In retrospect, he said, he'd used the diagnosis as an excuse to do something he'd been wanting to do for years: to leave academia and to leave St. Agnes specifically. *That fucking snake pit!* he'd laughed.

He leaned forward and picked up a piece of bread from the basket in the middle of the table and passed the basket to me. I watched his fingers as he buttered his bread but could detect only a very slight tremor. He'd mentioned earlier that the doctors had eventually diagnosed his MS as benign, meaning very slow progressing, and that he'd been on an excellent treatment plan for years. He'd been very lucky, he'd said, compared to so many.

Behind him, I could see that the wall was covered with photographs of him and Hadid, their families and friends, and below that there was a bookshelf filled with cookbooks. It was a cozy kitchen, very rustic, yet modern, everything in neutral grays and whites, lots of reclaimed wood and natural stone, an enormous glass window that looked out on the perennial garden and the pool in the distance, the sweet bay trees that lined the far end of the property.

"Can I ask you something?" he said after a moment, putting down the bread he'd just buttered.

"Of course."

"Why now?"

"Why now?"

"Yes, why are you only doing this now? Why not twenty years ago?"

I shrugged. "Twenty years ago I was probably still too angry."

"And you're not now?"

"No," I said, "I'm really not."

He picked up the bread and looked at me evenly. "Really?"

Nobody ever believed me when I said this but it was true. I wasn't angry with my father in the way I'd once been, not like the way I had been in high school and college and throughout my twenties and thirties. Something had happened. Maybe having a child myself, or maybe just the passage of time, or maybe just the understanding that we're all inherently flawed, prone toward self-ishness and bad decisions, poor judgment. Mostly, though, I think that I'd just come to understand that my father had been sick. Perhaps very sick. Probably misdiagnosed, or undiagnosed. Certainly unmedicated. As for the years that had passed since then, they were harder to explain and forgive, but somehow I'd managed to, or if not forgive, then at least accept—accept that they were a mystery to me and therefore not for me to judge. Still, I could tell that Edward Bindley didn't believe me.

"Well," he said, after he'd taken a big bite of his bread and swallowed. "I don't know how helpful I'll be, Steven, but I'll certainly tell you what I know. I won't hide anything from you, I can promise you that." He glanced out the window at the pool, where sunlight was glinting on the still surface of the water, a blue raft floating languidly in the middle. "And I can tell you one thing for sure," he said. "Everything that Joseph Alors told you, you can go ahead and ignore that."

"Why's that?"

"Well, he hated your father," he said.

"Really?"

"Well, maybe 'hated' is too strong a word, but he envied him terribly. He used to complain about him to me all the time, all the attention he got. It was insufferable to him." He glanced out at the pool again. "Plus, I think he was in love with your mother."

"Really?"

"Yes." Edward laughed. "You never noticed?"

I picked up my wine and took a long sip, feeling suddenly unmoored.

"Don't worry," Edward said. "The feelings weren't mutual. I can promise you." He sat up in his chair and picked up another piece of bread. "Anyway, we all came in the same year—your father, Joseph, and me—so I was aware of it too. Your father's popularity." He paused then to cross his legs. "But it didn't bother me so much because I wasn't in the same department as him. I was in Classics. No one was comparing me to him all the time. No one was measuring me against him, you know? Not really. And besides, I loved him. I just adored your father. He was truly one of my favorite people. Just the sweetest man sometimes, and so funny. And really a brilliant teacher." He stared at me plaintively. "But I know there were other sides to him too, of course, sides I didn't see so much."

I said nothing to this but looked down at my plate and began to eat my salad.

"So what else did old Joseph say anyway?" Edward said.

"Not much," I said. "It was more what he implied."

"Which was?"

I put down my fork then and told him a little bit about the things Joseph had said about my father's book, how he'd had a chance to publish it but then how he'd decided not to, mostly out of stubbornness, how he'd basically sabotaged himself from the start.

"Sabotaged himself?" Edward rolled his eyes in disbelief. "I mean, yes, maybe later, after the verdict was announced. Maybe there was a little self-sabotage then. But not before. Not with his tenure case. It was your father who was sabotaged there."

I looked at him.

"And, as for the book, I can assure you that your father definitely wanted to publish that book. He was practically begging them at the end—he knew what was at stake—but there'd been some disagreements there earlier, and some issues with some of the peer reviewers, I think. He and I talked about this a lot, and I know he was distraught about it." He looked out at the pool. "But the thing is, it shouldn't have mattered anyway. Your father was already so accomplished, even without the book, especially compared to someone like Alors, who also didn't have a book, by the way." He shook his head in disgust, his emotions raw as if it had just happened last week. He picked up his wineglass and took a big sip.

While he'd been talking, I'd noticed a small stream of clouds moving across the sky, darkening it for a moment, and then passing. There was a terrace right in front of the swimming pool with chaise lounge chairs arranged around it in a symmetrical fashion, and when the clouds had passed over them, and then away from the terrace, the stones of the terrace seemed to glimmer in the sunlight. I slumped back in my seat and then crossed my legs.

"And how about Alors," I said after a moment, "do you think he was involved?"

"Involved?"

"Involved in sabotaging my father?"

"Oh," Edward paused and seemed to consider this for a moment. "I mean, yes, I've always suspected it, I guess. Alors and all of the other homophobes in that department." He picked up his glass again, and then leaned back in his chair with an impassive expression on his face. "You know that's what it was about, right? Your father and Deryck."

"That's why he was denied?"

"Yes. Why else?" He put down his glass again. "What other logical reason can you think of?"

I nodded, though I'd never considered this seriously as a possibility before, not as a root cause, at least. There had always been suspicions, of course, at least according to David Havelin, whispers in the hallway, and so forth, but never any direct evidence that he and Deryck had been involved, nor that anyone had condemned them for this.

"So you're saying Alors was homophobic?"

"It was 1984, Stephen. All those people were."

I nodded.

"No, the only thing your father was guilty of was falling in love." He looked at me. "And maybe trusting the wrong people. Maybe not being careful enough."

He looked down at his hands then, and I could see that the tremor was stronger now. "And he *was* in love," he said finally. "You know that, right?"

I nodded.

"And you know your mother knew it too."

I said nothing to this at first, but then finally acknowledged that I did. "We never really talked about it, though."

"Really?"

"Well, not in any great depth."

"Why not?"

"I don't know," I said. "I'm not really sure actually. We just never did."

Edward started in on his salad then, shaking his head as he chewed. When he finished a few bites, he put down his fork and stared at me again. "Well, he loved your mother," he said. "And he loved Deryck too. He loved them both. And he was very conflicted about it."

"He talked to you about this?"

"Yes. All the time." He dabbed his chin with his napkin. "David too."

"David Havelin?"

"Yes. He trusted David." He glanced out at the pool again. "There was a whole group of us who were out to each other, you see, but not out publicly. Your father and Deryck, me, Alan Hall in Admissions, a few other professors you probably didn't know. We had a sort of circle of trust, I suppose, an unspoken agreement among us, a kind of secret pact." He finished off the rest of the wine in his glass and then reached for the bottle to refill it. "It was a dangerous time to be out, of course, and your father and I were still married, for crying out loud." He laughed and shook his head, as if this was amusing to him. "It was a different time, you know? That's all I can say."

"And David Havelin was in this group?"

"No, no," he said. "David was very straight. But he was a friend to us. We all loved David."

He turned back to his salad again, and I waited while he ate some more.

"You should eat," he said when he finally looked up. "You've hardly touched anything."

I picked up my fork and speared a piece of salad. "Sorry," I said. "This is all just a lot to process, I guess." I poked at a few of the small leaves on my plate and then looked back at him.

"I'm sure it is," Edward said, plaintively. "And I hope I haven't upset you too much."

"No, not at all."

"I told you I'd tell you everything I knew."

"Yes, and I appreciate it," I said.

He pushed away his salad plate then and pulled the bowl of gazpacho closer to him, and as he picked up his spoon and put it in the soup I could see his tremor was much worse now, the gazpacho spilling over the sides. Finally, he put the spoon back down and put his hands on his lap.

"Some days are worse than others," he said, nodding at his lap.

"Sure."

"I'm sorry."

"There's no need to apologize," I said.

He slumped back in his seat then and sighed slightly. "Anyway," he said, "the thing is, Steven, you're kind of focusing on the wrong things here. You're focused on his tenure denial, but that was just a small part of it, you know? What was going on with your father—psychologically, at least—was much more complicated than just that, much bigger."

I nodded and sat there for a moment considering this.

"It wasn't just about the denial," he said. "I mean, it was on some level, of course, but that was just a very small part of it—the catalyst, if you will. It was really about so much else, you know?"

He leaned forward then and met my gaze.

"Anyway," he said, "what else can I tell you, Steven?" He sat up and composed himself. "What else would you like to know?"

"I don't know," I said after a moment, touching my glass. "I guess I'd like to know more about my father and Deryck."

"Like what?"

"Like how in love were they?"

"How in love?" He smiled. "Oh," he said. "They were very in love."

And for the next half hour, as we sat in his kitchen, finishing our lunch and drinking more wine, he told me more about my father and Deryck's relationship than I'd ever known. He told me how it all began, how it had started out as a casual friendship that fall Deryck arrived and then how it gradually evolved into something

more intimate over that winter and spring and of course throughout that summer when Deryck had been a constant presence at
our house. By the time Deryck was practically living in our cabana
house, things were very serious between them, Edward said, and
they often took day trips together to various parts of Orange
County and Los Angeles and often threw parties at Deryck's apartment near campus. Fun parties, Edward said, filled with beautiful
men and lots of booze. He talked about the fact that my father
and Deryck had had this whole other social life separate from
the social life my mother and father had, separate, that is, from
St. Agnes, and how most of the people they knew were younger
men that Deryck had befriended in various ways, few of them connected to St. Agnes or the academic world.

Later, when my father moved back in with us, Deryck was
apparently devastated, though they rarely talked to each other
or saw each other throughout that fall, even when my father was
living alone. Deryck was always trying to get my father to make a
firmer commitment, Edward said, and my father was always vacillating between the life that he'd built with my mother and me and
the life that he wanted with Deryck.

"In some ways," Edward said, "I'm not sure if your father really
knew what he wanted." He paused and picked up his glass. "Or
perhaps he just wanted too much." He looked at me then and
shrugged.

"And how about that spring," I said. "The spring after he was
denied?"

Edward nodded. "Well, it all started up again then, right?
Though perhaps more intensely." He stopped himself. "I'm not
sure if this is all stuff you really want to hear," he said.

"I don't mind," I assured him.

"I know your mother and you were very close," he said. "And I
know it was all very hard for her."

"It was a lot," I agreed, "for all of us."

Edward nodded again and looked at his glass. "Anyway, it got strange after that, I guess, and I don't know a lot of the particulars. I don't know that anyone does beyond your father and Deryck. All I know is one night I went over to Deryck's apartment—this must have been in May, right when everything was falling apart for your father—and your father was there, and it was very clear that they were breaking up. There was just an awkwardness between them that you could feel. A tension. There must have been about five or six of us there that night, just a small party, and after your father left I remember Deryck going into his bedroom and not coming out for the rest of the night. The rest of us eventually left, calling goodbye to him through his closed door, and the next time I saw him he was packing up his office in the English Department and heading back to Massachusetts, where he'd apparently already lined up another visiting position at Williams."

"Which eventually turned into a tenure track position, right?"

"That's right."

"And where he still is."

"Yes. Where he still is.

"The thing is," Edward continued, "it was never purely a physical thing with them, though I know that was a part of it. It was intellectual too. Perhaps more intellectual than physical in certain ways, if that makes sense. They thought very similarly, you see, your father and Deryck, and they had very similar tastes in literature and art, and of course they were both very brilliant, albeit in different ways." He paused. "And they were almost perfect complements for each other too. The way your father was so erratic and wild, and the way Deryck was so grounded and stoic. It could be pretty funny to hang out with them. I mean, they could be very funny together, as a couple. They played off each other well and teased each other a lot." He shook his head then and stopped himself again. "I'm sorry," he said. "Am I saying too much? You're looking uncomfortable."

"No, no," I said. "I asked, right?" But it was true that it was a lot to take in, a lot to process, even if I had imagined it many times myself, in my mind, and it was true that I felt bad for my mother, my mother who had adored my father and stood by him, my mother who had trusted him implicitly and believed him when he'd said that it was over. Believed him again and again. It was just hard to reconcile the man that Edward was describing with the man who had stood in my parents' bedroom and told my mother over and over how much he loved her (as my mother would confide in me years later), who had kissed her again and again in our kitchen and held her hand, who had reassured her of his devotion, his commitment, his love.

"And you're saying that someone found out about them then?"

"I mean, there'd always been whispers," Edward said. "But yes, I think one of them—" He stopped himself and looked down at his empty bowl, as if considering what he wanted to say next. "What I heard was—and this was just a rumor—but what I heard was that Deryck had confided in someone—it might have been Alors, it might have been someone else—and that whoever this person was told others in the English Department and that pretty soon everyone knew. It got around." He looked at me.

"And you think that's why they voted against him?"

"Everyone has their opinion," Edward said. "I'm just giving you mine."

I nodded and looked down at my hands. "And did you ever keep in touch with Deryck after he left?"

"I did," Edward said. "I did, and I still do occasionally. Not so much in recent years, but we've stayed in touch, stayed friends, yes."

I told him then about the many emails I'd sent to Deryck in the past few months, the letter that I wrote, the phone calls, how he hadn't responded to any of them.

"Well, can you blame him?" Edward said.

"What do you mean?"

"Well, consider what's at stake for him," he said. "He's been married close to forty years. He has grown children, grandchildren."

"It's not like I'm going to advertise it to his whole family."

"I know," Edward said, "but you have to understand Deryck. He's an unusual guy. In his mind, those two years at St. Agnes never really happened. Or parts of them happened and parts of them didn't. He put a lot of those memories away in a drawer somewhere and locked them up."

"You don't talk about it with him?"

"About your father? No." He shook his head. "No, not in a very long time. We don't even talk about St. Agnes really. Mostly we just correspond by email anyway. General news about our lives and stuff like that."

"So he just flipped a switch then?"

"I don't think anyone can just flip a switch," Edward said. "But some of us are better at compartmentalizing our feelings than others. All I know is that at a certain point Deryck made a decision to go in a different direction in his life. That's all I know."

"And you don't think it's strange?"

"I try not to judge people," Edward said and filled up his glass again. "We're all on our own journeys, right?" He passed the bottle to me, but I shook my head, explaining I had to drive.

For a while we sat there quietly, and then I said, "Do you think there's any chance you could get him to contact me?"

Edward narrowed his eyes.

"I know it's a big ask."

"I really don't think he will, Steven," he said, "if I'm being honest." Then he paused for a moment, as if considering it. "But yes, I can send him an email, I guess." He picked up his glass, and I could see the tremor again as he took a sip. "He's not going to meet with you in person, of course, but maybe he'll talk to you on the phone."

"Or Skype?" I said.

Edward narrowed his eyes again.

"I'd like to see his face," I said.

"Like I said, it's not likely," Edward said, "but I can try."

Before I left, Edward took me on a walk around his garden, pointing out the different flowers that he'd planted that fall and the previous summer, talking also about my mother and how she had always had the most impressive gardens, how he'd always envied her aesthetic. He seemed old as he walked, older than he'd seemed when he'd first greeted me at the door and shepherded me down the hallway to the kitchen, and I felt a sudden sadness then at the difficulty he seemed to be having climbing up the staircase to the house.

Later, as we stood outside my car in his driveway, I asked him the one question I hadn't bothered to ask him earlier, the most obvious question perhaps: whether or not he'd ever been in contact with my father since he'd left. He paused for a moment and then shook his head no. He said he hadn't, that he hadn't heard a single thing about him or from him since then.

"If he's still alive," he said, "he's certainly living under another name."

I nodded.

"Have you ever considered hiring a private investigator?" he said.

"Everyone asks me that." I smiled. "But the thing is, I think a part of me is still a little afraid of finding him, you know? I know that must sound strange."

"No, not at all," Edward said. "I think I can understand it." It was chilly out now, and Edward folded his arms across his chest, hugging himself. "Of course, at this age, there's a good chance there's someone looking after him, you know, at least if he's still alive. Have you ever considered that?"

"I have."

"How about your uncle," he said, "his brother? They were always very close, right?"

I told him then that I'd just seen him, that I'd just been out to Julian's and that there hadn't been a sign of my father anywhere. "He claims he hasn't heard from him in many years," I said. "Not in like a very long time."

"Hmmm," Edward said, thinning his lips and raising his eyebrows suggestively.

"What?"

"Maybe ask him again," he said and winked. He seemed now as if he was trying to tell me something without telling me something. "You never know, right?"

17

On the night my father received the letter denying his first appeal, I was out in the garden with my mother helping her plant delphiniums. This would have been early April, I think, a month or so before the end of the school year. It was a breezy night, the air cool and crisp, and we were both wearing sweatshirts as we worked. When my father eventually emerged from the house, I could tell he was in an agitated state. He stood by the grill and lit a cigarette and then read the letter over and over again underneath the light from the patio, as my mother and I looked on. At a certain point, he crumpled up the letter and shouted *fuck!*, so loud that a light went on in one of the neighboring houses, and then he turned around and disappeared inside the house. I looked over at my mother and she was squinting back at the house in a concerned way, biting her lip.

"I should go inside," she said after a moment, and I nodded.

She stood up then, put down her spade, and brushed off her jeans. Then I watched her as she walked back toward the house.

I don't think I fully understood what had just happened at that moment but I knew it wasn't good. I also knew that my father had been alienating more and more people at St. Agnes. There were the letters he'd been writing, but also there'd been a number of confrontations with various members of the faculty and administration, confrontations that I'd heard him describing to my mother in exhaustive detail over dinner or late at night when they'd thought I was sleeping. In all of these stories my father came across as the victim, not the aggressor, but I could tell, even then, that he was burning a lot of bridges, making a lot of enemies. On top of that, he'd recently begun to involve the students as well, recruiting one of his most devoted and talented to write a letter for the school paper about the injustice of his denial, getting others— almost a hundred—to sign a petition that was then handed over to Albert Doyle, the chair of the English Department, along with a letter requesting a reconsideration of my father's case. One day, there was even a small student protest outside the front steps of the English Department building, a protest organized by my father's most loyal and committed students, some of them holding up signs, others shouting imperatives and demands. I think that my father believed that the accumulation of some of these tactics might have an effect, but obviously it hadn't. Obviously it hadn't done anything but alienate the very people he'd been trying to persuade.

I stood up after a moment and looked back at the house, trying to surmise what was happening inside, but I couldn't see a thing. There was a light on in the kitchen but no movement, no sign at all of either of my parents. Finally, after a few minutes had passed with no sound from inside, I picked up the remaining delphiniums and placed them in the holes that we'd dug, making sure that the tops of the root balls were level with the soil. Then I sprinkled the ground with broadcast lime and wood ashes and gave the entire garden a good soak. It was a strangely quiet night, peaceful, and I sat there for a while in the garden, just waiting for some sign that it was okay to return. At a certain point I heard the sound of my father's voice, loud and booming from inside the house; then a short time after that I heard the sound of his car starting up in the driveway out front and taking off.

I knew where he was headed—the same place he'd been headed almost every other night that month—to Deryck Evanson's place. He wasn't even trying to hide it anymore, and my mother had long since given up trying to stop him. There were bigger things at stake, I guess, or maybe she'd just come to a point where she was too tired to try to protest anymore.

An exhaustion had settled in, I think, and I could see it in her face that night as I walked into the house and found her sitting down at the kitchen table pouring herself a large glass of wine. Her hands were still dirty from the garden and her cheeks and nose were smudged with streaks of dried mud. She lit a cigarette and regarded me, and when I asked her what had happened, she told me very briefly about my father's appeal, how it had been rejected, but then assured me that he'd still have a second chance to appeal the following fall, that not all hope was lost.

"But this is bad," I said

"It's not necessarily bad," she said. "It's just part of the process. Your father is just disappointed right now. That's all."

She looked at me and gave me a gentle smile. "By the way," she said, "Chau called."

"Just now?"

"Yes."

"Did he say what he wanted?"

"No," she said. "Just to call him back." She nodded at the phone on the wall.

"Okay," I said, "thanks."

I hadn't spoken to Chau in almost three months, not since that night at Brody's house, and I wondered what he wanted. It seemed strange that we'd gone so long without talking. It was the longest we'd ever gone since I'd known him, and it felt like a kind of deprivation, or perhaps a trial of endurance.

Later, as I sat in my father's office, the phone cord stretched across the hallway, the door shut, I felt a strange mixture of excitement and fear as I listened to the ringtone on the other end. I thought about Mai and what she'd said to me the last time I'd called, worried that she might pick up again, and I thought about Chau and the way he'd been ignoring me at school, the way he'd always look down at his feet when I passed him in the hall or quickly run and blend in with a group of his other friends. He'd started to dress more and more in the punk rock aesthetic, the same Black Flag and Suicidal Tendencies T-shirts, the same ripped jeans, his head shaved close in the back and on the sides, but long in the front, his bleached bangs pushed back behind his left ear. I heard that he'd been going to shows on the weekends too, at Ichabod's and Jezebel's, Social Distortion and Agent Orange and some of the other punk bands that were emerging at that time in Fullerton, bands that a lot of the kids at the middle school were starting to listen to then.

I worried that a part of him might have been fundamentally changed since that night at Brody's, that he wouldn't be the same person anymore, but as soon as I heard his voice on the other end of the line all of those fears seemed to vanish. He sounded the same as always, his voice just as familiar as it had always been, but also quieter that night, more reserved, even meek, reticent in a way that told me that something was wrong. I asked him if everything was okay, and after a long pause he told me that his mother had died the previous week, that she'd lasted longer than anyone could have expected but that it had finally happened. That's why he hadn't been in school, he said, and why he hadn't called me for a while. It had been a difficult few weeks, he said, and both his father and Mai were a mess. Then he added that the funeral had been the previous weekend and that he was sorry he hadn't told me. They'd had lots of relatives in town, lots of his mother's family, and it had been a pretty chaotic time. He said he hadn't been able to do much of anything lately, that he'd mostly just been staying at home, reading. That was it. Then he was quiet for a while. I was struck by the formality of his tone. There was a coldness to it, but I knew it was just a front, that he was just trying to keep the stronger emotions down, that inwardly he was devastated of course.

"So that sucks," he said, finally, and was quiet again.

I told him I was so sorry to hear about his mother but didn't know what else to say. I'd never known anyone who had lost a parent before.

"I don't know why I'm calling you," he said, "but I guess I'd like to see you."

"Okay."

"Do you think you could come meet me?"

"Tonight?"

"Yeah."

"Where?"

He was quiet again. Then he said he was at home now but that he'd be going over to Brody's later with Mai. He said that neither one of them could stand being in their apartment anymore, that their father was being impossible. I told him I'd have to wait till my mother left for her evening shift at nine and that it was kind of a long way to bike.

"I'll have Mai come get you."

"You sure?"

"Yeah," he said. "She'll do it. Trust me."

I tried to imagine what Mai would say to this but didn't press the issue further.

"We're going over soon," he said, "and she'll be by in like an hour to get you, okay? Just be ready."

"Okay," I said and then we both hung up.

· · ·

As it turned out, Mai didn't show up until almost ten o'clock. When she did, she was reticent, as Chau had been earlier, but perhaps more melancholy. She didn't seem particularly thrilled about the fact that she was picking me up, and after I'd told her I was sorry to hear about her mother, and she thanked me, she didn't say much else the rest of the way there. Mostly we just listened to the tape in her car—a mix of slow songs by bands like the Thompson Twins and The Psychedelic Furs—and watched the small houses on the backstreets get bigger as we moved closer to Sunny Hills.

At Brody's house, we found Brody and Chau sitting in the back by the lit swimming pool, drinking some type of fruit juice that I assumed was spiked with alcohol. When Brody noticed us, he sat up and waved in a jovial way, then motioned us over.

"My friend," he said to me, and I nodded. "What are you drinking, my friend?" he added, standing up then and walking over to the pool bar.

I told him I was fine.

"Oh, that's right," he said. "You prefer doobage, right?" He nodded toward the chaise lounge chairs where he and Chau had been sitting and where I now noticed there was a bong sitting on the ground between their chairs.

Chau lifted it up and motioned me over.

I didn't know if I should hug him or say something. It felt strange to suddenly be in his presence, to be standing there in front of him, looking at him, as if he might somehow be different now, changed by his mother's death.

He just smiled, though, and passed me the bong, and then a lighter. All around the pool, I now noticed there were little white candles in tiny glasses, as if this were a ceremony of some sort, a kind of mourning, and in the background, from the speakers above the pool bar, I could hear the faint sound of Pink Floyd's *The Wall*.

Mai walked over to Brody and whispered something into his ear and a moment later Brody looked over at us and told us to make ourselves at home, that his parents were away till Sunday. Then he said that he and Mai would be going inside for a while but to just call if we needed anything. Mai gave us both a stern look, as if to say, *don't embarrass me,* and then turned back to Brody, who quickly put his arm around her and led her inside.

When I turned back to Chau, he motioned for me to light the bong, and after I'd taken a hit and the world began to soften a bit, I felt suddenly grateful for the pot, relieved to have something to lighten the mood, to alleviate the awkwardness between us. I put the bong down on the ground in between the two chairs and then sat down in the chair next to Chau, saying nothing. The pool was a beautiful glowing blue, and there was a faint mist hovering above the water at the far end and in between the boulders at the edges of the waterfall, which was burbling now, quietly, in the distance.

I tried to think of something to say to him, something about his mother, but before I could, he stood up and walked over to the edge of the pool and peeled off his T-shirt and jumped in. When he reemerged a moment later, he pulled himself up onto the concrete edge and smiled.

"Come in," he said. "It feels good."

I can't remember how long we swam there that night, maybe an hour or so, but I remember that it felt amazing to be floating there in that luxurious pool, that pool that was nicer than any pool I would ever own, or that my parents would ever own, floating there on my back next to Chau, both of us stoned, staring up at the distant stars, these incredibly bright stars, the sound of Pink Floyd in the background, the sensation of being both weightless and grounded at the same time. The feeling of being both lost and locked in place.

Later, after we'd toweled ourselves off and put on our T-shirts, we walked over to a set of boulders at the far end of the pool and sat down on the edge, dangling our feet in the water. Chau had brought along the bong and a pack of cigarettes that Mai had left on a table near the bar, and after we'd sat down, he passed me the cigarettes and then handed me the lighter.

"Sorry I've been so out of touch," he said after I'd lit my cigarette.

"It's okay."

"I haven't been ignoring you."

"I know."

"It's just been—I don't know. It's been fucked up."

I nodded.

"It's been really crazy, you know?" He looked down at his lap then and crossed his arms. "And now Mai wants to take off," he said, "and my dad's freaking out, but I think she's probably going to do it anyway, you know?" He looked at me.

"What are you talking about?"

"She wants to go up to Humboldt State with Brody next fall. He just got in off the wait list."

"He's going to Humboldt State?"

"Yep."

"I didn't realize he was that old."

"I know," he said. "I told you he was lame."

Before this, I don't think I'd ever given much thought to Brody's age, but if I'd been asked I would have probably said he was closer in age to Mai—maybe fifteen or sixteen—not an eighteen-year-old, headed off to Humboldt State. Suddenly the fact that he'd given us alcohol and weed, the fact that he was dating a tenth grader, felt different.

"Is that even legal?" I said. "I mean, is she even legally allowed to do that?"

"I don't know," Chau said, "but I don't think she cares." He shook his head and looked out at the water. "Fucking Brody," he said. "He's going to ruin her whole life."

I looked up at the house where I could see a light was now on in Brody's room, could see shadows moving along the wall. I tried to make out their bodies, but it was too far away to see very much.

"And the other thing," he said, and I could tell now he was hesitant, nervous to say whatever he was going to say next. "And the other thing is now my dad wants to move too. Says he can't stand to stay in our apartment."

I stared at him. "Where to?"

"San Diego," he said. "That's where his brother lives, my uncle." He shrugged, then looked down at his lap, as if ashamed or guilty for having to share this news.

I stared down at my lap too, feeling suddenly gutted, stunned by the surprise of this, the pot somehow making it seem less real though. The next day I'd feel the sting of it harder, I'd feel the sting of it so hard I'd cry for several hours, but at that moment it just felt like one more disappointment in a spring of disappointments, another layer of my life being peeled away.

"I can still visit though," he said, reaching over and patting my shoulder. "It's not that far."

I nodded, though I sensed even then this would probably never happen.

"And maybe if things don't work out for your dad, you can move down there too. You and your parents."

I nodded again.

Earlier that night, while we'd been swimming, I'd told him a little about my father, about the fact that his tenure proposal had been denied, the fact that his appeal had been too, but I could sense he didn't quite feel the gravity of the situation—at least, the gravity of the situation for my father—the fact that it wasn't just about losing his job but about losing his whole identity.

"That wouldn't be for another year, though, anyway," I said, "even if it doesn't work out."

"What do you mean?" Chau stared at me, puzzled.

"I mean, even if he's officially denied, he still gets to work there for another year."

Chau shook his head at this, as if in disbelief. "I've never heard of that," he said. "You get fired from a job but then you still get to stick around for a year. A *whole* year." He shook his head again and then reached over for the bong.

After he'd taken a hit, he passed it to me, and I took one as well, although I already felt pretty high and was worried about getting too messed up. I looked back at the house and then closed my eyes and took in the chlorine scent of the air. I could feel the dampness of my shorts still, could hear the tape of *The Wall,* still playing on repeat.

When I finally opened my eyes again, I could see that Chau was rubbing at his eyelids, as if he'd just been crying, wiping at the side of his face with his T-shirt, then looking down at his lap.

I put my hand on his shoulder because it suddenly felt natural to do this, to touch him, though I knew I'd never be able to do this during the day, would never have the courage to. We sat there for a while in silence.

"It was so fucking trippy," he said finally, after I'd removed my hand. "She was there and then she wasn't, you know?" He was looking now at the palm trees in the shadows on the other side of the yard. "Mai was the one who found her, but I'd seen her that morning, before I'd left for school. We'd talked, and it was no different than any other day. She told me to get my bangs cut. She told me I looked like a freak. That was the last thing she said to me. She said: *look the way you want others to treat you.* Then I left for school, and, you know, that was it."

I said nothing to this, though I had a lot I wanted to say, a lot I wanted to tell him. I wanted to tell him, for instance, that I knew how much his mother had loved him, that I'd heard it in her voice, seen it in her face. He was her golden child, after all, not Mai—not Mai, who she had fought with constantly, Mai who had constantly challenged her—but I could see that he was holding on to that final moment—that final thing she'd said to him—as if it were some type of final word on their relationship. *My son, get your bangs cut. My son, you're a freak.*

I looked over at the house where I could now see Brody and Mai, standing at the sliding glass patio doors, looking out.

"We're leaving in like five minutes," Mai shouted. "It's a school night." Then she went back inside, and I could see Brody and her, walking around the kitchen, straightening things up, picking up the many abandoned fast-food containers and red plastic cups, putting everything in the trash, then wiping down the counters, everything looking very domestic in there.

"The thing is," Chau said after a while, "it could happen to any one of us. Or to anyone we know. Anyone we know could just suddenly be gone. Disappeared."

He reached over then and touched my hand, squeezed it, then let it go.

"Do you ever think about that?"

I told him I did.

He picked up his cigarettes then and shrugged.

"And the strange thing is," he said, "she'd told me the week before that she wasn't scared. She said that she wasn't scared of it because her family was beside her." He looked at me. "But I don't know if I'd feel that way. I think I'd be pretty scared, and I don't think that I'd want anyone I knew around me at all, you know?" He looked at me again. "Does that sound strange?"

I told him it didn't.

A moment later, the sliding glass patio doors opened again, and Mai appeared, looking out.

"Come on," she shouted, "let's go!"

. . .

I would see Chau once more after that. A random encounter in the hallway at school, in between fifth and sixth periods. This would be at the end of the school year, the very last week of school, in fact, and we'd make plans that afternoon to see each other one more time after that, one more time before he left. But something must have happened after that because I never did see him again, and the next time I called him, a week or so later, his phone number was already out of service, and he and his father were already moved out, already living down in San Diego.

Later that summer, I'd get a postcard from him, telling me how much he loved San Diego, how great it was, and how I had to come down and visit. Could I ask my parents? he'd asked at the end. But I'd be in a very different mental space then, unable to do much of anything, let alone write a letter, and I'd never write back to him, and he'd never write to me again either, and over time the distance between us would gradually grow, grow to the point that after a while it would begin to seem impossible that we'd ever find a way to bridge it.

Then, many years later, when I was in graduate school, and finally comfortable using the internet and search engines, I'd do a search for Chau one night and discover that he'd been killed in a drunk-driving accident in La Jolla just a few months before his seventeenth birthday, just about five years after that last time I'd seen him. There would be a small picture of him next to the article, and he'd look basically the same as always, albeit a little older and more clean-cut than the last time I'd seen him. The article would say he'd been an honor student and a track star, that he was survived by his father and his sister, Mai. I wouldn't be able to discern much else from the article, but from what I could gather, it had been the other driver, not him, who had been responsible. It would seem amazing to me at the time that this had happened and I'd not known of it, that no one had bothered to tell me, and the whole way home from the library that night, as I walked home along the quiet streets of campus, I'd feel disconnected from my body in a way I couldn't explain.

Later that night, alone in our apartment, I'd go out to the balcony to smoke a cigarette and end up staying out there most of the night, just chain-smoking and drinking from a bottle of Glenlivet that Alison had bought me for New Year's. I'd feel a sense of emotional displacement then, a strange disorientation, but it was only later, when Alison finally got home herself and came out to the balcony to find me, it was only then, when I saw the expression on her face, that I realized I'd been crying the whole time.

I don't know how Chau fits into this story but he does. He's all mixed up in my mind with my father and that crazy year and all of the unresolved feelings I still have about it all. I ended up sleeping with a few men in college, but it wasn't how I'd imagined it, and it wasn't like it had been with Chau. I was pretty sure I was mostly straight, although when I look back on Chau I can say without hesitation that he was my first love, the first person I'd ever desired, even before I'd known what desiring was. He was everything I'd ever wanted in a soulmate and a best friend—everything that Alison was too—only the problem was he wasn't real, or at least he'd begun to seem less and less real as time had passed, more of a figment of my imagination, a creation of my unreliable memory, an idealized version of something I wanted rather than something I had. He'd become memorialized, I think, as we often do with the dead, and in this way he'd become an unattainable ideal.

Still, I know that my feelings for him had been real, just as I knew that his feelings for me had been. I knew it in the way he looked at me, in the way he blushed every time he met my eyes. And I knew it even after he'd left, even after we'd stopped talking and corresponding, I knew even then that he was thinking of me, just as I was thinking of him. I knew it like I knew the sound of my own name, like I knew the smell of my own skin.

Later that night, as we drove back to our side of Fullerton, Mai blasted the radio and said nothing to either one of us the whole way home. I could see in her expression, her eyes, that a part of her was already checked out, already done with high school, already halfway up the I-5 to Humboldt State with Brody. Still, I watched her from the backseat as she drove, fascinated, as I'd always been, by her nihilism, her utter renunciation of everything her family stood for; and as we pulled up closer to my house and she put the car into park, I was surprised when she finally turned around and smiled at me, then said very quietly that it was time for me to get out.

Chau turned around then too, patted my hand, and told me to call him. I nodded and got out of the car and then started down the pathway to our house, feeling suddenly very high, but also strangely elated, and I remember everything after that feeling very surreal, the sound of Chau's voice trailing behind me, getting louder, *Hey, Steven! Hey Steven!* he was shouting, then turning around to see him dangling out of the passenger window, waving frantically.

Hey Steven! he shouted again.

And I stood there then, staring.

Listen, he shouted. *Listen up!*

Then he dipped back inside the car again to turn up the vol-

ume on the radio and a moment later I heard the famous opening guitar lick to "Edge of Seventeen," the rhythmic strumming,
and Stevie's voice coming on, low and powerful: *Just like the white
winged dove, sings a song sounds like she's singing. Ooh, baby, ooh, said ooh.*

Chau turned up the volume then so that the whole neighborhood could hear and then looked back at me, laughing. I can still
remember his smile at the moment, the glint in his eyes, the way
he was dancing as he dangled out the window.

It's your girl! he was shouting. *It's your girl!*

Then a moment later, Mai yanked him back inside the car and
turned down the radio and hit the gas, and just like that they were
gone.

18

In one of the last letters that my father wrote to my mother before she moved out to Berkeley to join him, before they married, he quoted a series of passages from Proust on the theme of death. Even now, thinking back on that time, trying to imagine it, it seems strange to me that he'd choose to conclude what had otherwise been a fairly romantic two-year correspondence on such an ominous note. Death would be the theme of that letter about Proust and it would also be a theme that he'd return to, or reference, in his other remaining letters. I'm not really sure what to make of any of it now, in retrospect, only that I remember discovering the letter after my mother's death, arranged chronologically among his other letters to her, and being chilled by the tone of it. There was something unusually grave and foreboding about it, but also strangely prescient, and though I can't remember all of the passages he quoted, there was one I wrote down in my journal and that I still return to from time to time, especially when I'm feeling low:

> People do not die for us immediately, but remain bathed
> in a sort of aura of life which bears no relation to true

immortality but through which they continue to occupy our thoughts in the same way as when they were alive. It is as though they were traveling abroad.

This idea of "traveling abroad," of death being a kind of travel, and of the dead not really dying for us immediately, these were things that I often thought about when I thought about my mother, or Chau, or other people in my life that I'd lost, and for a long time they were concepts I applied to my father when I thought about him, when I believed, as I did for a long time, he was dead.

I was trying to explain this to Alison the following day as we sat over lattes at Caffè Strada on the south side of Berkeley's campus. This was a café that we used to come to a lot in our early days in Berkeley. It was only about six blocks from our apartment and it was reasonably priced, and though it was often crowded with college students, it had a beautiful outdoor patio area that looked out on College Avenue and the School of Law across the street. It also had a wonderful energy to it, a kind of quiet urgency, all of these college students cramming for exams, writing papers on their laptops, quizzing each other with flash cards.

Alison always insisted that we sit outside, even when it was a little chilly, as it was that night, and she always ordered the same thing, a Strada Bianca (white hot chocolate with warm milk) followed by a latte. Earlier that day, I'd stopped by the apartment in Oakland that my friend had recommended, the rent-controlled sublet, and had been less than enthused. It was the type of place I might have been able to live in in my early twenties, but not the type of place I could fathom living in now. I'd spent the rest of the day wandering around the streets of Berkeley, dipping in and out of used bookstores and record shops, visiting old haunts, feeling discouraged and deflated.

Now, though, sitting across from Alison in the soft evening light of Caffè Strada, the slow-moving traffic on College Avenue, the steady flow of college students passing by wearing backpacks, heading home from their late afternoon classes, I felt suddenly refreshed, even optimistic. I picked up my latte and took a long sip, then smiled at her.

"So you're saying you feel certain that he's dead now?" Alison said, trying to decipher what I was getting at by bringing up the quote from Proust.

"No," I said, "I feel certain that he's not."

She stared at me then and narrowed her eyes in the way she did when she was confused by what I was saying.

"It's just a feeling I have," I said, and then I told her about the conversation I'd had with Edward Bindley and the way it had ended and the way that I felt he was hinting at something by encouraging me to contact Julian again, the way that it seemed he knew more than he was letting on.

"But this is something you could have figured out years ago," she said, "if you'd wanted to."

"I know."

"And it always seemed to me you didn't want to know, right? So that's changed?"

"I guess," I said. "I don't know."

She squinted at me again, but this time in a way that suggested she was irritated. She'd looked the same way when I'd told her about the prospect of talking to Deryck Evanson on Skype, an idea she didn't see the logic in, and when I'd mentioned the sublet and how untenable it seemed. I'd intended for this meeting to be a kind of mending of bridges, but I could see it wasn't going that way, so I tried to reset, picking up my latte again, changing the subject.

"So you said you had something you wanted to tell me," I said after a moment, calmly.

"I did?"

"Yes, earlier. When you texted."

"Oh right," Alison nodded, remembering. "It was nothing. I mean, it's probably nothing."

"Now I'm intrigued."

She smiled, but it was a weak smile, a tentative smile, a smile that told me I wasn't going to like what she had to tell me.

"So it's not good news?"

"I don't know," she said. "I mean it could be. Potentially." She looked out at the sidewalk, where a group of students were walking by, their heads pointed down at their phones, scrolling as they walked. "I got an offer," she said finally.

"An offer?"

"Yes. For a job."

I stared at her. "I didn't know you were looking."

"I wasn't. I mean it just kind of happened, I guess." She picked up her cup.

"Well, that's a good thing, right?"

"It could be," she said, "yes. It depends."

And that's when she told me what the job was, director of a public policy program at a major university, a definite promotion from the position she had now, and what the job paid, also a considerable upgrade, and then finally, very quietly, where the job was: Amherst, Massachusetts, at the University of Massachusetts, Amherst's Program for Public Policy. She went on to explain how the whole thing had just kind of happened randomly. A friend of hers from graduate school, Melody Ho, had mentioned her name to the previous director, a professor who was looking for a non-academic to replace him, someone with real-world public policy experience, someone who could guide and mentor these young undergraduates with nonprofit ambitions and goals. It was the type of work that Alison had been wanting to do more and more lately, and that she often talked to me about, teaching and mentoring the next generation, serving as a resource and an advisor rather than a rabble-rouser on the front line of change. She'd exhausted that side of herself, she felt, and wanted something different, something more directly influential and substantive.

When she finished she looked down at her lap and crossed her arms and neither of us said anything for a while.

I tried to take it all in, what she was saying and also what it meant. I sipped on my latte.

"I know it's a lot to think about," she said finally.

"So you'd want me to go too?"

"Of course," she said. "Of course I'd want you to go. Whether we're living together or not I'd want you to be there to be a part of Finn's life."

I nodded. "But not necessarily together?"

"What do you mean?"

"I mean, not necessarily living together."

She looked out at the buildings across the street, sighed. "That's not my decision to make," she said flatly. "That's a decision we need to make together."

"Together?"

"Yes."

"But what do you want?"

"It's not about what I want."

I looked at her. "Even so," I said, "what do you *want*?"

But of course I knew what she wanted. This was a once-in-a-lifetime opportunity for her, a chance to blend the two worlds she loved: the world of academia and the world of public policy. But still, I could see she was trying to be diplomatic, trying to hide her enthusiasm, trying to act as if this were just a strange coincidence and not something she truly wanted, not something she'd been hoping for for years.

"I mean it would be nice to finally own a home," she said sitting back. "That's something that would be possible there, with that salary. We could have a house, a yard. Think about how many years we've rented, how many years in apartments." She looked at me. "And there'd be the stability of it too." She rubbed her arms. "At this age, I can't say that's not appealing, especially with Finn getting older."

I nodded, bit my lip.

"And the schools there are pretty good too," she continued, "in the Pioneer Valley. I've looked into them a little." She looked down then, realizing perhaps that she'd shown her cards, revealed just how far along in the process she already was.

"I know you love California," she said quietly.

"So do you."

"But not in the same way. I'm not from here."

And she was right. She'd never had the same attachment to the state that I did, had never loved it as much. She had often talked about the possibility of leaving, had often questioned whether it was really worth the price of admission, the high cost of living.

"And also," she said steadily, looking down at her hands, "I think it would be good for us."

"For us?"

"Yes, and for you."

"What do you mean?"

"I mean, getting out of Berkeley," she said quietly. "For the obvious reasons."

And I knew what she meant, of course. It was not lost on me that I'd decided to settle down less than a mile from the neighborhood where my father had lived during graduate school, that I often passed the Department of English where he'd studied and earned his degree, that I was essentially living in the shadow of his most promising years, pursuing a career path that was undeniably similar to his, not as a scholar perhaps, but as a teacher of writing and language, as a person who worked with undergraduates. None of this was lost on me, and it was something that Alison and I had talked about often, and that I'd talked about with the various therapists I'd seen over the years, all of whom thought it was very interesting that I'd chosen to live here, that I'd made that decision.

"You've known for a long time that it's probably not healthy for you to be here," she said, glancing out at the street.

I nodded, and I thought then about the letter I'd written to Alison in the days before I moved out, the letter I left for her when I finally did, how I talked openly for the first time about my fear of abandonment, how I'd lived my entire life in a constant state of fear, worried that the people I loved most would abandon me, not wanting to ever relive what I'd experienced with my father, waking up one morning to discover him gone, and how I felt I was now somehow repeating the cycle myself, how in trying to avoid a certain outcome I'd unwittingly made it happen. I'd been closed off to her, I wrote, not because of disinterest but because of an almost overwhelming fear that I was one day going to wake up and find her gone. *That's what all of this is about,* I wrote. *That's what it is.* It was the most I'd ever written on the subject, or said, and I'd waited nervously for her reply, but her reply never came. The next time we spoke she simply said, *Thank you for the letter, it meant a lot,* and that was all.

Now, though, she was looking at me in an earnest way, as if she sensed what I was thinking, or as if she was recalling what I was recalling.

"I think it will help you to release it," she continued.

"It?"

"Whatever it is. Your anger."

I looked at her. "It's not anger."

This was an argument we had often. She was convinced I had unresolved feelings of anger toward my father and I was convinced I didn't, that I'd let those go long ago.

"You haven't tried to look for him in almost forty years."

"Because I haven't wanted to."

"Because you're still angry."

"I'm not," I said. "It's not about that."

I looked down at my hands and saw that they were gripping my knees now, that I was beginning to feel unmoored.

"You know, maybe that letter your father wrote about death," she continued. "Maybe it wasn't really about that."

"What do you mean?"

"I mean, maybe it was about fear, not death. Fear of what your father was about to get himself into by getting married, potentially having a family. Maybe it was about a kind of symbolic death, a realization that a part of himself was dying. Maybe that's what he was trying to communicate subconsciously to your mother, or maybe to himself."

I shook my head and looked out across the street at the School of Law, feeling dizzy, the students sitting around on the benches outside seeming suddenly like a dream.

"You know, I'm going to have to think about all this," I said finally.

"This?"

"This move. Or potential move. I'm just not sure I'm ready to leave California yet."

She eyed me steadily. "Well, it's not really your decision to make, Steven."

"What do you mean?"

"I mean this isn't really your decision to make," she said. "It's not about you." She looked down at her hands then. "None of this is actually about you."

. . .

Later that night, as I sat over a margarita at one of our favorite tapas bars in Berkeley, a place called César, right next to Chez Panisse, a restaurant that Alison and I had gone to for our last three anniversaries, I found myself revisiting a memory of something Alison had said to me years before. This was when we were both in our early thirties, years before Finn was born.

It was a warm night in early summer, a few years into our marriage, and I had just finished making us dinner and cleaning the apartment, something I did almost compulsively at the time, and Alison had looked up at me from the small table in the kitchen, where she was sitting, reading the paper, and smiled. *You know,* she said, putting down the paper, looking at me, *you don't have to work so hard to please me all the time, Steven. I'm not going anywhere.* She said this gently, with kindness, but it stopped me in my tracks. It was like she'd seen inside of me and revealed some shameful secret about me, some flaw in my psychology, that I did not do the things I did because I was a dutiful and attentive husband, but because I needed to do them, because I'd been conditioned to please, because it gave me a sense of power and control.

After that, I'd toned down my compulsive cooking and cleaning, but my abandonment issues remained, manifesting themselves in other strange ways, occasional bouts of jealousy and possessiveness, occasional periods of depression, and most recently, through the way I'd almost unconsciously pushed her away, created an emotional distance between us, started drinking.

I was thinking about this later that night in light of the comment she'd made earlier about me being angry. I didn't feel angry but that didn't mean I wasn't. Still, it didn't feel wholly true either.

Before I'd left Caffè Strada, I'd made this point again, that I didn't think that was it, that I didn't think it was about anger, and she'd just raised her eyebrows as if to say, *thou doth protest too much.*

Then she stood up and gave me a hug, and it surprised me the way she pulled me in, the way the touch of her hand on the back of my neck gave me shivers.

After that, I walked around Berkeley for a while by myself, just trying to clear my head, then gradually making my way down Shattuck Avenue to César. I was about a mile and a half away from my car at that point, but I didn't care. All I wanted to do was sit down and relax, have a drink.

César was crowded that night, and there was a line on the sidewalk outside, a wait even for a spot at the bar, so I put down my name with the hostess then walked over to an empty area of the sidewalk and checked my messages. There were two voice messages from Alison left earlier, before our meeting, and a short text from Edward Bindley:

Re: Deryck Evanson, he'd written. *It's a no go, I'm afraid. I'm so sorry, Steven.*

I stared at the message for a moment, feeling a wave of disappointment.

He won't talk to me? I wrote back.

No, Edward wrote back a moment later.

Any particular reason?

Doesn't think it would be a good idea.

I stared at my phone again, wishing I had Edward here in person to explain this.

Anything else?

There was no immediate response after that, but a few minutes later, after I'd been seated at the bar and served my first margarita, I received a fairly lengthy text from Edward explaining in detail the email he'd received, saying basically that Deryck had "unequiv-

ocally" turned down my invitation to talk though he'd acknowledged that he'd received my emails and my letter, my phone
messages. He said that he wished me well, truly, Edward wrote, but
just didn't think it would be a good idea to talk. He couldn't see
what good would come of it. At the end of the text, Edward added
that Deryck had also said he'd be willing to write to me if I could
give him an address. Did I have one to give?

I texted back the address of our apartment in Berkeley, though
I wasn't sure how much longer Alison would be living there.

Did he say when he'd write? I asked then.

No, Edward texted back. *And I wouldn't hold my breath. I really
wouldn't.*

This was what I was thinking about later as I made my way through
my second margarita, as I tried to make sense of everything that
happened that day, as I tried to work out all of the disparate
thoughts swimming through my head: the prospect of Alison and
Finn moving to Massachusetts, the fact that I had no place to live,
no place to even sleep that night, the fact that Deryck Evanson
didn't want to talk to me and probably never would, the fact that
that part of the puzzle would never be clear. The fact that I was
spending money I didn't have on margaritas I couldn't afford and
that everything around me seemed to be disappearing.

I ran my finger along the rim of my glass then tasted the salt,
looking up at the warmly lit shelves of high-end liquor on the wall
in front of me. The bartender was a pretty Argentinian woman,
probably mid-forties, and she'd been the one to warn me about the
margaritas earlier. One would be enough, she'd said. Two would
put me under the table. Three would be the absolute cutoff. When
she'd served me my second, she'd shaken her head and smiled
wryly, as if to say *I warned you,* then went back to her other cus-

tomers. Now the bar was even more crowded, my shoulders practically touching the two women on either side of me, the smell of
tapas filling my nostrils, a rich and strange combination of Kusshi
oysters and Chorizo Ibérico and spicy capicollo. I took another
sip of my drink, then scanned through the messages on my phone
again, searching until I came to the last one from Julian, sent two
days earlier. He'd wanted to see how my visit with Joseph Alors had
gone, and I'd never written back.

Now I pulled up a new text box and thought again about my
conversation with Edward Bindley, the way he'd smiled at me
before I left.

I think you know more than you're telling me, I wrote to Julian,
then sent it off.

A few minutes later, he wrote back: *?????*

I think you know more about my father than what you said.

There was a brief pause, a gap of about a minute or two, and
then Julian responded again with a series of question marks.

I think you know where my father is living, I wrote finally and put
down my phone.

To this, there was no immediate response. In fact, there was
no response at all for almost an hour. I finished off my second margarita then called an Uber to take me to one of the nearest motels
on University Avenue, a few minutes away by car, and it was only
then, as I was standing out on the sidewalk, waiting for my Uber,
watching the cars on Shattuck Avenue cruise by, it was only then
that I finally received the text message from Julian, a bright glowing message that pulsed dreamily, like a beacon, on my phone.

Let's talk, he'd written and that was all.

19

In the days that led up to my father's disappearance I remember everything feeling eerily calm. This was toward the end of May, the last few weeks of the semester, a period of time that my father usually spent grading his final papers or preparing his final exams or getting things ready for his various summer research projects. It was usually one of the busiest and most chaotic times of the semester, but that year it was oddly tranquil. One of the reasons it was oddly tranquil, of course, was that my father had not assigned any final papers or final exams, had not proposed any summer research projects. In fact, ever since he'd learned of his tenure denial, he'd done very little at all when it came to his job. From what my mother would explain to me later, my father had basically told his students that their attendance in his courses would be optional from this point forward, that they would not be expected to write any papers or take any exams or do any reading. They would not be expected to do anything at all, in fact, and in return they could all expect to get an A. As for himself, he couldn't be sure if he'd be attending class or not. It would all depend on how he felt.

All of this had been a form of silent protest, of course, as David Havelin had explained to me years later (that day we'd met for lunch at his apartment in Yorba Linda), but it was questionable how effective it had been and it was also a fairly risky path to take. He'd said similar things to my father at the time, given him warnings, but my father had ignored him, had ignored anything that stood in the way of what he wanted to do.

At the time, David had been over at our house quite a lot in the evenings—or at least on the evenings when my father wasn't over at Deryck's—and in many ways he'd been a kind of lifeline to my father, his main cheerleader and advocate, his primary source of information. He'd also been a wonderful friend to my mother, and the two of them had worked well together as a team, trying to calm my father down when he got upset, figuring out ways to reason with him.

I remember one night, in particular, when the two of them had spent half the night trying to convince my father not to attend a cocktail party on the other side of Fullerton, a party that was being held at the house of one of the college's vice presidents and that my father had been invited to (perhaps accidentally) and intended to join. I think my father's plan had been to use this opportunity to confront some of the college's administrators in a more informal setting and really get a sense of what they were thinking, what they truly believed about his case. I remember my father sitting at the kitchen table with a cigarette in his hand, waving it around dramatically, as my mother and David tried to reason with him, tried to explain to him how spectacularly this could fail, and then my father eventually relenting, giving in, acknowledging that they were right, then claiming that he hadn't really been that serious anyway, though of course he had been.

Later, after my father had retired to his study to work, I remember my mother and David sitting at the kitchen table and sharing a couple glasses of wine. I was lying on the couch in front of the TV, pretending to be asleep as *The Tonight Show* played on low volume in the background and my mother and David shared their concerns about my father. I remember my mother talking about the fact that my father had begun to use a Dictaphone almost compulsively to record his thoughts, how he burned through three or four tapes a day, how he'd begun to tape-record his phone conversations as well, or at least his side of them, and how he'd become meticulous about documenting everything. She talked about the fact that this had happened before, in the past, and how he'd seen various psychiatrists over the years, how he'd even been medicated at different points. This was one of the first times I could remember my mother talking openly about my father's mental illness, and it filled me with a strange sense of sadness and shame. Later, as my mother went on about my father's troubles, she talked about his low stress threshold and how what had happened to him that past spring had basically caused his mind to short-circuit, how what he needed right now more than anything was rest.

David had listened patiently, but said little, not until the end when he eventually agreed with my mother that my father needed rest, that he needed to step away from St. Agnes and everything that was happening there. If they could just convince him to finish the semester strong, to reconnect with his students again, to make amends with his colleagues, to teach these last few weeks of classes, then he'd have the entire summer to rest and recover, to reassess and re-strategize. He'd have a whole year to make a second appeal, to potentially apply for other jobs. Maybe not tenure-track jobs, but lecturerships and things like that. There was still a lot of time.

David was whispering as he said this, and I couldn't make out much of what he said after that, even as I was subtly trying to crane my neck around the end of the couch, but I remember my mother crying at one point and David reaching out to comfort her, touching her shoulder and squeezing it. It was strange to see another man touching my mother like that, even though I knew it was innocent enough, a gesture of kindness, and after a moment I lowered myself back onto the couch and closed my eyes.

Later, after my mother and David had both had another glass of wine, I remember my mother asking David if he wanted to crash in the cabana house that night, pointing out that it was getting pretty late. David had thanked her but declined and then the two of them had sat in silence for a while, the muted laughter from *The Tonight Show* filling the stillness of the house, the distant scent of the lasagna my mother had made earlier for dinner, still sitting out on the counter, and in the distance, down the hallway, the tap-tap of my father's typewriter.

After almost a full minute had passed in silence, my mother finally said, "I feel like I've lost him, Dave."

"You haven't lost him," David said.

But my mother said nothing to this. Eventually she stood up and sighed. "I feel like he's already gone."

The next morning, when I woke, I remember lying in bed listening to the sound of my father making breakfast in the kitchen, the mechanical whir of the coffeemaker, the faint popping of grease on the stove, the shrill ring of the toaster oven's bell. I could also hear him talking to someone on the phone, his voice low and serious. By then, I'd learned to detect the subtlest changes in my father's voice, the slightest signs of distress, and I could tell that morning that something significant had happened, that he was genuinely concerned.

By the time I came out to the kitchen, though, all of that worry seemed to have vanished. He was standing at the counter, sliding eggs onto a plate for the two of us, a generous side of bacon, toast. He smiled as he motioned me over to the table and asked me if I wanted to have fun today. I reminded him I had school.

He waved this comment away and said, "You didn't answer my question."

"Don't you have classes too?"

He shook his head. He was standing in a pair of white pants and a salmon-colored linen shirt, his hair slicked back with some type of product, his face cleanly shaven, his eyes wild. He waved his hand again as if his classes, his job, were simply a minor obstacle to the day's fun, an absurd impediment.

"Your mother's already at work," he said, "and I was thinking of going into Los Angeles to see a movie. Would you like to join me?"

I stared at him. I think he must have known that he had me because he smiled then.

"What movie?" I said.

At this, he laughed. "Well, that," he said, "that, my friend, is a surprise."

Had I known then that this would be the last day I'd ever see my father, I might have suggested we do something more personal, more intimate, than driving into Los Angeles to see a movie, but that's what my father had wanted to do and so that's what we'd done. All the way into L.A., I remember secretly hoping that my father was taking me to see *Splash* or *Sixteen Candles,* which had just come out the week before, perhaps as a surprise, a gift, though of course I should have known better. By the time we'd pulled off the exit in Santa Monica, he'd already told me the name of the film we'd be seeing. *L'Avventura,* a classic Italian art film by Michelangelo Antonioni, one of the greatest Italian auteurs, greater even than Fellini or Rossellini, he said.

It was a beautiful day, the sun high in a cloudless sky, the temperature cool, the mid-morning traffic in Los Angeles light, my father smiling as he drove, his eyes inscrutable behind his Ray-

Bans, his profile handsome, as always. I remember being aware of the fact that things were falling apart in my father's life, but I couldn't help getting caught up in his manic enthusiasm that morning, his frenetic excitement as he talked about *L'Avventura,* this cinematic masterwork, this film that was so far ahead of its time, that created an entirely new cinematic language. He talked about the fact that when *L'Avventura* had first premiered at Cannes in 1960 it had been met with catcalls and boos, people walking out of the theater; Antonioni himself had been brought to tears by the audience's reaction. Later, however, a public statement was made by some of the most prominent film critics and filmmakers of the time, declaring *L'Avventura* a masterpiece, one of the best films of the year.

It was a film of gestures and glances, my father said as we turned onto Wilshire Boulevard, of looks often not met. It was a film about characters who usually looked past each other or in the opposite direction, of characters who didn't really see or understand each other, who were often too distracted by other things. It was about the way we all have trouble communicating and connecting, he said, and I sensed then, as he said this, that he was talking about something else, or someone else. But best of all, he said, it was a mystery—he smiled then, knowing how much I loved mysteries—but different than other mysteries he'd shown me, different than, say, *Rebecca* or *Rear Window.*

"This is more of an anti-mystery," he said.

"What's that?" I said.

But he didn't answer at first. His eyes were focused on the road, the passing signs on Wilshire Boulevard. Finally, he patted my hand.

"You'll see," he said and smiled.

. . .

On the rare occasions our family went into Los Angeles, it was usually for an event of some sort—a concert, an art opening, a poetry reading, a film. That's how I knew when I saw the NuWilshire Theatre—a beautiful Art Deco theater right on Wilshire Boulevard in Santa Monica—that I'd been here before with my mother and father, perhaps to see *Persona* or *Nights of Cabiria* or *Pather Panchali*. In addition to showing a lot of obscure independent films, they ran a bunch of retrospectives here, my father explained, as we found a seat in the near-empty theater, like the one they were running currently on Antonioni. The theater was quiet, the only other people sitting near us were in the front row, an elderly couple and a man by himself. My father had bought us a large tub of popcorn and several boxes of candy—Junior Mints, Whoppers, Red Vines— as well as a couple large Cokes, which he'd almost dropped when we sat down. It was a long movie, he'd said as he passed me my Coke, we needed to stock up. Then he winked at me and pinched my arm.

It felt good to be close to him. Years later, I'd freeze-frame this moment in time—this quiet moment before the curtain went up and the movie started, this strange little lull in what was otherwise a fairly chaotic day, the two of us sitting side by side in the dark theater, elbows touching. Beneath me, I could feel my sneakers sticking to the theater floor and all around us I could smell the scent of stale popcorn, but for those brief quiet minutes it felt good to be next to him, to be in his presence, to be close to his voice.

Later, once the movie started, I remember him leaning in closer to me and taking my hand, a gesture so intimate it surprised me, then whispering to me to pay attention, pointing out the various symbolic arrangements in the film, the way the characters were positioned in relation to each other, the way they were positioned in relation to the land, the architecture, the way Antonioni liked to use symmetrical framing, the way he was always showing us the backs of people. The film was in black-and-white and the subtitles were often too quick to follow, but I remember liking the feel of it, the quietness of it, the emptiness of the landscape, the beauty of the architecture. At one point early in the film one of the characters uttered the line "There's nowhere to run," and from that point on whenever a character was confused or disoriented, or symbolically trapped, my father would whisper "There's nowhere to run" or "No way out," as if reinforcing some larger point about the film or perhaps about life, perhaps about *his* life.

Later, though, I began to notice his interest in the film waning, his mind growing distracted, as it often did when he was forced to sit for long periods of time in silence. At several points he leaned over and asked me whether I could remember if he'd locked the door to the car, and when I told him I couldn't, he grew restless and tense. Finally, he stood up and said that he needed to check, that he'd be right back, and then he disappeared up the aisle, moving so quickly he almost fell.

Meanwhile, the film itself was growing more cryptic, more bizarre. Early on in the film, one of the primary characters, a woman named Anna, goes missing, and for much of the film the other characters are wandering around the island where they've all gone on vacation looking for her, shouting *Anna?* or saying with puzzlement, *Where's Anna? Where's Anna?* In a more conventional mystery, there would usually be some answers to this question, or potential answers, clues, but two hours into *L'Avventura* it was becoming pretty clear that no answers were coming, that Anna would never be found, that her fate would remain a mystery. Years later, I'd learn about subverting the conventions of the mystery genre, of circumventing tropes, but at the time it just seemed bizarre to me, bizarre to me and sad. Why would someone go to the trouble of making a mystery, only to provide no answer to that mystery in the end? It seemed to make no sense.

. . .

When the movie finally ended, I made my way up the aisle to the front lobby, hoping to find my father there, only he wasn't. He was nowhere in sight. I looked around the alcove beside the concession stand, called into the bathroom, but there was no sign of him anywhere. I felt dull and slightly nauseous from all the popcorn and candy I'd eaten, and as I made my way out onto the sidewalk outside, squinting against the midday sun on Wilshire Boulevard, I felt suddenly disoriented.

Outside, the world felt different, altered by the dreamy existential cinematography of *L'Avventura*, the hypnotic soundtrack, the characters' ennui. Every face I met seemed dissociated, distant. I searched around the small crowd of people congregating on the sidewalk outside the theater, waiting for the late afternoon show, and finally spotted my father standing under the marquee, leaning against the wall and smoking a cigarette.

When he noticed me, he smiled and motioned me over to his cool little spot in the shade.

"Did you like it?" he said.

I told him I did.

"Monica Vitti," he said, raising his eyebrows. "Hm?"

"Yes."

"Amazing, right?"

I nodded.

He ashed his cigarette and then looked into my eyes with a strange intensity. He seemed very pleased about something. "I'm so glad you got to see it," he said. "I really am." Then he pushed my hair to one side and kissed my forehead. "And I'm so glad you liked it." He pulled me toward him, and I was confused once again by his sudden affection.

As I leaned back against the wall of the theater, my father

smoked in silence, and I thought about my mother back in Fullerton and what she was going to say when we got home, when she learned that I'd skipped school, when she learned that my father had encouraged this. I watched the people on the sidewalk as they made their way slowly into the theater, moving in pairs, or small groups, chatting quietly, their movements almost trancelike. When I turned back to my father, though, he wasn't watching these people. He was staring out across the street, strangely.

After he'd finished his cigarette, he dropped it on the ground, rubbed it out with his shoe, then lit another.

"What are we doing?" I said.

"What do you mean?"

"What are we doing right now?"

"We're waiting."

"For who?"

"For friends."

"Which friends?"

But my father didn't answer. He looked out across the street, his expression dull. "There's something I have to tell you," he said finally. "And it's not something I want to tell you, believe me."

I said nothing to this but watched as he took another long drag on his cigarette.

"But maybe it can wait till later."

"What is it?"

But he shook his head. "No, let's wait on it. Okay?" He shielded his eyes from the sun and then peered across the street again, his expression growing impatient.

Finally, he turned to me and talked a little more about the film, the beauty of the cinematography, the poetic quietness of it, all of the literal symbolism. He asked me if I'd figured out what he'd meant by anti-mystery, and I told him I thought so.

"Did it bother you," he said, "that they never found Anna?"

"No."

"Why not?"

"I don't know," I said. "I guess it just seemed like part of it, you know?"

He smiled.

"It was right there in the beginning," he said, "that very first scene."

"What?"

"No way out," he said. "I kept telling you."

In the distance, across the street, I could now see Edward Bindley and Deryck Evanson standing on the sidewalk, waving at us, as if they'd just materialized out of the ether, as if my father had somehow willed them to be there. They were both standing beside Deryck's car, a red Renault, and both were wearing white pleated pants, like my father, and bright pastel shirts.

My father waved back at them casually, and it was only then, when he waved to them, that I realized that they'd been the friends we were waiting for, that this day had not been about me after all.

"You want to go to a party?" he said, waving.

But he was already moving across the street by then, already running. He didn't even hear me when I said no.

20

The house we went to that day has only ever existed to me in dreams. I know now that it was a real place, a real place that existed in 1984, but I have never been able to find it again. Even in high school, when I used to drive around the winding hills of Hollywood, looking for familiar landmarks, houses or street signs that might seem recognizable, that might jog my memory, I never found it. I'd end up circling around and around for hours, but never with any luck. Later, I'd try to retrace my steps and realize I was lost. I'm sure by now it's been torn down, built over, that not even the basic skeleton of it remains, but when I close my eyes I can sometimes still see it: this elegant mid-century modern home, perched in the heart of the Hollywood Hills, overlooking the canyons, with sweeping, panoramic views of the valley, the reservoir, the Griffith Park Observatory, even all the way down to the ocean.

The entrance to the house was modest, I remember, a fairly nondescript driveway that sloped sharply down to the flat-roofed home, everything around it obscured by a thick wall of hedge, the house itself flanked on both sides by two palms.

Deryck was the one who'd learned of the party, who'd been invited and who knew the host, and I remember the three of us following him as he walked up to the door, knocked lightly, then pushed it open, as if he'd been here before, which he probably had.

The entry to the foyer was a narrow room of stone walls, but once you turned the corner the house opened up into a cool and airy floorplan, a series of light-filled rooms that all connected to each other, creating a seamless flow to the house, a wide expanse of white walls, long rectangular windows, lots of sleek, practical furniture, everything imbued in a calming palette of blues and whites, bringing a sense of serenity to the place, an almost Zen-like quality. On the far side of the house, in the main living area, an entire wall of glass sliders looked out onto the swimming pool area and the patio, and beyond that, to the canyons and the city below.

Everyone at the party seemed to be out by the pool, so we followed Deryck out there, watched him from a distance as he spoke to the host, gave him a hug, then waved us over. I stayed back while my father and Edward went over to meet the host, a tall, white-haired man, then watched all four of them as they made their way over to the wet bar and mixed themselves drinks. At that point there were probably only about ten or fifteen people there, a small gathering, and the vibe was mellow, people lounging in the pool, sunning themselves on chaise lounge chairs, standing in small groups talking and smoking. A song by Joni Mitchell played faintly on the outdoor speakers, and I could hear the light tingling of wind chimes in the trees.

I walked over to one of the empty tables by the pool and sat down. In the distance, beyond the edge of the property, which was lined with bougainvillea and agave and tall pampas grass, you could see the entirety of Los Angeles, even a small sliver of the Pacific Ocean in the far distance, faint and glimmering. The sky that afternoon was still cloudless, and there was a light breeze, blowing my hair. I leaned back in my chair and looked around the property. As with all of the indoor spaces, all of the outdoor spaces had the same simple, sculptural lines, almost as if they had been designed to replicate the same geometric patterns and shapes as the inside, and the whole effect—the symmetry of both the indoors and the outdoors, the unity of the entire house—was strangely calming. I leaned back farther in my chair and closed my eyes.

A moment later I heard a voice coming from behind me. "My dad said you needed a suit."

I turned around and looked up to see a boy of about fourteen or fifteen wearing a Led Zeppelin T-shirt staring at me. His blond hair was longish and pushed back behind his ears. His nose was dusted with light freckles.

"A bathing suit," he said. "You can borrow one of mine. Come on."

He spun around then and started back toward the house, moving at a quick gait, his arms swinging purposefully, his long blond hair bouncing in the breeze, catching the sunlight for a moment just as he darted around the side of the house and down a small shady path on the edge of the property. Though I was a little taken aback, I eventually stood up and followed him, moving quickly myself, spotting him just as he was slipping into a sliding glass door on the side of the house, a sort of secret entrance to his bedroom.

Unlike the rest of the house, with its clean, symmetrical lines and minimalist aesthetic, this boy's bedroom looked pretty normal, a pretty typical teenage boy's room, dimly lit with piles of clothes in the corner, a velvet, glow-in-the-dark Pink Floyd poster above the bed, a pink fluorescent lava lamp, a desk cluttered with loose-leaf paper and comic books. Perched right in the middle of the room was a low table, and right in the middle of this table was a green plastic bong, just like Brody's, sitting right there in the middle of the room for anyone to see. When the boy caught me staring at it, he smiled, then turned to his bureau, fished out a pair of blue swimming trunks, and tossed them to me.

"Your parents don't mind that you smoke?" I said, nodding toward the bong.

"It's just my dad and Jeffrey," he said and shrugged.

I looked at him.

"I kind of have two dads," he said, turning back toward the wall without explaining. "I'm not really sure where my mom is right now."

He turned all the way around then, so that he was facing the bed, and I realized that this was so I could change. I quickly dropped my pants and slid off my Vans and stepped into the bathing suit, all the while trying to process what he was saying, what it meant. It was only then that it occurred to me that almost everyone I'd seen outside at the party was male.

When the boy turned around again, he looked me over and nodded. "So what's your name?" he said.

"Steven."

"Steven," he said, "I'm Kai." He reached out his hand and I took it. Then he went over to his desk and started sorting through the clutter. When he looked back up a moment later, he smiled, as if surprised to still see me there, standing in his room.

"How old are you, Steven?" he said finally.

"Fourteen."

"Really?"

"Yeah."

He looked at me dubiously. "You feel like smoking out?"

He nodded at the bong, and I said nothing, but a moment later he walked across the room, packed the bowl, and handed it to me. I picked up the lighter on the table and took a small hit, pulling only a little smoke into my lungs, then handed it back to him.

After he'd taken a hit himself, I asked him why he wasn't in school today either, and he said he didn't have to be in school whenever he was shooting or auditioning. He just had to meet once a day for an hour with his tutor.

"You're an actor?" I said.

He shrugged but didn't answer.

"Have I seen you in anything?"

Again, he was evasive. He looked down at his desk again, as if he was searching for something he'd misplaced, then finally walked over to his stereo and put on some music, something light and dreamy that I'd never heard before, synthesizer music without words. He sat down on the floor then, and I did the same, and we sat there for a while like that, Kai flipping through a comic book and me staring up at the posters on his walls, mostly posters of rock bands from the 1970s—Steely Dan, Aerosmith, Cheap Trick. He didn't seem to want to talk, and I didn't want to disturb him, though it seemed strange to be spending time together like this when I barely knew him. After a while, I felt my mind drifting back to the film I'd seen earlier, *L'Avventura,* and the cryptic comments my father had made afterward. I wondered what it was that he needed to tell me but couldn't, wondered what any of this was about. I leaned back on the floor and closed my eyes and lay there for a while, my mind drifting. At one point I looked up and saw that Kai was standing up to put on another record, dusting off the record sleeve with his hand.

I told him I should probably get back to the party now and he nodded without turning around.

Then, as I was standing at the door, he glanced back at me. *"The Fall Guy,"* he said.

"Huh?"

"You asked what I've been in. I was in an episode of *The Fall Guy* with Lee Majors, but it never aired."

I nodded, then I turned back to the door and let myself out.

By the time I got back to the pool, the party had grown considerably and the sun was lower in the sky. I saw my father and Deryck, sitting at the far end of the pool, talking, and Edward Bindley sitting by himself in the shallow end, drinking a daiquiri out of a tall glass with a straw.

When Edward noticed me, he smiled and motioned me over, and then I sat there for a while with him, my feet dangling in the water. The party had grown considerably, as I said, and the energy of it was different now, more lively, louder, though it was still mostly men. Men sitting together in the pool, men standing together underneath the cantilevered patio cover, men sipping drinks by the olive trees on the edge of the yard, men lighting cigarettes and laughing. I leaned back on my elbows and watched the sunlight shimmering on the pool's surface, the slow movements of the guests, the lazy rhythm of the party settling in, everyone sundrunk and drowsy in the late afternoon heat.

On the other side of the pool I could see my father and Deryck still talking, their feet dangling in the water like mine, my father refilling his plastic cup with more white wine, using the bottle they'd brought down to the pool with them, Deryck motioning for him to stop, to slow down, then my father laughing, even as the wine began to spill over the edge, licking the excess off his fingers before downing the entire cup in one gulp, then reaching for the bottle again and refilling it to the top, passing it to Deryck and telling him to do the same.

I looked over at Edward Bindley and saw that he was watching too, his eyebrows furrowed with concern. At one point Deryck looked over at Edward and held up his hands, as if to say, *what can I do?*, and Edward just nodded. Then, perhaps in an effort to distract me, he started talking to me about the fence on the edge of the property, asking me if I knew what it was for. I glanced over at the wire fence on the edge of the cliff, just beyond the bougainvillea, but told him I had no idea.

"It's to keep out coyotes," he said. "If you didn't have one of those, they'd come right up."

I nodded.

"You ever seen a coyote, Steven?"

I told him I'd seen a couple over the years, though never up close. I'd definitely heard them in the hills of Orange County.

"I don't think they'd hurt you necessarily," he said, "but I wouldn't want to chance it, you know?"

I nodded again.

Across from us, I could see that my father was now smiling, that Deryck was too, that everything seemed to have settled down over there, though I still sensed something was wrong, had sensed it all day. I'd sensed it that morning when my father was on the phone, had sensed it after the film, and I could sense it now as my father stood up and headed back toward the house, probably in search of another bottle of wine.

I followed him with my eyes, watched him as he disappeared inside one of the sliding glass doors then made his way over toward the kitchen. On the other side of the house, I could see the main living area through a tall wall of glass, the white-leather couches, the steel side tables, the small armchairs made of teal upholstery, the elegant wall sculptures and paintings. At the far end of the room, a group of men were standing in a circle passing a joint, and after a while I noticed them disappear down one of the side hallways. My father was not among them. He was still back in the kitchen, as far as I could tell, talking with another group of men. I glanced over at Deryck, and he smiled plaintively, his eyes full of warmth.

Then I turned back to Edward and he was looking at me the same way, a look of pity.

"I'm sure it must be difficult," Edward said after a moment, "being at a party with all grown-ups."

I shrugged and told him I was used to it.

"Yes," he smiled. "I imagine you must be." He pulled out his cigarettes and lit one. "You know, I can't remember my own parents ever throwing a party," he said, "if I'm being honest. I'm not sure that they even had friends." He laughed, shaking his head, and drew on his cigarette.

In the distance, my father was now reemerging from the house, holding a bottle of wine and moving cautiously across the lawn, watching each step, as if afraid of stumbling and dropping the bottle. When he reached Deryck, he looked over at us and waved jovially, then sat down on the edge of the pool and dangled his feet in the water again. Without looking up, he filled up one of the plastic cups with wine for Deryck, and one for himself. Then I watched Deryck as he put down his cup on the side of the pool and pushed it away, as if to suggest he wouldn't be drinking anymore. My father ignored this and turned to light a cigarette.

"You know, I love the garden here," Edward said, as if we were still in the middle of a conversation, "but I still love your mother's more. You know?"

I nodded and looked out at the small succulent garden beside the pool, and beyond that at the lavender and salvia and blue-gray agaves on the edge of the yard, the neatly manicured lawn that wrapped around the side of the house, dotted with paradise palms and desert grass. In the far distance, above the edge of the cliff, you could see the sun beginning to set now on the horizon, the sky darkening.

"Welcome to Monday night in L.A.," Edward said, motioning around the party, the crowd that was still growing. I looked over at my father and Deryck but they were no longer talking. My father was staring down at his feet in the water and Deryck was pretending to look off at something else in the distance. After a moment, my father drained his glass of wine and filled it up again, while Deryck continued to look away, and then a short time after that Deryck stood up and walked back to the house by himself, leaving my father alone.

My father filled up his glass again, took a sip, then looked around. I turned back to Edward.

"Did something happen today?" I said.

"What do you mean?"

"I don't know," I said. "Like, did something happen today with my father?"

Edward narrowed his eyes but said nothing.

"Like with his job or something?" I said. I explained how I'd overheard my father talking on the phone that morning, how he'd seemed concerned. How he'd seemed unsettled all day. I told him about the things my father had said to me outside the NuWilshire Theatre, about how strange he'd been acting lately.

At this, Edward looked away evasively and drew on his cigarette. He said nothing for a long time.

"Was he fired or something?" I said.

Again, Edward said nothing, but looked at me this time. "No, he wasn't fired," he said and glanced over at my father, who was still looking down at the pool, his shoulders hunched.

"But?" I said.

"But nothing, Steven," he said. "This is something you should probably be talking about with your father."

But I think he could see then that I was frightened, that I needed something, and that my father was clearly in no state to give it to me.

I glanced over at my father and saw that he was trying to stand up now, but having some trouble, going about it very slowly and methodically. Around him, people were moving aside to give him space. Finally, he got himself into a standing position and started back toward the house. I asked Edward again to tell me what was going on, and he shook his head and sighed.

"I don't want to be the one to tell you this," Edward said. "I really don't."

"Please," I said.

"Steven."

"Please," I said again.

And so he did. Looking down at his hands the whole time, he told me how my father's contract hadn't been renewed for next year, how his year of grace had been rescinded, and how he'd no longer be working at St. Agnes as of graduation.

I sat there for a long moment, taking this all in.

I looked at him.

"You said he wasn't fired," I said.

"Well, it's not quite the same thing," he said, but I could see as soon as he said this that he understood it was.

"Why?" I said.

"Why what?"

"Why wasn't it renewed?"

He looked at me.

"He wasn't teaching his classes," he said. "There was lots of other stuff too. But that was the main thing."

"I thought he had a contract though. I thought they'd already given it to him."

"They did," he said. "And that contract had terms." He touched his glass. "One of the terms was that he had to continue to teach his classes."

I looked down at my hands then. "So what does this mean?" I said. "We're going to have to move now?"

"I don't know, Steven," Edward said, glancing over at the wet bar, the crowd growing there. "I don't know." He tried to put his arm around me, but I moved away.

"Why are we even here?" I said. "Why are we even at this stupid party?"

Edward had no response to this.

I looked over at the house again, but it was too crowded now to see all the way inside. Still, I could see that they were turning on lights now, illuminating the kitchen and the living room.

"So did he just find out this morning or something?" I said. "Is that what that phone call was about?"

"I don't know," Edward said. "Maybe officially, yes." He looked down. "But Steven—" He paused. "Steven, I think he's always known that this was going to happen."

It's hard for me now to remember what happened after that, the exact chronology of things. All I know is that at one point I ended up lying on the floor in Kai's room with Kai, watching the film *American Gigolo* with Richard Gere, and that shortly after that several other kids from the party came in to join us, three boys who were around Kai's age and a girl who was maybe about sixteen or seventeen, all six of us lying on the floor in the dark, staring up at the tiny color TV on Kai's bureau, the dialogue barely audible because the party outside was so loud, the grown-ups laughing, the music blaring, everyone dancing. It must have been about eight or nine o'clock by then, maybe later. I'd taken another hit from Kai's bong and time had become fluid. I remember lying there on the cold floor of his room, staring up at the images on the screen, the faces of the actors, but not comprehending anything, not really being there, in fact, my mind drifting elsewhere now: to my mother, and to our house, and to the very real possibility of having to leave California, having to move now and follow my father wherever he wanted to go next. I can't remember ever again feeling such intense anger toward another person as I did toward my father at that moment. If he had been there in the room with me, I would have hurt him, I felt sure. I would have harmed him physically, just as he had harmed my mother and me, just as he had deprived us of the life he had promised us and could have given us, that he had selfishly taken away from us simply by acting in his own self-interest at every point along the way, simply by being himself.

This is what I believed at that moment and what I'd believe for many years afterward, and for the longest time no one could convince me of anything else. But that was the moment it began, lying there in the dark, in that strange beautiful house in the Hollywood Hills. That was the moment my anger first bloomed.

As for what happened after that, the rest of the evening seemed to move by in a blur. I know that at one point a few of the kids had to leave, their parents stopping by Kai's room to pick them up, and that by the end of the night it was just Kai and me and one of the other boys, lying on the floor in the dark, watching *Blue Thunder*. Outside in the yard, the party was beginning to slow down a bit, the music getting quieter, people starting to leave. At one point, I stood up to go to the bathroom, and as I wandered down the hallway in search of the bathroom door, I remember hearing the sound of Deryck Evanson and Edward talking inside one of the bedrooms at the end of the hall. I slipped inside the bathroom then and closed the door behind me, and a short time after that I heard the sound of Deryck and Edward closing the bedroom door behind them and heading back to the party.

I sat there for a while in the bathroom, just listening, but it was quiet outside now. In the far distance, outside in the yard, I could hear the faint sound of people laughing, others splashing in the pool, but the hallway itself was silent. I stood up and washed my hands, then headed down the hallway in the opposite direction of Kai's room, toward the room where Deryck and Edward had been talking. The door to the room was still closed, and I stood there for a while before finally turning the knob and peeking in.

Inside, it was dark, the room lit only by a small bedside lamp, but I could make out the unmistakable shape of my father's body, sprawled out on the bed, his upper body completely naked, his lower body still wearing the white pleated pants he'd been wearing all day, his face buried in one of the pillows. I walked over to the wall-mounted bed and sat down beside my father, watched his breathing, the steady rise and fall of his chest. I could smell the acrid stench of vomit coming from somewhere but saw no evidence of it anywhere, no plastic bowl or bucket beside the bed. I touched my father's shoulder and shook it, said his name, but he didn't stir. I said, *Come on, wake up, Dad,* but again nothing. His face still buried in the pillow, he looked like a child, a grown-up child, and though the room was quiet, and my body was perfectly still, I was not thinking peaceful things, I was thinking, *I hate you, I fucking hate you,* and then at one point I was saying it out loud, just a whisper at first then louder, *I hate you, fucking hate you,* my eyes staring at his shoulders, the back of his head, but my voice steady, even.

I have no idea if my father heard me that night, if he heard me but simply decided not to move. All I know is that a moment later I heard my name being called from the end of the hallway, and then I was standing up and rushing to the door, peeking out to see Edward Bindley and Deryck Evanson standing at the far end of the hall, dressed in their optimistic colors, staring at me.

"Hey Steven," Deryck yelled, holding up his car keys, waving. "Come on. We're going to take you home."

In the end, it would take my father almost two days to get back to Fullerton, but I would never see him again. Not after that. My mother wouldn't allow it, wouldn't allow me anywhere near him, nor him anywhere near me. Not after what he'd done. Not after he'd taken me out of school for the day, driven me into Los Angeles without telling her, taken me to a party in the Hollywood Hills, then proceeded to get so drunk he couldn't drive me home. She could forgive a lot of things about my father, but she couldn't forgive that, couldn't forgive him putting me in that type of danger, or taking that type of risk with me. When I finally got home later that night—it must have been around one or two in the morning— I remember the look of both fear and relief in my mother's eyes. I had never seen her so frightened, nor so relieved. She had been up half the night crying, had been on the phone with the police, the campus security at St. Agnes, our friends and neighbors. When I finally walked through the door, she kneeled down in the hallway and hugged me so tightly I could barely breathe, could barely feel my arms, while behind us Deryck and Edward stood in the doorway watching, apologizing. Whatever they said to her that night, though, my mother didn't hear. She was too preoccupied, too consumed by relief, her voice low like a whisper as she pressed me toward her, as she said my name again and again, over and over, repeating it in my ear like it was a mantra, or a prayer.

I remember that moment so vividly, even now, that image of my mother embracing me, just as I remember earlier that night, on the long drive home to Fullerton, sitting in the backseat of Deryck Evanson's car and feeling such a profound sense of sadness and fear, confusion. In less than a month from then, my father would officially disappear, would officially take off without any explanation of where he might be headed or when he might be back, and from that point forward there would no longer be any evidence of his actual existence—no phone number, no permanent residence, not even a record of his car—but I didn't know any of that then. All I knew was that something had shifted irreversibly in my life, something had been fundamentally altered, and I remember having that feeling so intensely that night, just sitting there in the backseat of Deryck Evanson's car, staring out at the fading lights of Hollywood in the distance, listening to the low staticky hum of the car radio, everything around us feeling muted and surreal, distant.

I remember the 101 being mostly empty that night too, only the occasional vehicle ahead of us or behind, and the car itself being quiet, neither Edward nor Deryck trying to sugarcoat anything or ignore what had happened. I appreciated that about them then, and I appreciate it about them now, the fact that they showed me that decency, that kindness. And I appreciated also the way Deryck would turn around from time to time to check on me in the backseat, his eyes gentle and warm, the way he'd occasionally ask me a question, and the way later, when I finally stopped answering him, he reached into his glove compartment and pulled out a mix tape of songs by Stevie Nicks, a mix tape that he said he'd made for me a long time ago but forgotten to give me, and then put it into the cassette deck, the song "Sleeping Angel" coming on quietly in the backseat, Stevie's voice low and yearning. I realize now that this was an act of kindness, an act of empathy, and I think I must have realized it then too, because I didn't say anything at first. In fact, I waited for almost the entire song to finish before I finally asked him to please turn it down, and then to turn it off, before I told him that I didn't listen to that type of music anymore.

21

There's a photograph of my father holding me in the hours after I was born. In the photo, my tiny body is bundled up in a little blue swaddle, and my father's face is ecstatic, beaming. In another photo, taken just a few minutes later, he is staring lovingly into my eyes, only now there's something different in his expression—a hesitation? An ambivalence? Does he see something he doesn't like? For years, I used to study those two photos as if they contained some secret roadmap to my relationship to my father, or to his feelings toward me.

Now they sit in a box with a couple dozen other photos of him; photos of him as a child, as a teenager, as a college student, photos of him at Berkeley, photos of him with my mother when they were young and first married, photos of him as a young professor, as a loving friend.

What are these photographs now though except brief glimpses in time, fleeting moments that add up to nothing, that tell you nothing, really, tiny pieces of a puzzle that's always shifting and changing and never quite complete.

Sometimes I spend hours looking at these photos; other times I put them away for months.

Still other times I put them so far back in my closet that it would seem almost impossible to ever find them again, but of course I always do.

I always know exactly where they are.

There's still so much about my father I will never know, so much that remains a mystery, but there are also other things that I've learned about him since starting the trip, small details and anecdotes that complicate him, that add new layers.

I've learned, for example, that he used to make his own clothes in high school, or tailor secondhand clothes he bought at the thrift shop in town, that he always wanted to appear meticulously dressed, polished, and always did, even though they never had money, his family, even though they never had anything close to the latest fashions or trends. I learned that he believed that the way the world saw you was the way the world treated you, which was why he never showed the world anything, why he never had friends over to the house, for example, or girls, never dated girls long enough for them to expect this of him, to expect an introduction to his family or his home. Later, in college, as a reinvented Dartmouth student, he hid from his classmates the fact that he was on scholarship and spent much of his scholarship money in the service of perpetuating this myth, buying oxfords and khakis from the Dartmouth Coop, wearing leather penny loafers like the ones his roommate wore, buying a subscription to the *Yale Law Journal,* even though he knew nothing of law. "When I went up to visit him his freshman year," Julian said, "he looked like a Vanderbilt or like some guy who'd just come from Choate. It was kind of uncanny, you know, how studied it was."

Later, though, he gave up all these affectations and became a truer version of himself, or at least a version of himself that was closer to the version I'd known: bookish, articulate, passionate about literature and art, a little shy, but also incredibly charismatic when he wanted to be. The one friend of his from college that I was able to track down described my father as an introvert but also mentioned that he was heavily involved in the drama productions on campus, that he even cowrote a musical with another friend, a kind of parody of Gilbert & Sullivan, that earned rave reviews in the campus paper. Julian confirmed this, saying that my father had always been involved in theater productions, even in high school, that he even thought my father might have met my mother because of a play that he was in, that he believed that they'd first met backstage after a performance through a mutual friend. "And of course, once he met your mother that was it," Julian said. "He was focused on two things. Your mother and books." Julian told me this the night that I'd stopped by his house on my way up north. He'd also talked about the way that my father had charmed my mother's parents, especially her mother, my grandmother, how they both adored him. "I think they thought he was going to save her," he said. "I think they thought he was going to give her this incredible life."

This would be a recurring theme in the stories about my father: the way that others seemed to believe in him unconditionally and also the way that others were drawn to him. When I spoke to Edward Bindley he talked a lot about the English Department secretaries and how much they'd loved my father, how much they'd loved to talk to him and tease him for forgetting things. He was always leaving his umbrella in the classroom, he said, or forgetting to turn in his office hours or mixing up people's names, and they thought that was hilarious. "But he was kind to them too," he added. "I found out later on that every year during the holidays he'd buy them all gifts, and nobody else in the department did that. He was the only one."

In the boxes he left behind were hundreds of pages of student teaching evaluations, and they all said similar things about my father: how he was one of the most generous and compassionate professors they'd ever had, how they'd appreciated his kindness and sensitivity, his empathy and understanding. They talked about how most professors tended to talk down to students but how my father was different, how he spoke to them honestly, as equals, how he really seemed to care about them. These were all things I'd witnessed myself, of course, on the few occasions my father had brought me onto campus and allowed me to sit quietly in the back of the classroom while he taught, the students leaning forward with rapt attention, my father speaking to them in a calm and gentle voice, listening to them with patience, understanding, taking their ideas seriously, honoring their thoughts. It was a side of him that I only ever saw in his classrooms, though, never at home, never with me.

"They would have done anything for him," David Havelin said to me that day I'd visited him at his apartment in Yorba Linda. "And they were just distraught when he left. Just sick about it." David talked to me about other things too: how my father used to write a funny satirical column in the student paper that the students just adored, how he started a film series devoted to campy horror films from the 1950s and how he used to screen these films himself for the students, sometimes even making them popcorn or buying them pizzas, sitting in the back row of the small theater on campus where he showed them, laughing along. Even Joseph Alors had to acknowledge my father's popularity with the students, his kindness and compassion. In a follow-up email after our meeting, he told me a story about a mutual student of theirs, a boy from New Mexico who was distraught over the fact that he couldn't go home for Thanksgiving because he didn't have enough money and how my father had bought him a round-trip bus ticket and then paper-clipped the ticket to the back of the student's midterm when he handed it back. *Your father never said a word to me about it,* Joseph wrote at the end. *I only found out about it later from the student.*

Almost everyone I spoke to seemed to agree about my father's generosity, his kindness, but as with everything else about my father, the collected sum of the stories about him were filled with contradictions, half-truths:

He was frivolous with money, according to my mother, and yet he'd set up an incredibly generous college fund for me, which he contributed to religiously, every month, for the first twelve years of my life. He was quick-tempered according to his colleagues, and yet incredibly patient according to his students. *He can be so funny and charismatic in class,* wrote one of his students in a teaching evaluation, *and yet he's always so shy and skittish when I pass him in the hallway. Almost like he's scared of me.*

Insecure and confident, narcissistic and selfless.

Easygoing and jovial, according to one person, but shy and withdrawn, according to another; a good sport with a great sense of humor in one situation, overly sensitive in another.

And it was true in other ways too. He loved both my mother and Deryck; he loved both his students and me, and yet he was different with all of us, each one of us got to see a different side of him, a different piece of the puzzle. Which one of us got to see the true side of him? Well, that's always been the question.

He's been such a wonderful mentor to me, writes one student in their teaching evaluation, *almost like a friend.*

Writes another: *He's an inspiring teacher no doubt, I can see why everybody loves him, but sometimes I wonder if he even sees me, if he even knows that I'm there.*

I had hoped in writing this that the picture of my father would become clearer but it hasn't. If anything, it's become murkier, more elusive, all of the disparate memories and stories working against each other, telling different truths, but not one central truth, and all of them collectively tainted by the unreliability of memory.

And then add to these memories one more: an image of my father at seventy-five in a wheelchair, his mind mostly numb from medication, his frail body hidden by a thin blue robe, his eyes cloudy with disinterest.

Imagine an image of him so opposite my memory of him that it doesn't even register as my father.

Even though I've prepared myself for weeks, even though Julian has told me several times that it's going to be a shock, and even though I've told myself not to expect much, not to expect anything, really, even despite all of this, I am still stunned, speechless.

Here, at an assisted living facility in Portland, Oregon, I feel that I've come to neither an end nor a beginning but rather to a strange detour that I never could have imagined.

When Julian first described the facility, he'd made it sound almost cushy. He'd talked about the courtyard and garden, the arts and crafts studio, the fitness center, the daily bus trips into Portland, the organized events. He'd talked about the on-site psychiatry and counseling, the art and work therapies, the café and bistro. He'd made it sound like a place where someone would want to live.

But this was not a place where someone would want to live.

The hallways painted an antiseptic beige, like the hallways of a hotel, the residents wandering around listlessly, or sitting in small groups, quietly, not seeing each other, a somnolent, slow-moving energy filling the hallways, the social center, everything benevolent and positive on the surface, but underneath a strangely calm and funereal lull.

That's how it had seemed to me, at least, when I first arrived, but that might have just been me projecting too. It might have been a very different type of place altogether. It's impossible to say now. All of it is still a blur.

Earlier, I'd sat in my car in the parking lot for almost three hours. I'd sat there and wondered if this was something I wanted to do. Around the grounds of the facility, which looked like the grounds of a large apartment development, were mountains, the Cascade Mountains to the north and Mount Hood to the east, and in front of them lots of green fields. The facility itself was a long-term mental-health assisted living facility where my father had been living since 1998, according to Julian, and where Julian had been overseeing and funding his care since he'd discovered him.

Before that, my father had lived in various parts of the Bay Area: Modesto, Redwood City, Santa Clara, the Castro. He'd developed late-onset schizophrenia in the mid-1980s, according to Julian, the beginnings of which we'd witnessed, and eventually regressed to a point that Julian didn't want to talk about, that he didn't think would be helpful to describe.

How he'd spent those years before Julian tracked him down was also somewhat vague, Julian only saying that I didn't want to know about it, that he didn't think it would give me much peace.

And when I pressed him on it later, he remained firm, saying again that I should trust him on this one. "Just trust me on this, Steve," he said, "okay?"

I know this is the part of the story that I'm supposed to draw out and tell dramatically, that I'm supposed to imbue with emotion, but I can't because there was nothing particularly dramatic about it. I wish I could tell you that my father recognized me, that he understood who I was, but he didn't, in part because I didn't tell him who I was, in part because I asked the nurse to introduce me as a friend, a friend who was just going to sit with him for a while in his room, but even if she had told him who I was, I'm not sure it would have registered anyway. That's how heavily medicated he was, that's how out of it. Julian had warned me about this too, that some days he was more communicative than others, but it was difficult to see firsthand, difficult to witness.

For almost an hour we sat there together and said nothing. We sat there and said nothing, though it felt good to be in his presence again, to take in the scent of him, to feel a closeness to him.

I remember studying his face in the late afternoon sunlight of his room. It was the same face but also not the same face at all. It was the face of someone who had been through a lot, who had lived a very hard life. That's how I'd describe it to Alison later in the airport before I flew home. As I said, I would have never recognized him had I passed him on the street.

"A very hard life?" she'd said.

"Yes, a very hard life."

"And why the wheelchair?" she asked.

"Psoriatic arthritis," I said.

She was quiet for a very long time, and then she said, "I'm so sorry, honey, but I'm glad you found him."

I said nothing.

"Steven?"

I hadn't realized until she said this just how badly I was shaking.

· · ·

If this part of the story seems incomplete to you, unfinished, it's because it exists that way in my mind, as a series of fragments, snapshots, vague images. It happened so quickly, just a two-day trip and a one-hour visit, that I almost wondered later if it had happened at all, if I'd imagined it.

I know at one point, though, I took his hand, I took his hand and squeezed it, but he didn't move. And I'd like to think I spoke to him too, but I can't remember if I did or if I just imagined I did. I'd like to believe I said *I miss you* or *I'm sorry,* but I can't be sure of these things.

There was one thing, though, that I do remember, a curious thing. There were no books in his room. Not a single one. There was a TV, a dresser, some floating wall shelves decorated with potted plants, some wall art that looked like something Julian would have given him, a west-facing window with a view of the fields, but not a single book. This seemed amazing to me. That my father would live in a room without a single bookshelf, a single book.

Months earlier, I'd learned from Julian that my mother had known about the facility too, though not until a few years before her death. Before that, my father had been adamant about neither one of us ever knowing where he was, and Julian had always tried to respect this, but then at one point, during a weekend visit with my mother a few years back, he'd felt compelled to tell her—he couldn't say why it was then and not earlier, only that he'd been carrying the guilt of not telling us for years—and my mother had been deeply upset by it, of course, angry with Julian, as I was too the night he'd told me. This was the night he'd called me while I was standing outside César, the tapas bar in Berkeley. I'd canceled the Uber and taken the phone to a quiet bench on Shattuck Avenue and sat down. He said that he'd asked my mother if she'd like to have the name and address of the facility, and she'd taken a few days to think about it but ultimately said no, though she contributed generously to my father's care from that point on.

"She'd made peace with his absence a long time ago," Julian had said. "I think it was too hard for her to open that door again." And, of course, they'd talked about me too. This was shortly after Finn was born, and my mother was sensitive to this, sensitive to the pressures I was under. He said that she'd asked me hypothetically several times if I'd be open to seeing my father if she was ever able to track him down, and I'd unequivocally answered no, that I wouldn't. I was still very angry then, Julian said, though I don't remember being as angry as he suggested.

"Do you remember her asking you this?" he'd asked.

I told him I did, though I only remember it seeming random, strange.

Before her death my mother had made Julian promise to tell me if I ever asked, and he promised he would, though he couldn't explain why he hadn't that last time I'd visited, why he'd panicked and said nothing.

"Maybe I was just afraid of how angry you'd be," he said.

And I told him I was, because I was at that moment, very angry, but that I knew I wouldn't be forever, and then we'd hung up.

Before I'd left the facility that day, I remember stopping by my father's room one last time to look in on him, not knowing if I'd be back but hoping I would be. He was sitting by the window then, looking out, and he seemed peaceful, even content. I decided not to disturb him or say goodbye but just to watch him for a while. It was probably four o'clock in the afternoon then, sunlight filling the room. It all felt so surreal still, but I also felt somehow lighter, and I was glad I'd made the visit.

In the letter that Deryck Evanson had written to me a few weeks earlier, he'd talked about the importance of forgiveness, how it was important for me to understand that what had happened to my father had not been his fault and how it was important to forgive him, that not forgiving him would carry its own weight and that weight would never leave me.

It was a beautiful letter in many ways, eloquent, honest, though it was also very cautious. He said nothing of his own involvement with my father, for example, nothing of his love for him, only that it was very sad what had happened to him, what had happened to his mind.

Walking out to my car that day, I remember looking back at the facility and thinking that it was perhaps not as bad as I'd originally thought. It was certainly a lot better than a lot of the other places I'd imagined my father ending up: buried on the side of the road, homeless on the street. It was maybe even, as Julian suggested, a good place for him to be at this point. I couldn't say, and still can't now. As I mentioned before, much of that trip is still a blur, but I remember sitting in my car for a while afterward, staring back at the facility in the late afternoon sunlight, thinking of my father inside, staring out at the fields, and how peaceful he'd looked, how seemingly content. I thought about what his days must be like right now, his nights, what types of thoughts might be going through his mind. Finally, after about a half hour or so, I started up my car and pulled out of the lot, heading back down the rural highway toward Portland, thinking about something that Julian had said to me the last time we spoke, that night I'd talked to him on the sidewalk outside César, that night he'd told me everything. I'd been asking him how he went about finding my father, and he'd just paused for a long time and then he'd said, *You know, he wasn't actually that hard to find, Steve,* his voice suddenly soft. *It was just that nobody—well, you know, nobody ever really wanted to find him. That's all.*

What do you mean? I said.

Just what I said.

And I realized only then, as he said this, and as I stood there in the fading light of Shattuck Avenue, that he was right.

Part
4

22

In the imagined life, so much is different.

In the imagined life, my father gets tenure. In the imagined life, Deryck Evanson disappears at the end of the year and our lives return to normal. In the imagined life, my father gets better, gets help. We continue to live in the same house for many more years.

In the imagined life, I have a strange and often challenging father, but I have a father. All through middle school and high school. All through college. I have a father who appears on my wedding day, a father who is there to meet his grandson when he's born, to have the type of adult conversations he always promised me we'd have. Conversations about literature and film and all of the things he was passionate about, things I would later become passionate about as well. In the imagined life, we have an adult relationship; I learn more about him, he lets down his guard a little bit, lets me in. He continues to struggle with his mental illness, but by the time I'm in college there are incredible medications that help to balance him out, and by the time I'm married to Alison, he's more or less stable. In the imagined life he becomes old and mellowed out, but not passive. Not sedated. He turns his adventurousness inward, toward his scholarship and his work. He achieves great things.

I often thought about this imagined life when I was growing up, sometimes almost compulsively. Lying in bed at night, in those years after my father disappeared, I used to picture what our lives might have been like had things gone differently, had my father gotten tenure, had my parents stayed together. In many ways, it was a futile exercise, and yet it was still a thing I did, in the same way one might revisit a poor decision over and over again, even though in doing so nothing is changed, no solace is found.

On the wall in front of my father's desk in his study, he'd left us a small piece of paper with the following quote from Proust:

The true paradises are the paradises we have lost.

I always took this quote to be an apology of sorts to my mother and me, an acknowledgment of how he'd failed us, though it's very possible he meant for it to mean something else entirely.

My mother left it up there until the day we finally moved, just as she left his books exactly where they were, his files neatly organized in a metal filing cabinet in the corner of the room, his papers intact, as if she expected him to return one day to retrieve them, which of course he never did.

In many ways, that was the hardest time for both of us, that period of time right after he vanished. I remember my mother spending a lot of time out of the house or by herself, and I remember wishing she was around more and wishing she could see the type of pain I was in, wishing she would ask me about it without me actually having to tell her. But of course I'm sure she knew the type of pain I was in. She just didn't know how to talk about it yet because she was in pain herself. And so instead she'd show me her love in other ways, pulling me toward her often, hugging me at random moments, and the two of us would continue to exist in a kind of implicit silence, each of us grieving privately, in our own way, never talking about my father or what we'd lost.

Later, after we'd moved out of the house and into an apartment, the silence seemed to grow stronger, our orbits further apart. I know it was very hard for my mother to live in such a small space, after being accustomed to a house, and I know it was especially hard for her to lose her garden. I'd find out later on that we could have had a small garden had we taken a ground-floor unit but my mother had felt it was too dangerous, especially given the fact it was just the two of us; and so she'd forgone the possibility of a garden and would not have a garden again for many years after, not until I was out of college and she was living in Costa Mesa. And though this might seem like a small thing, I don't think it was a small thing for her. In many ways, I think it was one of the hardest things of all, at least in a symbolic sense, the fact that she could no longer do the thing she loved to do most.

As for me, I started to spend a lot more time away from my mother after that, after we'd moved into the apartment. I was already beginning to embrace the same punk rock ethos that Chau had embraced the year before, finding it a necessary and important outlet for my anger; and though I tried to convince myself I was fine, I was not fine at all. I was consumed by a kind of quiet rage, a nihilism that would follow me all the way through middle school and high school and even into my first few years of college. Even now, I still feel guilty for the way I acted during those years and especially for the way I'd reacted to the news that my father had gone missing, when my mother first told me, the way I'd just looked at her and shrugged, as if to say *who cares,* then walked out of the room, leaving her all alone to deal with the fallout by herself. I wish I could have been a better son to her then and I wish I could have told her honestly how I was feeling because the truth was I was very concerned about my father. The truth was, for most of middle school and high school, I used to lie in bed at night, worrying about him, wondering where he was, working through the various scenarios in my mind: that he'd gotten involved with the wrong people, that he'd met with foul play, that he'd killed himself in some remote location, that he'd gone through some elaborate process of reinvention. By morning, though, my fears would be replaced once again by anger, resentment, and I'd be back to my original conclusion, that he hadn't died in some tragic way, but had simply abandoned us, in which case, I told myself, it didn't matter what had happened to him.

I realize now, of course, that my mother loved my father deeply, that she never stopped loving him, all the way up till the end of her life, and I know that I loved him too, intensely, that I still love him now, though he barely resembles the man I remember, and yet I still have trouble answering Julian's question, or implied question: Why hadn't we tried harder to find him?

I know that my mother did try hard in the beginning, that she made several trips into the city, that she spoke to all of his remaining relatives and friends, that she filled out a missing person's report, but I also know she was protective of me, and aware of my anger toward my father then and perhaps a part of her worried about what might happen if we actually did find him, if we brought him back into our lives. Perhaps over time it became easier just to live with the not knowing, to not open that door again, to try to move on the best we could with our lives.

As for me, I know that at a certain point I had to give up on the hope of him returning because that hope was going to crush me if I didn't let it go. It was just so much easier to be pessimistic, to assume the worst, to believe that he'd abandoned us, or that he'd taken his own life, because to believe the opposite, to be optimistic, was just excruciating.

And so began a period of self-medication and denial, a period of heavy drinking and drug use, that I recognize now as a period of intense grieving. This would have been during my freshman and sophomore years in Tucson, a period of time that I don't like to think about very often these days, though people who knew me at that time would probably be surprised to learn that I'd been unhappy.

It was a period of time when I was out at the bars in Tucson six out of seven nights a week, when I was always in search of a party, a person who was willing to extend the night a little longer. And what seems strange to me now is that it was during this time, a time that I think of now as my most self-destructive, that I first met Alison and fell in love with her, that the two of us began to date.

In retrospect, of course, I think that one of the main reasons I fell in love with Alison so quickly was the fact that she was one of the first people I could talk to openly about my father. In the past, I had always been too afraid of unloading on my girlfriends, or my friends, or even on my mother. I always worried that it would scare them off or simply be too much, but Alison was one of the first people I could talk to openly about him, one of the first people to make me feel comfortable enough to do this.

We were living on the same hallway at the time, the same hallway of the same dorm, and though we had nothing in common in a superficial sense—she was an activist who never drank, who went to bed early on Saturday nights—we had so much in common on a deeper level, including a deep love of literature and film, a commitment to social causes, a belief in being kind to people above all else. I remember sitting with her in her dorm room late at night, the two of us just sitting there cross-legged on her floor, the sound of R.E.M. playing on her stereo in the background, the smell of the incense she always used to burn back then, and I remember talking to her about things I had never talked about with anyone else, things I had never dared to utter, and I remember her just sitting there and listening to me, not trying to fix anything or offer advice, not even trying to make me feel better, just listening, and I can't explain how important that was to me at the time, how she changed the entire trajectory of my life, how she probably even saved me.

I was thinking about this the day after I'd returned from Portland, the day after my strange and somewhat confusing reunion with my father, as I sat on a small grassy hill near Fisherman's Wharf with Alison and Finn, looking out at the water on a sunny, cloudless day in San Francisco.

It was windy as usual, but the temperature was warm and people were out in droves, walking their dogs, playing Frisbee, laying out large blankets and setting up picnics. Behind us, you could see the tourists in Ghirardelli Square, and in front of us the Bay, the water choppy and rough, the faint shape of Alcatraz in the distance.

It was hard to believe but neither of us had been to Fisherman's Wharf in years, not since Finn was born, at least. I think in some ways we always felt it was too touristy, not the type of thing an actual Bay Area family would do, but now that we were leaving—Alison had taken the job at UMass, had already begun to send our stuff ahead of us—we wanted to do as many of these types of things as possible, just so that Finn would at least have memories of having done them, just so that when somebody asked him, a Bay Area native, if he knew what Fisherman's Wharf was, if he knew what Ghirardelli Square was, he could at least say yes.

Earlier we'd gone to Begoni Bistro in Chinatown, one of our favorite old haunts, a place we used to go to a lot when we were younger, and afterward we'd walked around for a while in North Beach and Russian Hill. All afternoon Alison and Finn had been teasing me about the vaguely insulting fortune I'd received in my fortune cookie at Begoni Bistro, a kind of mixed message that had them both in stitches, and all afternoon I'd been pretending to be wounded, hurt by their teasing, though of course I wasn't. The fortune had read, *Not everyone is meant to soar,* and for some reason they'd found this very funny, even hilarious, the veiled insult perhaps, or maybe just the subtle harshness of it, I'm not sure. All I know is that they had been teasing me about it relentlessly all day. *I guess not everyone is meant to soar,* Alison had said, shaking her head, as I tried unsuccessfully to parallel park on Mason Street. *Guess not everyone is meant to soar, huh, Dad?* Finn had echoed when I'd forgotten my wallet in the car and had to run back to get it. And now they were saying it again, as I wiped at the black coffee I'd just spilled on my jeans.

"I guess not everyone is meant to soar," Alison said, smiling.

"That's right," Finn said, patting my shoulder, "but it's okay Dad, we understand," and then looking at Alison and laughing, the two of them sharing a conspiratorial wink at my expense. I looked at them and shook my head, pretending to be wounded again, pretending to be hurt, though of course it was nice just to see them laughing again, nice just to have the three of us all together.

It had been almost a month now since Alison and I had reconciled, since I'd moved back in, but we were still taking things slow, not rushing anything. It was a delicate time, in many ways, but also a good time. Alison had stopped working by then and was already shifting her focus toward her new job, toward our new lives in Massachusetts, and I was trying to focus on myself, trying to get better for my family, as I'd put it to the therapist I'd been seeing. This involved, among other things, doing exercises designed to release the trauma I'd been storing in my body for years, exercises designed to heal me, and it also involved going to regular therapy sessions and giving up drinking, both things I'd done since the day I'd moved back. Most recently, though, it had also involved writing about it, something I'd never done before, writing about everything that had happened back then as a way of trying to release it, or confront it, or both, and in certain ways this had been the most effective part of the whole process, something I'd never imagined before, just keeping a daily journal, writing down my thoughts.

And through this process too I'd learned how to revisit some of those memories from my childhood in a way that wasn't traumatic or triggering to me, and through my conversations with the therapist I'd also come to see how what I'd been doing with Alison these past few years, withdrawing emotionally and drinking heavily and pushing her away, was all part of the same cycle, the same pattern I'd been repeating for years in different ways, that the emotional distance and the pushing away was coming from the very same place as the neediness and the desire to please, that they were two parts of the same fear. This was all stuff that I'd been talking about with the therapist at length and with Alison too, Alison who had picked me up that night at César when I'd called her in tears after getting off the phone with Julian, after learning of my father's whereabouts, Alison who had taken me home that night and allowed me to stay, allowed me to stay on the condition that I would start going to therapy and stop drinking and that I would be more present in every way, which I had tried to be and which I believed I was. It was a gradual process, though, this whole thing, and all I knew now was that the writing was helping. The writing was maybe the best part.

.   .   .

I was explaining this to Alison later that afternoon, as we leaned back on our blanket on the grass, and Finn played on the small beach at the edge of the Bay, just in front of us. Finn was out of earshot, and so I'd been talking to her about my father, about the strangeness of my visit, but also about how I'd been writing about it already, how I was already beginning to get some perspective about it simply by writing in my journal. If acceptance was the last stage of the grieving process, I said, I felt like I was maybe getting closer to that.

"And how about forgiveness?" she said.

I shrugged. "I don't know," I said. "I think so. I know I'd like to forgive him." I propped myself up on an elbow. "But it's complicated, you know?"

"Even now?"

"Yeah, even now."

She nodded. "And how about yourself?"

"Have I forgiven myself?"

"Yes."

A few days earlier, just before I'd left for Portland, I'd told her for the first time about the words I'd said to my father the last time I'd seen him, how I'd told him I hated him, and how I was more convinced than ever that he'd heard me, how I didn't know why but I just felt it. She'd reminded me that I'd been a twelve-year-old boy at the time, a twelve-year-old boy who was probably very scared and confused, but I told her it didn't matter, how it was a weight I'd been carrying inside me privately for years, how it was something I'd never fully reconciled. Now, though, I took her hand, and nodded.

"I think I have," I said, "in certain ways, yes. As much as I can for now, at least."

I looked out at the water, the ferryboat headed out to Alcatraz Island, the sun getting lower in the sky.

"I think the thing I still worry about, though," I said, "is that one day I'll end up becoming just like him, you know? I still worry about that. That one day Finn will look at me in the same way I looked at him."

Alison stared at me.

"That could never happen," she said. "You're nothing at all like him."

"But sometimes I feel like I am," I said. "I see that selfishness there sometimes, things you point out to me."

"We're all selfish, Steven," she said. "Everyone is." She stared at me. "Look at me. I'm asking my whole family to move across the country to a very cold place where we know absolutely nobody just because I want a job there."

"That's not selfish," I said. "The very nature of your work is the opposite of selfish."

"But that doesn't mean I'm a completely selfless person."

I nodded.

"You need to be easier on yourself sometimes."

I smiled. "And so do you."

"That's true."

She looked out at the water then herself, a smile spreading across her face, a faint recognition of something, then closed her eyes.

A moment later, she nestled back into me, and I put my arm around her, and we lay like that for a while, her head resting on my chest. In the distance, I could hear the sound of somebody playing acoustic guitar, a street musician perhaps, a rhythmic strumming, and I closed my eyes too and listened to it for a while, pulling Alison closer to me and Alison letting me, not resisting. I could feel our chests rising in unison, our breathing synchronized, could feel her fingers intertwined with mine, a familiar feeling, and for a while I could feel a calmness washing over me.

"All of that anger," I said quietly, my eyes still closed.

"I know."

"And all of those years of me telling you I wasn't."

"And yet you were."

"I was. And you knew."

"I did." She pushed the hair away from my forehead, kissed it.

"I'm sorry," I said and took her hand, but she just squeezed mine back and said there was no need to apologize.

"If it makes any difference," I said, "I think I'm ready to let go of that too."

"Good," she said, "I'm glad."

She nestled in closer to me, and I pulled her in tighter, my eyes still closed.

"It was just so weird, though," I said after a moment, rubbing her back, "the fact he didn't even recognize me, you know?" I was thinking now of my father again, drifting back to our visit.

"I'm sure."

"And I don't know what I wanted to say to him, but I did want to say something."

She was quiet.

"I think in some small way I just wanted to let him know I hadn't forgotten him."

"I think he knows that."

"You do?"

"Yes," she said. "I do."

And I opened my eyes then and saw that her eyes were open now too, that she was staring right at me. I looked down at the beach, where Finn was still playing, and then out at the water, the expansiveness of the Bay, the sun even lower now in the sky, touching the horizon, everything getting quieter, darker.

After a moment, Alison slid out of my embrace, stood up and brushed off her jeans, then started down to the beach to see Finn, saying she'd be right back. From where I lay, I watched them playing there for a while in the sand, Alison now helping Finn with his castle, Finn now laughing.

I lay back on the blanket again and sipped my coffee, looked out at the water, the waves.

It was strange to consider, but only about eight miles to the north, just across the Bay, was Sausalito, where Stevie and the rest of Fleetwood Mac had recorded *Rumours* in 1976, and to the east, just about thirteen miles or so, was Berkeley, where at that very same time my father, mother, and I had lived in a small studio apartment off College Avenue, as my father finished up his dissertation and applied for his very first teaching jobs. It was also where Alison, Finn, and I lived now, if only temporarily, and where we'd built a life for ourselves as a family. In certain ways it seemed like everything in my life was always coming back to this place, to these same ten or twenty square miles, and yet, in a matter of weeks, we'd be leaving it, we'd be leaving it for good.

This was both a sobering thought and a comforting one. There was the possibility of the unknown, of course, the excitement of our new lives, but there was also now the understanding of what we were leaving behind, of what would be lost.

And I thought then about something Alison had once said to me.

This was shortly after I'd moved out, as we were talking one night over coffee. I'd been talking to her about something related to my father, I think, or perhaps my mother, I'm not sure. All I know is that at one point she looked up at me kind of sadly and shook her head. *This place is full of ghosts for you, Steven,* she'd said, waving her arms broadly, as if to indicate not just Berkeley, but the entire state of California, the entire West Coast, and in certain ways, I realized then, she was right. The ghost of my mother was still here, the ghost of Chau and all those memories of him, the afterburn of all those years, the ghost of my father, or at least of the man I remembered from that time, the ghosts of all of my father's friends and colleagues, all of those people's younger selves, they were all still here, all still flickering, and though I've been trying hard to remember them, to dream them back up through my writing, to preserve them on paper as they were at that time, they're also still receding now too, falling further and further into the past, growing fainter with each passing day.

I looked down at the beach again and noticed that Alison and Finn were now looking up at me, waving. I waved back to them, and then sat there for a while, watching, everything around us luminous now, golden, the world suddenly still.

California. They've always said the quality of light here is different and maybe that's true. I knew I was going to miss it. But for now, we had another few weeks, and who knows how much longer after that as a family, we weren't putting any expectations on anything, just approaching it day by day, but today, today had been a good day, and that's all I was thinking about as I looked down at Alison and Finn on the beach, the sunlight shimmering on the water behind them, their bodies silhouetted against the bright orange sun in the distance, the image bringing back so many memories of my own parents from our early days in California, those long lazy days on the beach, only back then I never understood what anything meant, or what might happen next, whereas I understood right now, as Alison and Finn looked up at me, waving, beckoning me on, that they were wanting me to join them, that they were wanting me to come down and play, and so after a moment I stood up and started down the small grassy hill toward them, moving so quickly, so briskly, I didn't even realize until I'd reached them, until I saw the expressions on their faces, I'd been crying.

Acknowledgments

To my wonderful agent, Terra Chalberg, for her unwavering encouragement and support over the years and for her early belief in this book, and to my brilliant and generous editor, Diana Tejerina Miller, for her guidance, advice, and insights, and for her tremendous care with every aspect of bringing this book into the world. It is a gift to get to work with both of you.

To the many people at Knopf who played an important role in the life of this book: Jordan Pavlin, Reagan Arthur, John Gall, Serena Lehman, Suzanne Smith, Fred Chase, Nicole Pedersen, Matthew Sciarappa, Elka Roderick, Morgan Hamilton, and Soonyoung Kwon.

For help with research, many thanks to archivist Cheri Pape at the Fullerton Public Library and Bill Evans, owner of Black Hole Records in Fullerton.

To Trinity University, and specifically the Department of English and the School of Arts and Humanities, for your continued support, generosity, and kindness. And to my colleagues and students at Trinity, you are a constant source of inspiration to me. It is an enormous privilege to get to work alongside you.

To the many writers and friends who were also sources of inspiration for me as I wrote this book, but especially to Holiday Reinhorn, Jonathan Blum, and Amber Dermont, the three writers who are muses for me always, even when they don't realize it.

To my extraordinary mother and to the memory of my equally extraordinary father, the two of you were never far from my thoughts as I was writing this book. To my wonderful siblings, Mike and Di, you are both blessings in my life. And finally, to Jenny, Charlotte, and Alex, thank you for your patience, love, and laughter. You are all fire (as Alex would say) and you are my whole heart.

A NOTE ABOUT THE AUTHOR

Andrew Porter is the author of the story collections *The Disappeared* and *The Theory of Light and Matter* and the novel *In Between Days*. A graduate of the Iowa Writers' Workshop, he has received a Pushcart Prize, a James Michener/Copernicus Fellowship, and the Flannery O'Connor Award for Short Fiction. His work has appeared in *One Story, Ploughshares, American Short Fiction, Narrative, The Southern Review,* and on National Public Radio's *Selected Shorts*. Currently, he teaches fiction writing and directs the creative writing program at Trinity University in San Antonio, Texas.